STAR TREK®
THE ORIGINAL SERIES

book one

‹ERRAND of VENGEANCE›

THE EDGE OF THE SWORD

Kevin Ryan

**Based upon STAR TREK®
created by Gene Roddenberry**

D0057801

POCKET BOOKS
New York London Toronto Sydney Singapore

An *Original* Publication of POCKET BOOKS

POCKET BOOKS, a division of Simon & Schuster, Inc.
1230 Avenue of the Americas, New York, NY 10020

STAR TREK is a Registered Trademark of Paramount Pictures.

This book is published by Pocket Books, a division of Simon & Schuster, Inc., under exclusive license from Paramount Pictures.

ISBN: 0-7434-4598-8

First Pocket Books printing July 2002

10 9 8 7 6 5 4 3 2 1

POCKET and colophon are registered trademarks of Simon & Schuster, Inc.

For information regarding special discounts for bulk purchases, please contact Simon & Schuster Special Sales at 1-800-456-6798 or business@simonandschuster.com

Printed in the U.S.A.

For Natasha and Tania

Acknowledgments

I would like to thank Gene Roddenberry and all the producers, writers, actors, artists, and other creative people who have brought the Klingons to life. This book owes particular debts to two people. First is *Star Trek* writer and producer Ronald D. Moore, who has told so many of the wonderful Klingon tales. Second is Marc Okrand, who created the Klingon language and who has illuminated so much of Klingon culture and history. His three books, *The Klingon Dictionary*, *The Klingon Way*, and *Klingon for the Galactic Traveler*, are great fun and were indispensable to me as I worked on this tale. Thanks also to the Klingon Language Institute for their very helpful translation work.

Thanks to my editor, John Ordover, who had the idea for this cool, new take on *The Original Series* and for his many indulgences.

Special thanks are in order to Michael Okuda, who provided much technical assistance with great patience and quickly answered all emails that began with "Is it possible to..." or "What would happen if..." Many of the good parts of this book and in the two that will follow came from Mike's advice and suggestions.

I also want to thank Michael and his wife, Denise Okuda, for their incredible books *The Star Trek Encyclopedia* and *The Star Trek Chronology*. They are won-

ACKNOWLEDGMENTS

derful reference books, and I wonder how *Star Trek* writers and fans ever got along without them. The Okudas have made the *Star Trek* universe richer and more fun for all who work and play there—and especially for those fortunate enough to do both. *Star Trek* would not be the same without them. I also thank them for their friendship and support.

Thanks to my wife, Paullina, for her thoughtful comments and suggestions. And thanks to my children, Natasha, Misha, Kevie, and Tania, for their great patience.

bortaS nIvqu' 'oH bortaS'e'

("Revenge is the best revenge.")

—KLINGON PROVERB

Prologue

STARBASE 26
FEDERATION SPACE

THE KLINGON TENSED as he felt a hand grasp his shoulder. His instincts were to turn sharply and meet the challenge, but he forced himself to endure the insult and relax.

Finally, Kell turned slowly to see an Earther next to him. The Klingon almost shouted out the traditional Klingon greeting, "What do you want?", yet his training held. Instead, he made a grimace—*no, a smile,* he corrected himself mentally.

Willing himself to relax, Kell looked at the Earther next to him—or the human, as they called themselves. He was young and wearing the red tunic and ship's scr vices insignia of a security officer, just as the Klingon wore himself. The Earther's face had the peculiar combination of eagerness and softness that Kell had seen in some of the other new security personnel he had seen.

"Hey, relax," the Earther said. "I hcar that the captain rarely eats new recruits anymore."

Kell started. In the Empire he had heard many tales about that particular Earther, but...

Then the Earther beside him cackled—*no, laughed,* the Klingon corrected himself, realizing that the man was joking.

"Seriously," the Earther said. "You look like you're preparing to walk into an ion storm."

The Klingon smiled again and forced the tension from his shoulders, adopting the Earther slouch he had perfected in his training.

"You're right," the Klingon said noncommittally.

"On the other hand, everybody's a little nervous." The Earther gestured around the transporter room to the other four new security officers. "Did you hear what happened to the guys we're replacing?" the Earther asked, lowering his voice and leaning closer to the Klingon.

Kell cringed inside. No Klingon warrior would whisper, hiding his words from others nearby. Yet for this cowardly and weak Earther, such behavior was second nature.

Forcing his revulsion down, he simply said, "No."

Lowering his voice even further, the Earther said, "Well, I heard that some sort of a shapeshifting creature sucked their brains out *through* their faces. Of course, that's not what the official log says, but..." Then the Earther shrugged, which Kell recognized as a gesture of, among other things, ignorance. "You can't believe everything you read in an official log—Federation security, you know. The creature tried to do the same thing to the captain," he added.

Now the Klingon was interested. "What happened?" he asked.

"No one knows, but the captain was the only one to survive meeting it face-to-face. Somehow the creature died during the attack. They say the captain killed it with his bare hands. Of course, that's not what the official log says, but…"

"You can't believe everything you read in an official log," the Klingon said seriously. The Earther smiled and then laughed again, swatting Kell on the shoulder once more. It took all of the Klingon's self-control not to kill him.

"You're all right," the Earther said, holding out his hand. "I'm Luis Benitez."

The Klingon shook the Earther's hand, which felt cold to his touch.

"I'm Jon Anderson," Kell said, flinching inwardly at the lie. It was not the first he told on this mission and he knew it would not be the last.

"I'm from Earth," Benitez offered.

"I'm from Sachem IV," Kell said. He was glad to see no recognition in the Earther's eyes. "It's a small agricultural colony." That much was true. The real Jon Anderson had been targeted for replacement by the Klingon Defense Force because he was from an out-of-the-way Federation colony that had produced no other Starfleet personnel. That reduced the chance that the Klingon now wearing Anderson's face and carrying his identity would run into anyone from Anderson's "home."

Kell was spared further interaction with the human when two starbase officers walked into the transporter room. One he recognized as a junior administrator in a gold tunic that the Klingon had seen when he arrived. The other wore a red tunic and stood behind the transporter console.

The junior administrator spoke. "Please take your positions on the transporter pad." As the new security officers stepped up to the platform, he said, "I hope you realize how lucky you are. Many of us would gladly give up two steps in rank to go where you are going."

Kell stood at attention like the other recruits and faced the officer, who nodded once at them. "Good luck on the *U.S.S. Enterprise.*" Then the Klingon felt the transporter beam take him.

Chapter One

THE BEAM DEPOSITED THEM in another, similar but smaller, transporter room. This one had a single operator and an officer wearing a red tunic with a ship's services insignia. By the single gold braids on the man's cuffs, Kell could tell that he was a lieutenant. For a long moment the Earther just stared at them. Then he spoke.

"Welcome to the *U.S.S. Enterprise.* I'm your section chief or squad leader, Lieutenant Sam Fuller. I've reviewed your records. You all have excelled in your training—otherwise you wouldn't be serving on this ship under Captain James T. Kirk. Now before we go any further, I have a simple question for you. How many old Starfleet security officers does it take to fire a phaser?"

The Klingon heard the light titter of Earther laughter around him from the other recruits, but he noted that Sam Fuller didn't smile. He merely looked at them expectantly.

"Anyone?" Fuller asked when the group quieted down.

5

Finally, a very earnest-looking Earther female next to him spoke up. "Just one, sir. Starfleet security officers of any age do not require assistance for such a simple task."

Fuller considered her for a moment, then shook his head. "No, that's not it, but I will spare you further guessing. It's a trick question, because—and listen very carefully—*there are no* old *Starfleet security officers.*"

More laughter from the group. Kell was so surprised that he nearly joined them—there was a very similar Klingon proverb about *old warriors.*

"I'm glad you're amused, but the truth is that security has the highest mortality rate in the service—higher even than careless starship captains. Of course, there are compensations. We also have the lowest pay." Then, for the first time, Sam Fuller smiled.

"You remember the words of the great Zefram Cochrane, Starfleet's mission is 'to boldly go where no man has gone before.' Well, going boldly is a risky business. It is the business of Starfleet and the Federation that we serve. Getting a whole bunch of different races together is risky. Meeting new races is risky. And protecting the ideals of the Federation and the lives of its members is risky. But as our captain says, risk *is* our business. It is the business of Starfleet and the Federation we serve. No branch of the service takes greater risks or pays a higher price than Starfleet security. And, as far as I'm concerned, there is no higher calling in Starfleet or the Federation. Now, does that make any of you nervous?" Sam asked.

"No, sir," the Klingon and the group replied in unison.

"Well, it should, but here in security we are not very high on common sense, so you'll fit right in. Now, as your first duty officer, it is *my* duty to swear you in as members of Starfleet and the crew of the *U.S.S. Enterprise.* Before I do, I'll offer you one last opportunity to step back on the transporter pad and go back to Earth, your colony, your space station, or wherever it is that you call home. You can take your expensive Starfleet training and find any number of nice safe posts in the private sector. Bear in mind there is no shame in doing so; in fact, you would be showing remarkable intelligence and foresight."

He paused for a moment, looking over the group. "Anyone?"

Kell looked around. None of the recruits motioned to go. That surprised him in a race renowned for its cowardice. He could only surmise that there were dire consequences for the ones that actually tried. No doubt they and their families would suffer.

"Since it looks like you are all going to stay, I will ask you to repeat after me: I solemnly swear to uphold the regulations of Starfleet Command as well as the laws of the United Federation of Planets, to become ambassadors of peace and goodwill, to represent the highest ideals of peace and brotherhood, to protect and serve the Federation and its member worlds, to serve the interests of peace, to respect the Prime Directive, and to offer aid to any and all beings that request it."

The Klingon repeated the oath with the group, though it burned his blood to do so. For him, taking an oath falsely—even an Earther oath—was a compromise of his honor that he shuddered to make. As Fuller spoke, Kell hated the weak and treacherous Earthers even more for forcing him and the Klingon Empire into this position.

When the oath was finished, he stood in silence with the others.

"Congratulations and welcome aboard," Fuller said.

At that moment, the doors to the transporter room opened and two Earthers stepped in. One was wearing a red tunic and the other command gold. Kell recognized that one immediately: it was Captain James T. Kirk. A dozen thoughts ran through the Klingon's head at once—he had heard many tales in his Klingon Intelligence training of Kirk's treachery, his cowardice, his deceit—but those thoughts were interrupted when Fuller snapped to attention himself and said, "Captain on deck."

The Earther was smaller than Kell had expected, only slightly taller than Kell himself.

Kirk casually put a hand on Fuller's shoulder. "At ease, Sam," he said. Kell had been surprised when his fellow recruit, Luis Benitez, had done the same to him. Such contact was unusual for Klingons, unless it was a prelude to a fight. And for a captain of a ship to behave so familiarly with someone so far below him in rank was unthinkable.

"Recruits, I present Captain James T. Kirk and Security Chief Giotto," Fuller said.

"Scared any of them off, Sam?" Kirk said with what Kell recognized as humor in his voice.

"Not yet, Captain, but I will keep at it," Sam said.

"I'm sure you will," Kirk replied. Then he turned to the recruits. "Welcome to the *Enterprise*. I look forward to getting to know each of you in turn. For now, I'll trust you to Lieutenant Fuller's capable hands."

Then, with a nod, the captain left the room with Giotto next to him.

"At ease," Fuller said, and the Klingon allowed himself to relax for the first time, or at least to give the appearance of relaxing. His heart was pounding in his chest from his close encounter with Captain James T. Kirk. Though he knew that all of the tales about Kirk could not be true, he was just as certain that he had just been in the presence of one of the greatest enemies of the Klingon Empire.

"Now, for the next six weeks of your orientation, as your section chief I will be responsible for each of you. You will train together, eat together, and serve together. I will not accept anything less than your best at all times, and I expect you to never do anything that will embarrass your captain, this ship, or its history."

With that Fuller took the group on a short tour of the vessel, stopping first at engineering, which the Klingon was amazed that personnel not directly responsible for ship's systems were still allowed to see. No doubt the lax security was an example of the bizarre combination of arrogance and weakness that defined Earthers as he understood them.

Then they saw the enormous hangar bay and something called an arboretum—a strange place where the Earthers kept plants, *intentionally.* There was also a large room the Earthers allocated to what they called *recreation.*

Then, in the upper section of the ship, he saw sickbay, where injured and sick Earthers convalesced in weakness instead of simply dying with honor as Klingons did.

"We can't see the bridge," Fuller said. *Finally,* the Klingon thought, *the Earthers show some sense.*

"The bridge is restricted to officers on duty," Fuller continued. "But I'll see that each of you spends at least one shift there in the next few weeks."

Impossible, Kell thought. *Giving access to the ship's core systems and personnel to new recruits—one of whom is a Klingon living under their noses. The Federation will deserve their fate when they fall to the Empire.*

Still, Kell was amazed at the scale of the ship. He had toured a decommissioned Klingon cruiser and had seen nothing near the same amount of open space. Granted, the Klingon ship was about three-quarters the length of the starship and, thus, was half the internal volume—all while maintaining a larger crew.

On the Federation vessel, everything he saw, from crew's quarters, to storage areas, to corridors, to science labs—which would never have had such a prominent place on a Klingon vessel—was much larger than anything he had seen on a Klingon warship. Of course, he reminded himself, the Federation maintained that their vessels were not warships, but *exploratory* vessels.

That notion, he knew, was at the heart of the Federation's greatest deception: It called its own gross imperialism *exploration*. Meanwhile, every year the Federation annexed world after world, becoming a greater and greater threat to the Klingon Empire. Still, they seemed to take great care to maintain the deception of scientific study and exploration—even among only themselves, going so far as to allocating large areas to sensors and scientific equipment.

Finally, the tour was ended and Fuller turned to the recruits. "You'll have plenty of time to further explore the ship in the next few weeks. Since you have your room assignments, your first test of your knowledge of the *Enterprise* will be to find your cabin. Dismissed."

"What room are you in?" Luis Benitez asked the Klingon.

Before he could answer, another voice called out, "Jon Anderson." Kell had been trained to respond immediately to his Earther name and turned to see a red-shirted officer approach him. "I need to speak to you, Anderson," the man said.

"I'll catch up with you later," Benitez said, turning away.

Up close he saw that the man was a security officer, tall with yellow-colored hair—blond, the Earthers called it, though the Klingon people didn't have an equivalent shade or even a word for it.

The Earther officer smiled at him. "I'm Ethan Matthews, I need a moment with you," he said, leading Kell away from the others.

The Klingon barely had time to wonder if he had been found out when the Earther turned to him, instantly serious and said, *"betleH 'etlh,"* or The Blade of the Bat'leth.

Kell was so surprised to hear his native language spoken on this Federation ship that he started in surprise. The incongruity of hearing it spoken by an Earther—*no, not an Earther,* he corrected himself. *A Klingon and an Infiltrator like me.*

We are betleH 'etlh. *And like that honored blade we will weaken our foe with a thousand cuts before the point of the weapon, the great Klingon fleet, delivers the killing blow.*

The Infiltrator who now called himself Matthews noted the recognition on the Klingon's face. *"Yes, we share the same warrior blood behind these soft and hated faces,"* Matthews said in Klingon. "Come with me," he said, leading Matthews into an empty cargo room.

"I did not know there would be another on board already. Are there still more?" Kell asked, glad for the opportunity to speak Klingon.

"We must continue in their weakling *English,*" Matthews said in the Earther tongue, nearly spitting out the word. "I could not resist when I saw you, but they are not as stupid as they look and we do not want to raise questions. It is only us, brother. But I do not think we will need any assistance to fulfill our mission."

"You have our orders?" the Klingon asked, then he

looked around nervously. "Is it safe to speak openly here?"

Matthews grinned a surprisingly human-looking grin. "They may not be as stupid as they look but they are just as soft and careless as they seem. There is no surveillance of the crew."

Kell could not contain his surprise. "I had heard that might be true in our training, but I thought perhaps just officers escaped..."

"It is true for all. The Earthers seem determined to aid in their own destruction," Matthews said.

"Our orders then?" the Klingon asked.

"Our orders are clear and the task will be painfully simple: We are to kill Captain James T. Kirk."

"But his personal guards?" Kell asked.

"*We* are his personal guards," replied Matthews. "I have been here two months and I already have the next landing-party rotation with the captain."

"I will be pleased to hear it is done, but I regret that I will not be able to share in the glory of that deed," the Klingon said.

Matthews smiled. "There will be many glorious opportunities for both of us, do no worry. And it is pitifully easy to earn their trust. For now, just go to your room and complete your training. We will speak again."

Kell nodded and followed Matthews out the door. They entered the corridor a few steps behind two technicians in red overalls. Matthew laughed and put a hand on the Klingon's shoulder.

"I'll see you later," Matthews said with a perfect imitation of Earther good humor in his voice.

Kell did his best to mimic the tone. "Yes, later," he said, and headed for the turbolift.

* * *

The Klingon entered his quarters and saw that no one else was inside, though there was a Starfleet duffel bag on one of the room's two beds. Once again, Kell marveled at the size of the space given to two of the newest and lowest-ranking crew members on the ship. He wondered how many officers on Klingon vessels could boast accommodations like this. Then he reminded himself that it was just this kind of excess that made the Federation cowards as soft as they were.

Kell put his duffel bag on the empty bed and unpacked the "personal items" given to him by Klingon command. There were civilian clothes that he assumed had been owned by the real Jon Anderson. These, he placed in a *dresser* he found for storage.

On a shelf behind his bed, he placed Anderson's few books, a collection which included a copy of a title that the Klingon had already read: *The Starfleet Survival Guide*. Klingon Intelligence had secured a copy. Incredibly, no raid or covert operation was required to acquire it. The remarkably careless humans sold the book to the public. Any Klingon trader was able to simply purchase it in virtually any Federation world or base.

On top of the dresser, Kell placed photographs of Jon Anderson's mother, an older brother, and a father, now deceased.

Anderson's family actually closely mimicked the Klingon's own family, a mother, an older brother, and a father, who was dead. The similarity was not accidental; it kept him from betraying himself with a careless mention of his family.

But as far as Kell was concerned, the differences between his family and Jon Anderson's were far greater than the similarities. While Anderson's father and brother were merchant officers on cargo ships, his own father and brother were warriors who served with honor in the Klingon Defense Force. And his father had not died in a simple accident like Anderson's—the Klingon's father had died fighting Starfleet cowards twenty-five years before in the Battle of Donatu V.

A high-pitched three-note whistle sounded in the room and a female voice came over the intercom. "Ensign Jon Anderson to the briefing room. Captain Kirk is waiting for you." The message repeated one time and went silent.

Kell's blood went cold. In an instant, he saw his dreams of revenge disappear. In that instant he knew the Starfleet cowards were not as stupid as they looked. *How could they be?* the Klingon joke went.

Perhaps there was surveillance of the crew, and he and the Infiltrator called Matthews had betrayed themselves in their brief discussion.

There was nothing to be done now, he realized, but accept his fate with honor. And perhaps before he died he would be able to strike a blow for the Empire, as he had no doubt that his father or brother would do.

The Klingon straightened his back and exited the room. He took the turbolift to the briefing room's level and found it with minimum difficulty. He paused for a moment outside the door. Captain Kirk was inside and with him—Kell was sure—were a group of guards. Perhaps Matthews was there already, in custody. From what he had heard about Kirk, the Klingon was sure that the captain would perform his own interrogations. *So be it,* he thought. *Perhaps the Earther will get careless and give me an opportunity to fulfill my mission.*

Steeling himself, Kell stepped in front of the door, which opened automatically. Without looking, he stepped inside. What he saw in the room surprised him more than a room full of wild *targs*. Kirk *was* in the room, and he appeared to be alone. Most astonishing, he was facing *away* from the door, studying a data padd.

For a moment, the surprise of seeing the captain with his back to a door outweighed all other thoughts. How foolish and trusting the Earthers were. No Klingon commander would turn his back on a door, even if only his crew was on the other side—*especially* if his crew was on the other side.

The captain gave him a quick glance and said, "One moment, crewman," then went back to his padd.

That gave the Klingon a moment to wonder where the guards and interrogation devices were. And why was the captain so relaxed? How often did he learned that a member of his crew was a Klingon agent?

Kell remembered that the recruit called Benitez had said the captain had used his bare hands to kill a brain-devouring creature that had killed a number of security officers. Perhaps, in his arrogance, Kirk thought he was invulnerable. That thought reminded the Klingon that Kirk was in fact vulnerable, right now. He had his back to Kell. Was it a trick? Was the captain baiting him? Goading him? Showing his contempt for the Empire by dismissing him as a threat?

But perhaps the Klingon could land a blow; he had studied enough Earther anatomy during his training to know that a single, strong blow to the back of the neck could be fatal. But that would mean striking him in the back. Many Klingons would not hesitate, he knew. But his father had been a follower of Kahless the Unforgettable and his mother had instilled Kahless's teachings into her two sons. "A battle should be face-to-face. Anything less is an insult to a Klingon's own honor."

That thought kept him from seizing his chance, and then as quickly as it came the chance was gone. The captain put down the padd and turned to face him. "Come in, crewman," Kirk said, gesturing to a seat across from his own. "Have a seat."

When the Klingon hesitated, Kirk said, "That's an order," and smiled.

He's toying with me, Kell thought as he took the offered seat. He set his face, determined not to give the Earther the satisfaction of seeing him squirm.

"I think you have set a record," Kirk said.

"Sir?" the Klingon replied, maintaining the charade.

"I don't think that any member of this crew has managed to disrupt the ship's business to the extent you have after only half an hour on board," Kirk said evenly.

"I do not know what you mean," Kell said. It was a lie, but a lie that was part of his training. Still, he felt a pang at the dishonesty; after all, Kahless had once fought his brother for twelve days because his brother had lied and brought dishonor to his family.

"But to be fair," Kirk said, "the disruption began before you even arrived."

So that was it. Kirk and Starfleet had known about him and the Infiltrator program before he had even arrived. He knew he had very little time now. He and Kirk were still alone. There was a chance to kill him in an honest and honorable single combat—if such a fight was possible with an Earther. It was what his father or brother would do, he knew.

Then again, his father and brother had brought honor to his family by becoming warriors, while he had been rejected by the Klingon Defense Force and had been assigned to *intelligence* work. Until he had the opportunity to volunteer for the Infiltrator program, he had thought he would languish in his encryption/decryption post for the rest of his life without ever doing anything to avenge his father or join his brother in serving the Empire in its battle against its enemies.

"Two weeks ago, to be exact. That was when the disruption began," Kirk said.

Kell noted again that he was slightly shorter and more slender than the captain. His relatively small size was one of the things that kept him from being a warrior. For years he had cursed his body. But his size had made him a candidate for the Infiltrator program. And now he was face-to-face with Kirk and in a position to rid the Empire of its hated foe—something no proper warrior had been able to do so far.

Perhaps Kirk was bigger and had some hidden advantages, but in a moment he would know what it was like to face someone with a Klingon warrior's blood.

Despite the coming battle, Kirk kept his tone neutral, perhaps even friendly. "Does the name Gabrielle Anderson have any meaning to you?" he asked.

"What?" the Klingon asked, dumfounded for a moment.

"Gabrielle Anderson, you *do* know her," Kirk said.

"Why, she's…she's…" Kell said, trying to figure out Kirk's game.

"She's your mother," Kirk finished for him.

"I don't—" the Klingon began, but Kirk cut him off.

"I know her name because I have received no less than twenty messages from her in the last two weeks. It seems you have not contacted her in four months and she is convinced that Starfleet has kidnapped her son."

"I don't understand," Kell said. Then he did: The real Jon Anderson's mother was contacting the captain asking about her son.

"Then I will make it very clear for you. You have not written to your mother in four months. As a result she's been sending regular subspace messages to me urging me to make sure you contact her when you arrive. I make it a rule not to get involved in my crew's family situations. However, in this case I am talking with you so you can take the appropriate action necessary to insure that the captain of this ship can keep his messages restricted to ship's business."

Kell stared at Kirk, for a moment too surprised to respond.

"In other words, write your mother, that's an order," Kirk said with what might have been a smile on his face. "Is that clear?"

"Yes, sir" was the Klingon's muttered reply.

Then the door opened and an officer wearing a red uniform entered the room.

"Captain," the officer said.

"Scotty," Kirk replied, then turned his attention back to Kell. "That will be all, crewman, you are dismissed."

The Klingon got up from his seat and headed for the door as another officer entered the briefing room.

Chapter Two

DR. McCOY WAS THE LAST of the department heads to arrive. Kirk smiled inwardly. He supposed it was the good doctor's rebellion against meetings of any sort. Normally, Kirk would have ribbed him about it, but not today. This meeting was too serious and included all the security section chiefs as well as the department heads.

"I have just received a level-five security alert from Starfleet Command. For now the details will remain restricted to department heads and security section chiefs," Kirk said.

"So we have a serious Federation security situation that we have to keep *secret,* Captain?" Dr. McCoy asked.

"Complaint, Bones?" Kirk asked.

"Just an observation, sir," the doctor replied.

Kirk continued, "As you all know, twenty-five years ago Starfleet forces fought the Klingon fleet to a standstill at the Battle of Donatu V. The outcome of that battle was inconclusive, and there have been no conflicts as serious since then. Now Starfleet Intelligence has reason to believe that the Klingons are planning a major offensive."

The captain turned to his Vulcan first officer, who was seated at his customary place in front of the computer console at the captain's right.

"Mr. Spock," Kirk said.

The Vulcan brought up a graphic of the Donatu system on the viewscreen on the wall.

"Since the battle, some in Starfleet have maintained that another major confrontation with the Klingon Empire was inevitable," Spock said.

"Command knows what the Klingons are thinking?" McCoy said.

"While Starfleet Intelligence can only conjecture about the Klingons' state of mind, there is no doubt as to what they are doing." Spock tapped the console and brought up a star map of Klingon space. He walked over to the viewscreen. "And what they are doing is executing a massive military buildup."

"Long-range sensor scans reveal large energy readings here and here," he said, pointing to two systems near the Klingon homeworld of Kronos. "Detailed analysis suggests they are two new facilities to build warships. Starfleet Intelligence has also detected several large-scale maneuvers involving a significant proportion of the Klingon fleet."

"War games?" McCoy asked.

"More like training," Security Chief Giotto said.

"Precisely," Spock said. "Training for a large-scale conflict involving virtually the entire Klingon fleet."

"In other words, war, gentlemen. War with the Federation," Kirk said.

Kirk saw that the faces around the briefing room table were troubled. He knew how they felt.

"How long?" McCoy asked.

"Within the year, but not likely to come in the next six months, given the ongoing nature of the construction program," Spock replied.

"The *Enterprise* will be ready, Captain, but will Starfleet?" Scotty asked.

"Starfleet is marshaling its resources as Federation diplomats work to improve relations with the Klingons. If the diplomats do their jobs, the conflict will never happen."

"And what do we do if they don't?" Lieutenant Uhura asked.

"For the moment," Kirk replied, "we are to remain alert and to remain close to the border between Federation and Klingon space. For now, Scotty, Starfleet is suspending upgrades that will take major systems offline for more than twenty-four hours. Lieutenant Uhura, your department will work with Starfleet Intelligence's encryption department to help intercept and review messages from within the Empire. Mr. Giotto and security section chiefs, your personnel are to maintain a constant state of readiness. And we are all to be on alert for unusual lapses in security. There have been reports of unprecedented breaches: acts of sabotage, codes being compromised, and the disappearance of Starfleet personnel. None of these have been definitively traced back to the Klingon Empire, but Starfleet doesn't seem to believe in coincidences."

"Aye," Scotty said. "Tha' sounds wise."

Kirk scanned the room to see if there were any questions. Section Chief Sam Fuller spoke up. "As you know, Captain, my father served during the Battle of Donatu V, sir." Kirk nodded. Sam's father had also served with Kirk on the *Farragut*. He had heard stories about the battle from Sam Fuller, Sr. "What I'm saying is, if it happens, it's going to be bad. How soon before we can tell our people what we're up against and what might be coming?"

"I don't have an answer for you, Sam. For now, Starfleet has ordered that this information remain classified. I don't know when that will change, but the quieter we keep this situation, the more maneuvering room the diplomatic corps will have."

Kirk scanned the room one final time. "Dismissed," he said, then added, "Mr. Spock, Dr. McCoy, please stay behind."

Kirk watched as the others filed out.

"This could get bad, Jim," McCoy said, when the three men were alone. "And it looks like there isn't much we can do."

"We hope for the best, even as we prepare for the worst," Kirk said, but the doctor was echoing the captain's own frustrations. Just weeks ago, the Federation was threatened by a Romulan incursion into Federation space. The *Enterprise* happened to be there and was able to stop them. The single Romulan vessel, which had been testing Federation defenses, had been destroyed. They had won a battle that prevented a war.

This time, if the Klingons really launched an all-out invasion, the combined might of the *Enterprise* and the other ships in the fleet *might* be able to repel the Klingons.

Then again, they might not.

The doctor was watching the captain closely. He raised an eyebrow and spoke Kirk's next thoughts aloud. "I hate to trust the future of the Federation to a bunch of diplomats."

Kirk looked to Mr. Spock. "I have to agree with the

doctor," the Vulcan said. "The level of military buildup and mobilization we are seeing in the Klingon Empire shows a strong commitment to their plans. And in the best of circumstances, even simple matters of diplomacy with the Empire have proven difficult. I see the situation as very grave."

That was it, Kirk thought. The situation was dire, so much so that even Dr. McCoy and Mr. Spock were in agreement about that fact.

The Klingon returned to his quarters to find the Earther Luis Benitez inside, lying on one of the beds. Kell's surprise nearly overcame his training, and he barely kept himself from calling out in Klingon. He chided himself for that. To survive a meeting with Kirk, only to reveal himself to this recruit.

He held himself for a moment, remembered the proper Earther response, and said, "What are you doing here?"

Luis smiled and said, "I live here. I could ask you the same question, you know."

Of course, the Klingon thought, *he is my… roommate.*

"How is that for a coincidence? I'm glad, though. I was worried about who I might get stuck with…you never know," Benitez said.

"I was worried as well," Kell said truthfully.

Benitez sat up, "You're still a little stiff, but we can work on that. You're on the *Enterprise,* you've made it. The hard part was getting here."

The Klingon sat down on his own bed. He did not have to feign his exhaustion. He had not slept the previous two nights in anticipation of the beginning of his mission.

"Did you get to look around much?" Benitez asked.

"No," Kell replied. "I had to take care of a...family matter."

"Would you like me to show you around?" Benitez offered. "The closest mess hall was not on the tour."

The Klingon's stomach rumbled at the mention of the mess hall. He had not eaten recently either. Nevertheless, he shook his head and said, "No." Perhaps Benitez would go on without him.

"That's fine, we can stay here and get to know one another."

Kell felt his blood cool but made a smile and said, "Fine." It was not, but he did not see any way out now.

So he lay down on his back on the Earther mattress. It was soft, too soft. He wondered how the Earthers were able to rest on them.

"Have you heard about the invasion?" Benitez asked.

That got the Klingon's attention and he turned his head to Benitez. "No, I have not."

"Yeah," the Earther whispered conspiratorially—a painful reminder of his inferior nature. "We're getting ready for something big. I've been hearing about it for weeks."

"Really, I had not heard anything," Kell said.

"Starfleet is on extra alert. We're getting ready for an attack, a major attack by the..." The Earther lowered his voice even further. "Romulans."

"But didn't the *Enterprise* repel a Romulan attack just weeks ago?" the Klingon asked.

"Yes, that's what the official report says, and I bet it's true, as far as it goes. But supposedly the Romulans have been preparing their revenge. There's some sort of buildup going on in the Empire."

The Klingon marveled at both how right and how misguided the young Earther was. He relaxed and put his head back down on the small mattress—*no, pillow,* he corrected himself.

As Benitez continued, he closed his eyes. "I also heard there was more to the incident with the Romulan ship. A lot more..."

Kell heard the Earther continue, but soon the words ran together and he found himself drifting into sleep.

Chapter Three

STARFLEET COMMAND HEADQUARTERS
SAN FRANCISCO, EARTH

ENSIGN WEST WAITED OUTSIDE Admiral Justman's office. Typical of high-ranking officers, the admiral kept him waiting.

West was impatient to get on with it. A meeting between a fleet admiral and a recent Academy graduate was unusual. And while he had almost gotten used to unusual attention at the Academy, he had never liked it.

This situation threatened to be more than distasteful, however. West was awaiting his first assignment, and he did not want anything interfering with his plans.

"The admiral will see you now," a pleasant-faced older woman said, gesturing to the doors.

Ensign West stepped up to the doors, which slid open, revealing the admiral's office. It was large and had a good view of San Francisco Bay. Otherwise, the office was surprisingly spare. The only decorations were a Starfleet emblem on the dark blue carpeting and a few images of ships and starbase facilities on the walls. A couch and a chair sat around a small table by the large window.

The admiral stood up and smiled at him. Not the polite smile of a high-ranking officer greeting a new ensign, but a warm and friendly smile. West was immediately on his guard and remained at attention in front of the admiral's desk.

The admiral stepped around his desk to approach him. "At ease, Ensign," he said, putting a hand on West's shoulder. "Have a seat." He led West to the couch facing one of the far windows. As West sat, the admiral took a seat in the chair and was now facing him across the low table.

He is giving me the view, West thought. Was the admiral trying to impress him? Why?

"I knew your father, son," the admiral said, and West felt the hairs on the back of his neck bristle. Yet he was sure he had hidden his reaction. He had certainly had enough practice doing it.

"You did, sir?" West responded evenly.

"Yes, and I met you once before, though you were probably too young to remember. In fact, I served with your father. We fought together in the Battle of Axanar, under Captain Garth."

West was not surprised. At the Academy he had met many people who had served with his father.

"Like the rest of the Federation, I owe Captain Garth and your father a great deal. And in your father's case, I wouldn't be here if it weren't for him."

There it is, West thought. The admiral was another one of his father's admirers.

"How is your father?" the admiral asked.

West mustered a polite smile. "He's fine," he said. He assumed it was true. His mother would have told him if his father were not.

The admiral's face set. West waited for what was coming.

"Lieutenant, I know you are wondering why I asked you here and I won't keep you waiting," the admiral said. "A post has opened up here with me at Fleet Command, I would like you to fill it."

Lieutenant West could not contain his surprise. "But, sir, I had requested—"

"I know you requested a post on a starship, but as you know, Lieutenant, only a small percentage of Starfleet Academy graduates ever serve on a starship, let alone for their first assignment," the admiral said.

"Sir, with all due respect, I graduated in the top three percent of my class. It is an unwritten rule that cadets at the top five percent of the class usually are assured—"

"Stop right there, Lieutenant. Please do not cite unwritten rules to me. They are not worth the paper they are not printed on. Starfleet policy guarantees no specific assignment to anyone, regardless of Academy class rank. And I am very well aware of your standing in your graduating class. In fact, according to my report," he continued, pulling out a data padd, "you might have graduated valedictorian if not for some demerits earned in your last year for...well, let's call it a conduct situation stemming from your disagreement with Starfleet policy."

The admiral took a second to read from the padd. "And while I'm on the subject of disagreements with Starfleet, I am particularly interested in your senior thesis that challenged the wisdom of Starfleet's handling of the Battle of Axanar, which many people credit with preserving the Federation.

"I quote: 'While no one can question the brilliant strategy and tactics used in fighting the battle by Captain Garth and those in his command, a close look reveals that the conflict was a direct result of flawed Starfleet policy.' You also take Starfleet to task for not including a single officer in the Fleet Command chain whose primary training is xenosociology or xenoanthropology, your own specialty. According to your thesis, 'the continued deficiencies in this area are irresponsible in the extreme and will only result in more serious conflicts with alien races and greater and greater threats to Federation security.' " The admiral put the padd down. "Your work received a lot of attention in this building, Lieutenant," he said.

Through force of will, West kept his expression neutral and said nothing.

"And not everyone was happy with what you had to say. What was your father's response to the material?" he asked.

"We did not discuss it," West said truthfully. Even by the most broad definition of the word, you could not call their exchange a discussion.

The admiral's face registered surprise, then a flash of understanding.

"Then can I assume that the refusal of my request for a post on a starship is being denied as a form of punishment?" West said, struggling to keep the anger out of his voice.

"I can see how you would think so, but no, it is not a punishment. Just the same, your request is being denied. I need you here," the admiral said.

"With all due respect sir, I am a xenoanthropologist. I am more of a scientist than a command-track officer. My training and abilities would be best put to use on a starship. Surely there are better candidates for—"

The admiral cut him off with a wave. "There are many command-track officers who would give two steps in rank to get posted to my staff, but I don't need them, I need a xenoanthropologist. Anything less would be"— the admiral paused for effect—"irresponsible in the extreme."

Lieutenant West felt all his resolve and anger melt away and he sank back into the couch. He had just been outmaneuvered by an admiral.

After a long moment, he asked, "Do I have a choice, Admiral?"

"No, Lieutenant, you do not. You are now my special adjunct and I am putting you in charge of a highly classified project," the admiral said.

"Sir, I am only cleared for—"

"As of right now, your security clearance is top-level. What I am about to tell you is highly classified." The admiral took a moment to collect himself, then said, "We are facing war with the Klingon Empire in the next six to twelve months."

West had to review the admiral's words in his mind to be sure he had heard them correctly. "Certainly there are tensions," he said finally. "But that is expected of any two powers—"

"We are facing war, Lieutenant. You will see the intelligence reports, and I think you will be satisfied that they are accurate. God knows I wish they weren't."

"Admiral, if we are really facing war, I doubt I would be much help," West said.

"On the contrary, Lieutenant. You are exactly what I need. You see, I am qualified and ready to defend the United Federation of Planets with force, and Starfleet has quite a bit of force to muster. As you know, I served at the Battle of Axanar. I also served at the Battle of Donatu V against the Klingons. I have seen more than my share of fighting. What I need from you is a solution, a way to avoid the fighting. Put your ideas to the test, find me something that the diplomats are missing. And do it before we start down a destructive path, Lieutenant."

"Sir, there are qualified xenostudies personnel in the diplomatic corps," West said.

"Yes, and if they fail to resolve the situation, Starfleet is the last line of defense. I want war to be the absolute last resort," the admiral said, waving off any more comments from West.

"You will have all the resources you need, much more than you could expect on a starship, and the chance to make a real difference. In your thesis you wrote, 'In the future, understanding should become the most important weapon in Starfleet's arsenal.' Well, that future begins today, Lieutenant West. We need some understanding, and we need it fast," the admiral concluded.

West managed a nod.

A few moments later, Yeoman Hatcher escorted a stunned Lieutenant West to his new office.

He sat down at a computer terminal and called up the intelligence reports on the current Klingon situation.

Kell woke with a start to the sound of the red-alert klaxon, followed by a female's voice confirming the "red alert." He was instantly awake and sitting up.

He heard Sam Fuller's voice over the intercom. "Anderson and Benitez, report to the armory."

Instantly on his feet, the Klingon realized that he was already dressed. He had fallen asleep the previous evening and had never awakened. He turned to see his roommate struggling into his uniform. Looking at him, the Earther said groggily, "Where did Fuller tell us to report?"

"The armory, hurry," Kell said. He had a moment to

wonder if the Klingon invasion had begun. Such speculation was useless now. Until he knew for certain, his duty to the Empire lay in maintaining his ruse of being a Starfleet officer.

Benitez was dressed now and hurrying out the door behind the Klingon. "The armory..." the Earther said, looking around. "Wait, it's..."

"This way," the Klingon said, taking the Earther firmly by the arm and leading him to the right. The armory was on their deck—where most of the security department was quartered—and he had taken care to memorize its location. They ran toward it.

The corridor was full of crewmen hurrying to their duty posts. Whatever was happening was serious.

"Intruder alert," the com voice announced and repeated between red-alert klaxons. That told Kell that the alert was probably not the result of a Klingon action. There would have been signs of a battle before a Klingon party could have boarded the starship.

In an odd way, that simplified matters. For now, he was to act like a Starfleet officer. As they approached the armory, Kell realized that his heart was pounding hard in his chest and his face felt flush with the anticipation of the heat of battle.

He wondered if this was what his father felt during his campaigns, or what his brother felt during battle on his battle cruiser. He had only a moment to note the irony that the first time he felt the heat of battle in his blood was when he was wearing the face and uniform of a Federation coward. He wondered how he would explain that to the spirit of his father and of Kahless when he met them in the afterlife at the River of Blood that stood at the entrance of *Sto-Vo-Kor*.

At the entrance to the armory, he saw Matthews exit

with a phaser pistol in hand and race down the corridor. Inside, he saw Fuller, who was barking orders at two of the other new recruits. The recruits left with phasers in hand, and Fuller turned his attention to Benitez and the Klingon. "Anderson, Benitez, listen up. We don't have much time. We have unknown aliens at several locations on board the ship," he said, handing them each a phaser pistol—which Kell recognized as a Phaser II weapon.

"We do not know what kind of weapons they have, but they seem to be resistant to phaser fire, so set your weapons to full. I'm going to take a team to engineering via the turbolift. You are our backup, I want you to take stairs and access ladders in case the lifts fail. With any luck it will be over when you get there. Now let's move." He raced out of the armory with three security officers the Klingon did not recognize behind him.

Kell led Benitez across the corridor to the ladder on the wall. One deck down, they took a main corridor to the rear of the saucer-shaped primary hull. This put them right above the dorsal that connected the primary hull to the engineering hull. The Klingon knew it was nine decks down to engineering. They made two decks quickly on the stairs but became stuck when they saw bodies lying on the stairwell.

Pulling Benitez into the corridor, he shouted, "We'll have to use the ladders!"

The Earther looked unsure for a moment. "They need help," he said, pointing to the four crewmen lying on the stairs and landing below.

"Orders first," Kell said brusquely. "And I suspect they are beyond help."

The Klingon took a moment to orient himself, then headed for an access ladder nearby. On the ladder, Kell realized he could grab the outside of the ladder and slide most of the way down. Benitez followed him.

The next ladder was quicker, but after that he saw that the ladders were not lined up, owing to the roughly diagonal shape of the dorsal that connected the hulls. At each subsequent deck, they had to dash a few meters down the corridor to reach the next ladder.

With his heart now thundering in his chest, the Klingon found the process maddeningly slow. By the time they reached engineering the battle might well be lost. And if it was lost in engineering, the ship would not survive long. And that meant his mission would be over before it had begun.

He allowed himself no regret, because he realized that the Empire would still be served if Kirk and the *Enterprise* were both destroyed.

One more deck to go, and then they would be at engineering. He heard Benitez's labored breathing, then realized he was breathing just as hard.

He landed on the deck and waited for the Earther to do the same. When Benitez was on the ground, he looked at the Klingon and said, "On three?" Kell could see that the Earther was frightened, which he had expected from an Earther. But, like Kell, Benitez had his phaser out and seemed ready to do his duty anyway. That surprised the Klingon.

No doubt the famous Starfleet cowardice would show itself soon enough.

"One," the Earther said.

"Two," Kell said.

"Three," they said together. They simultaneously turned and stepped out of the small alcove that held the ladder. They came out pointing their weapons and found the deck empty, and silent.

It was just a few meters to the doors of engineering. They crossed them quickly, taking positions on opposite sides of the doors.

This time the Klingon did the count silently with his fingers. On three, the two men turned from their protected position and stood in front of the doors, phasers out. The doors slid open.

Once inside, Kell saw that the deck was darkened, with low-power emergency lights providing the only illumination. When his eyes adjusted, he realized they had indeed come too late. He saw two technicians slumped over their consoles, while a security officer lay on the stairs leading up to a second level. Two more security officers lay on the floor near a mesh fence, which stood at the rear of the deck and sealed off a large chamber.

In the dim light, it took the Klingon a moment to place the face of the man on the stair: It was Sam Fuller.

That was when he heard the sound. It came from their right and he instantly realized that the sound was not mechanical. It was also not something a Klingon would make, or an Earther for that matter.

A creature, Kell guessed. Some sort of alien.

Then the sound came louder than before. It was a roar, only louder and more guttural than anything he had ever heard. It made him shudder and he wondered what the creature that made that sound would actually look like. When another roar sounded, closer this time, he realized that he would find out very soon.

Sparing a glance to his Earther roommate, he could see that Benitez's face revealed the same combination of fear and excitement the Klingon felt himself. So Earthers knew something of the heat of battle. Perhaps Benitez would avoid his race's well-known tendency toward cowardice long enough to be of some help.

The creature roared again, this time farther away. Kell placed the sound a few meters to his right, somewhere between the large engineering consoles. There were two consoles, which were spaced less than two meters apart. Each console was perhaps three meters by two and about two high.

Another roar.

"He doesn't sound so tough," Benitez said, flashing a nervous smile.

The Klingon's answering smile came easily and automatically. "We will see," he said. He gestured for Benitez to approach from the left, while he moved to the right.

"Remember, the creature is resistant to phaser fire. Aim for the head," he said.

Benitez nodded and both men moved out.

Kell felt his own fear as a nearly tangible thing in his chest. He remembered Kahless's words: "Only a fool never feels fear. A true warrior uses his fear, then conquers it as he conquers his foe."

Now he knew his fear was keeping him alert to every sound and movement in the room. He could hear and see Benitez moving to the rear of the consoles as he took his own place. If they moved in unison, they could catch the creature between them. Even if it was resistant to phaser fire, he doubted it would stand for long against two sustained blasts.

Reaching the first console, he crept alongside it for just two strides until he was able to peer around the corner, down the accessway that separated it from the other console. There was nothing there. A moment later, he saw Benitez's head peer out from the console on the other side.

The two men nodded to each other and each moved down the length of his console. The Klingon peered around the far corner of his console and again saw nothing but Benitez's face looking back at him.

Listening carefully, he could hear a soft rustle. The creature was close, but that was all he could tell. Was it avoiding them or just playing with them? Had it slipped between the two consoles and was now hiding on the other side?

Kell nodded to Benitez, and the two men inched back along the outside of their respective consoles. The creature was very likely waiting for them at the end.

They would have only one chance to catch it in their phaser fire. Of course, for that to happen both men would have to fire simultaneously and not miss. If either of them missed, the other would likely feel the pulse of a phaser set on full. The result would be the same as a direct hit with a Klingon disruptor: instant disintegration.

Kell knew he was trusting his life to a Federation coward, but he would not shirk from this fight and be guilty of cowardice himself.

So when he came to the end of the console, he called out to Benitez, "On three.

"One.

"Two.

"Three."

The men came around their corners with phasers leveled, ready to fire. The Klingon barely had time to remove his finger from the firing plate when he saw that there was no one there but his Earther partner. From the look on Benitez's face, he saw that the Earther had come equally close to blasting him.

Then both men heard something bolt up the main aisle in the reverse direction from the way they had come. Acting together, they jumped into the center aisle in time to see the creature dart around the far corner to the right.

"He's playing hide-and-go-seek with us," Benitez whispered.

Kell didn't know that Earther game, but gathered enough from the name. He nodded.

"We can't afford to wait any longer or we will end up like them," the Klingon said, gesturing to the fallen crew members on the floor. Then he holstered his weapon and gestured for Benitez to do the same.

"Give me a lift," he said. Benitez immediately complied, lacing his fingers together to make a foothold for the Klingon.

Kell stepped into the Earther's cupped hands as Benitez lifted. The Klingon's hands gripped the top of the console. He began hoisting himself up. Then Benitez lifted again, pushing him up even higher.

Quickly scrambling to the top, Kell grabbed his phaser and leaned his head over the side. He pointed to the far corner of the console where he guessed the creature was now hiding. He raised himself to a crouch on top of the console and stood at the edge, keeping his Earther partner in sight below him.

At the edge of the console, he slowly took a large step onto the next console. For a moment, he stood above the deck, straddling the two consoles. Then he pushed off with his rear foot and leaned forward onto the next console. For a moment, he lost his footing and came down heavily.

The creature must have heard that, he thought. He spared a glance to his right and saw Benitez looking at him with concern. He nodded to the Earther and resumed his crouching position.

Standing at the edge of the console, he saw that when

he stepped onto the other side, he would be within full view of the creature that was, if Kell was correct, hiding just below it.

If he were to succeed, he would have to act immediately. And if he were to survive, Benitez would have to do the same.

The Klingon took two steps to the end of the console, making no effort to conceal himself. He allowed himself a moment to peer down at the creature, which was a large reptilian, with an impressive musculature, a long snout, and large fangs.

Kell didn't hesitate; he treated the creature to a roar of his own. The alien looked up, and as it did, Benitez appeared from around the corner of the console.

Jumping over the creature, the Klingon continued his roar as he spun around and fired his phaser as he descended. He released the phaser's firing plate for a moment as he hit the deck, hard.

Allowing himself only a moment to recover, Kell reaimed the phaser and fired again, this time at the creature's face. The creature reared up, looming over him for a moment, then shuddered when Benitez's phaser beam slammed into its head from the side.

The Klingon's continued fire drove the creature back into the console, where it crumbled into a heap.

Incredibly, it did not disintegrate under the steady barrage of dual phaser fire. It simply lay on the deck.

The two security officers held their fire for a moment, and Benitez moved to Kell's side.

The Klingon prodded the creature with his foot, taking in its reptilian features.

"You were right," the Klingon said to Benitez. "He was not so tough."

Then, suddenly, the room lights came back on and he

heard a strange sound behind him. Kell spun around to see Fuller and the other four "dead" crewmen striking their hands together. *Applauding,* he remembered it was called.

"End simulation," Fuller called out.

The Klingon took his breath in heaving gasps and still felt his heart pounding in his chest and blood heating his face. He stared at Sam Fuller, who approached him with a smile on his face.

Reaching out a hand, Sam patted Kell on the shoulder. Still in the heat of battle, the Klingon flinched and barely held himself from striking back.

It was just a simulation, he thought, forcing himself to relax.

He saw that Benitez was smiling even though he was flushed and breathing hard as he received congratulations from two other crewmen.

"Nicely done, Mr. Anderson, Mr. Benitez," Fuller said.

Making a smile, the Klingon said "Thank you, sir" in unison with his roommate.

Then Kell examined his phaser.

"Modified for training purposes," Fuller explained. "And a good thing too," he added, turning his attention to the "creature," which was struggling to its feet. Without the heat of battle and with the lights on, the Klingon could see that the creature was no more than an Earther in a costume, some sort of rubberized polymer. He could see the seams where the rubber was fitted together. He also noticed that the joints were unnaturally wide with the rubber skin bunching and buckling around them.

The simulated creature pulled up on its own head, which came off after a few tugs to reveal a yellow-headed Earther.

"Are you okay, Lieutenant Kyle?" Fuller asked.

"Just getting a little warm in the suit, sir," Kyle replied.

"Gentlemen, I give you your intruder, Mr. Kyle. But in this suit we call him the Dragon."

Kyle nodded.

"And this," Sam said, pointing to an officer, "is Lieutenant Commander Scott, chief of engineering. He has graciously loaned us both the engine room and Mr. Kyle."

"Well done, lads," Lieutenant Commander Scott said.

"Not the best time we've ever seen," Fuller said, "but pretty close. Most recruits play a bit more cat-and-mouse before they think of heading to the top of the consoles. A nice, coordinated effort, men. Now, get back to your quarters and get cleaned up. I need you to report for your first full day of training in one hour."

Chapter Four

KLINGON BATTLE CRUISER *D'K TAHG*
KLINGON SPACE

JUNIOR WEAPONS OFFICER KAREL shut off the computer terminal in disgust. Still no response from his brother. There were, however, several increasingly frantic messages from their mother. She had not heard from Kell in months.

Karel's messages to Kell's commander in Klingon Intelligence had also gone unanswered. His apprehension grew.

When his brother had failed to get a proper post in the Klingon Defense Force, Karel had been disappointed for him. Yet part of him was relieved. Kell had neither the size nor the native aggression to make a successful warrior. Had he gotten posted to a Klingon warship, Karel had no doubt that his brother would have soon fallen victim to the natural and violent process of promotion and succession aboard ship.

He thought Kell would be safe working in the encryption division of the Klingon Defense Force on Qo'noS. He might die of boredom, but he would live.

Karel did not fear his own death. He stood ready to welcome an honorable end at any moment. Yet he found that he did not wish the same honor for his brother. Karel knew he was being selfish, yet he would not deny the truth. Anything less would shame the memory of his father and would shame Karel in the eyes of Kahless the Unforgettable.

At the moment, honor demanded action as well as truth. His mother was due an explanation of the whereabouts of her son. Karel would find out the truth. He was certain that his brother was safe. But Klingon Intelligence command was absurdly secretive, in a way that Karel found distasteful.

Over a month ago, he had spoken to Gash, the weapons officer and Karel's direct superior. Gash had assured Karel that he would make inquiries, yet weeks had passed with no information.

To speak to anyone higher in the command chain would be a grievous insult to the weapons officer, no less than an accusation of incompetence in dealing with simple matters.

He would have to speak to Gash again.

At the end of his duty cycle, Karel approached the weapons officer, who met him with the traditional Klingon greeting. "What do you want?!" Gash barked.

Karel looked up and kept his eyes steady on his superior officer. Gash was large by Klingon standards and at least half a head taller than Karel, who himself was taller than average.

"I still await news of my brother," Karel said evenly. He dared not falter in his gaze or the set of his body. Gash was a harsh commander and harsher still when he saw weakness.

Recognition flashed in Gash's eyes.

"The *noncombatant* brother who serves in the *intelligence* division," Gash said with undisguised disdain.

Karel refused to be baited.

Yet.

"You said you would make inquiries," Karel responded, spitting out his words.

"I did," Gash spat back. "I also said I would contact you when I had information."

"I have waited long enough," Karel said.

Gash considered him carefully for a moment. "I have no information," he said, but Karel saw something in his eyes that he could not identify at first. Then it was clear: Gash had faltered for an instant because he was lying.

"You will have to wait longer!" Gash shouted, and turned away.

Karel's blood burned.

No true warrior would lie, and Gash had worn the untruth in his eyes. Karel had known that Gash was no follower of Kahless, who taught that a warrior's honor demanded truthfulness.

Karel considered his next move. He was not finished with Gash, but that consideration was secondary. He would deal with his superior soon enough.

For now, he had to learn the truth about his brother. After seeing the lie in Gash's eyes, he was no longer certain that his brother was safe.

Thirty minutes after his first drill on board the *Enterprise,* the Klingon was sitting at a table in a mess hall with Benitez. He had a basic knowledge of Earther foods from his training by Klingon Defense Force Intelligence and had ordered eggs, potatoes, and toast with coffee. He would have preferred an Earther dish that he actually found acceptable, but he knew from his brief time on the starbase that *meat loaf* was not considered appropriate for breakfast. And he could not afford to draw unnecessary attention to himself.

The food was hot, but Kell was put off by the fact that it was not moving. He much preferred live food, with a few exceptions—like *rokeg* blood pie if it was very fresh.

Still, the food was tolerable, but the coffee he could not stomach. He simply found it bitter and unpleasant. Benitez, however, was drinking his second cup with relish.

"I thought we were finished. There we were, the two newest guys on the ship against an alien that had wiped out six seasoned officers in engineering. Then you start screaming. What was that anyway?"

"The creature roared to scare us," Kell said.

"It worked on me," Benitez replied.

"Yes, such sounds can be very disconcerting to an enemy. I simply gave him"—the Klingon searched for the right idiom—"some of his own medicine. Something my instructor taught me."

"Instructor?" Benitez asked.

"My…martial-arts instructor at home," Kell said. In fact, his instructor had been his brother, who had learned the art of *Mok'bara* from their father.

"More than just farming going on back home, huh?" Benitez said.

"At times," the Klingon replied.

"So anyway, you start hooting and leap out of the sky at the creature like Flash Gordon and—"

"Who?" Kell said.

"You know, Flash Gordon, the hero," Benitez said.

The Klingon searched his memory of Earther and

Starfleet heroes. Flash Gordon held no meaning for him.

"You've never heard of Flash Gordon?" Benitez asked.

Kell decided to tell the truth. He saw no other choice. "No," he said. "Is this Flash Gordon from Earth?"

Benitez smiled broadly at that. "Yes, he's from Earth, centuries ago. A great hero, who almost single-handedly repelled an alien invasion, a bunch of them actually."

The Klingon was appalled at the gap in his knowledge of Earth history. If he was able to make a report to command, he would have to alert Klingon Intelligence to investigate this figure. Kell realized that his face must have betrayed some of his concern.

"He's not real, just in stories—you know, comic books and the old-style movies," Benitez said finally. "Boy, you must not have gotten out much at home, what with all the farming and yelling at each other in martial-arts class." Benitez grinned widely.

"We should report to training," the Klingon said.

They went to a multipurpose room on the same deck as their quarters. The room had been set up as a classroom with twelve forward-facing chairs. There were already a few new recruits milling about the room. Two of them Kell recognized as being from the group who had beamed over with him.

Benitez obviously knew them and led the Klingon over. "Hi," Benitez said, and Kell wondered when the Earther had had time to get to know them.

"Hi," the female said. "Didn't we beam over together?" she asked.

"Yes," the Klingon said.

"Leslie Parrish, Philip Becker," said Benitez. "This is Jon Anderson."

They both held out their hands, and Kell shook the female's hand first, then the male's. The Klingon marveled that Benitez had already met and formed a friendly relationship with these people.

"You can call him Flash," Benitez added

"Flash?" Leslie Parrish said, and all three Earthers smiled.

"Why Flash?" Becker asked.

"I just gave him that name. If you saw him in action during the drill you would understand," Benitez said.

Kell noticed that the room was filling up and the recruits were beginning to take their seats.

"We'd better sit down, we'll talk more at lunch," Benitez said, and the four took seats next to one another. The Klingon wondered if he could avoid another meal with his Earther peers. He was worried about the possible complications of social relationships. On the one hand, such relationships might expose him. On the other hand, if he avoided them completely he would draw unwanted attention to himself.

A crewman in a gold shirt with lieutenant's braids on the sleeves entered the room. The Earther was older than the new recruits, but by how much Kell was not sure—he found he had trouble estimating the age of most humans he met.

"I'm Lieutenant Finney, records officer on board the *Enterprise*. And for this training and orientation period I will be your instructor. This is a job I take very seriously and one I have been doing for more than ten years. I taught for years at Starfleet Academy and I have students at almost every level in the service, including the captain of this ship."

A murmur arose from the recruits at that, and the Klingon heard Benitez suck in air in surprise.

"Now, taking my course does not guarantee you command of a starship—nothing can do that—but it does guarantee that you will have a few things to think about next time you go charging off against the unknown."

Then Lieutenant Finney pointed to Becker and said, "You, tell me why we're all out here, why Starfleet does what it does?"

Without blinking, Becker replied, "To boldly go where no man has gone before."

Lieutenant Finney fixed his stare on Becker. "You memorized that very well, but it's only part of the answer. For the whole answer you need to know more about the history of Starfleet and the Federation, and that is what I'm going to teach you."

"Are you sure?" Kirk asked Lieutenant Uhura, leaning over her station on the bridge.

"The message is real, sir," Uhura replied. Then, before he could ask the question, she added, "Whether it is actually from Dr. Korby is something else. I can tell you that it originated from the sector of space that contains the Exo system."

Kirk nodded. Exo III was the location of Korby's last mission five years ago. It was also the site of his disappearance.

"Any red flags in the signal, Lieutenant?" Kirk asked.

"No, sir. It matches standard Starfleet protocol for an automated distress signal. Because it's only a fragment and because we have not received a live response to our own hails, it's impossible to further authenticate it."

"Have Mr. Spock and Dr. McCoy heard the fragment yet?" Kirk asked.

Uhura nodded. "I routed the message immediately and tagged it a priority one. They should—"

She was interrupted by the opening of the turbolift doors and the appearance of both Spock and McCoy.

"Affirmative, sir. It looks like they've heard the message," Uhura said.

"Is it true, Jim? Did we just receive a message from Roger Korby?" McCoy said, excitement in his voice and on his face.

"Well, we received the message you heard, but I'm not convinced it's Korby," Kirk said.

That caused Spock to raise an eyebrow. "Based on what evidence, Captain?" Spock asked.

"Based on my feeling that something doesn't seem right. It's been five years. Exo III is uninhabitable and two expeditions there failed to find Dr. Korby," Kirk said.

"Do you *feel* that this might be an intentional effort to divert the *Enterprise,* Captain? Perhaps a Klingon trick?" Spock asked.

"Sorry, Mr. Spock, even my best hunches are rarely that specific," Kirk said.

Kirk could see tension in Dr. McCoy's face. "Everyone is a little jumpy, but Jim," he said, "if there's even a chance that Korby is alive..."

The captain nodded. The stakes were high. Korby had virtually invented the field of archeological medicine. His work was required reading at Starfleet Academy.

"Bones, I know what finding Dr. Korby would mean, but Exo III would take us away from the Klingon border," Kirk said.

"But we haven't been ordered to patrol the border. All we have is a vague warning that something might happen months from now," McCoy said.

"Spock?" Kirk said.

"The loss of Dr. Korby was a great loss to Federation

science," Spock said. "The *Enterprise* is the only ship in the sector. If they are alive, we do not know how long Korby and his group can survive, especially since the odds against them surviving this long are astronomical."

"Do you think it would be worth the risk, Spock?" Kirk asked.

"Impossible to calculate the risks with so many variables, but I would be inclined to follow our only hard information—Dr. Korby's message."

Kirk studied his first officer and chief medical officer. Both Dr. McCoy and Mr. Spock were in agreement, for the second time in one twenty-four-hour period. That was something. Of course, it made sense. They were both scientists and both had an interest in Korby's field.

Studying the two men, Kirk saw real concern on Dr. McCoy's face, tension and...something else.

"There is something you should know, Captain," the doctor said, hesitating for just a moment. "Nurse Christine Chapel knows Dr. Korby."

"*Knows,* Doctor?" Kirk could see that there was something McCoy wasn't telling him.

"They were engaged when he disappeared," the doctor said.

Kirk heard the sharp intake of Lieutenant Uhura's breath.

First Spock and McCoy in agreement, now this, Kirk thought. Well, he wouldn't hold up science, or the significant personal interest of a member of his crew.

"We'll make for Exo III, but I will not authorize a full-scale search-and-rescue operation without actual contact with Korby's party. Doctor, please prepare sickbay. I'm sure anyone we find will need to spend at least some time there. Mr. Spock, please assign a landing party that will include you, myself, and some security people."

Kirk turned his attention forward, catching the doctor's and Lieutenant Uhura's smiles with his peripheral vision. He only wished he could share their enthusiasm.

"Mr. Sulu, lay in a course for Exo III, warp five," Kirk said.

Chapter Five

LIEUTENANT FINNEY'S CLASS took the whole morning. And as Kell had feared, after class Benitez insisted that the four of them take lunch together. They took a table in the dining room nearest their quarters.

"Flash here is from a farming colony," Benitez offered to the table.

"Sachem IV. It was not a very interesting place," the Klingon added.

"Not very interesting," Parrish said. "Try growing up in a mining colony and living underground."

"I'm from Earth," Becker said. "It's actually pretty interesting." Both Becker and Benitez found that funny and laughed together.

Their laughter was cut short when the intercom came on. "This is the captain," the voice said, and the room fell completely silent. "The *Enterprise* has set a new course for the planet Exo III to effect a rescue mission.

We will arrive in fourteen hours. Duty rosters and landing party assignments have been posted. Kirk out."

Benitez was the first to break the silence, "Rescue mission...I wonder if this is it."

"What?" Becker asked.

"Have you heard the rumors? Something big is going on with..." He lowered his voice. "...the Romulans," Benitez said.

For the rest of the meal, Benitez led the conversation about the possibility of a Romulan invasion. Kell was relieved. It meant he did not have to spin lies about his past or answer any questions that might betray him.

After lunch, they went back to their impromptu classroom in the recreation room for tactical instruction. When they entered the room, an Earther he recognized was standing at the head of the class.

"Sit down, recruits, and hurry, you are all late," Lieutenant Commander Giotto said.

The Klingon quickly took his seat, as did the other officers. One of the recruits raised his hand and said, tentatively, "Excuse me, sir, but I don't think we are late."

"Of course you are," Giotto said.

"But sir, class was scheduled to begin at fourteen hundred. It is just that now," the officer said.

"Yet I was here ten minutes early, ready to teach you. Therefore, class started ten minutes ago, and, thus, you are all late."

Kell could see that the recruit was now indignant. "But, sir, that's not fair."

"Fair!" Giotto said. "Excuse me, where did you get the idea that this job was fair? It's not. Consider this the first thing I have taught you. Now, the fact is that I was early and none of you anticipated that. Some of you might see that as unfair, but the wise ones will see it for what it is: an object lesson of life in Starfleet security. Every day, on starships across the known galaxy, we lose security officers because they failed to anticipate some unforeseen event or circumstance. Mr. Jawer here would say that is not fair, but those officers are still dead.

"Right now, I'm going to give you something you may never get in the field. A second chance. You now know something about me—at least some of the time I am early for class. I suggest you use that knowledge tomorrow. I also suggest that you cultivate your instincts, because I would bet a month's pay that one or more of you had the feeling that they should get here early but disregarded it because you knew that class began at a fixed time. Next time you have a feeling of that sort, do not disregard it. An ability to identify and follow your instincts may mean the difference between a short, tragic career and a long, successful one. Of course, there are many good officers that followed the book and trusted their instincts and died anyway. It may not be fair, class, but it's true.

"Now, to get back to the reason we are all here, strategy and tactics in the field..."

Kell listened with great interest. Since he had been placed in intelligence work by Klingon Defense Force command, he had been allowed no training in combat. It meant his career would be extremely limited, with little chance of advancement and even less respect from the Klingon service.

Two hours later, the class moved together to the gymnasium, where they changed into clothes for physical training. The clothes were loose and comfortable, making movement easy. This, of course, went against the Klingon philosophy of heavy, often binding clothing that made the challenge of physical activity greater.

"Fall in line," Fuller said. "Already today, you have been drilled, you have learned a thing or two from Ben Finney about what we're doing out here, and a bit about how to think on your feet from our commanding officer Security Chief Giotto. Now I'm going to help you master one of the most basic survival skills you will need: self-defense in a hand-to-hand combat situation. I use the term *hand* loosely, because you may one day use these skills against opponents that have tentacles, prehensile tails, or something else they use for up-close fighting. I had one foe who used the power of his mind to disintegrate me."

"Disintegrate you, sir?" Benitez asked.

"I recovered due to the intervention of his parents, who were pretty steamed at him," Fuller said, smiling.

The chief looked at the openmouthed confusion of the assembled recruits and said, "Look up Thasians in the ship's log. Now, before I begin, I will answer the question you are probably already asking yourself: Didn't I cover this in my Starfleet training? The answer is that, yes you did. However, your Starfleet training was the beginning of your training, not the end. The saying goes that Starfleet Academy instruction is the tip of the iceberg, or just ten percent of the training you will receive in your career. The rest you get in the field or in continuing training you receive while on duty.

"Now I need one volunteer for this first exercise," Fuller said, looking at the six recruits in front of him.

Six hands went up, but the Klingon waited the longest before raising his. There was no point in calling attention to himself.

"Excellent. You, Mr. Anderson, step forward."

Kell stepped onto the pad with Sam Fuller, who smiled at him. "You remember your self-defense training? Well, Mr. Anderson, I'm going to charge you and I want you to try a simple throw."

The Klingon reviewed his study of Earther self-defense techniques as taught by Starfleet. Though he had never studied them formally, he had read the data-bank information that was no doubt gained from interrogations of Starfleet officers.

As Fuller charged, he acted automatically. Leaning forward with one hip, he grabbed the section chief and, using the Earther's momentum, tossed Fuller over his hip.

The section chief didn't fall as much as roll back to a standing position.

"Good, Mr. Anderson. A competent execution of a simple movement that will be very effective against most untrained attackers. The problem is that some of the beings you will face will have training, or a natural strength greater than a human's. And in that situation you need the two things that separate the winners and the losers, or the living and the dead, and they are greater speed and a greater sense of balance. Balance and speed can allow a smaller or weaker combatant to defeat a larger or stronger one. Of course, in a situation where two opponents have equal training, but one is bigger, the bigger one will usually crush the smaller one. In those cases, I strongly suggest that you arrange to be the bigger combatant.

"Now, let's try that again, Mr. Anderson. This time, class, I will show you what someone with some speed and a pretty good sense of balance can do against someone without advanced training." Fuller looked at Kell and smiled. "Let's do this again. Try to throw me, but this time I will make it a little harder."

Fuller charged at the Klingon, who tried the same, fairly simple, traditional Earther maneuver. But this time, instead of simply letting himself be thrown, Fuller didn't put the weight into the attack. He lashed out with a fist, but kept his upper body back. Thus, when Kell tried to execute the simple Earther-style throw, Fuller was able to lean back and grab the Klingon by the shoulder. Pulling forward and using the Klingon's own weight, Fuller attempted a counterthrow.

The move was fairly simple. Most opponents would find themselves on the ground a moment later. But Kell was not most opponents and what he did, he did without thinking.

The Klingon allowed himself to be pulled forward, but instead of landing flat on his back, he curled his spine and pulled his section chief down with him. Kell used their combined weight to flip their positions and a fraction of a second later Fuller was on his back, with the Klingon on top of him.

Immediately, Kell realized his mistake and released Fuller, who took the opportunity to slip out from under him. A moment later, both men were on their feet.

The Klingon studied his superior for a moment and wondered what the repercussions of his actions might be. "I am sorry, sir," he said quickly.

"Don't be sorry, Mr. Anderson. You've had some additional training. That's fine. Let's see what you can do."

This time Fuller's attack was neither clumsy nor slow. He threw a closed fist from the center of his body, carefully keeping his weight back. Kell had a split second to wonder if Fuller was angry and was now seeking revenge. Before the thought was finished, his body had responded already by itself; he blocked the blow easily with his forearm and saw Fuller's other hand coming up before the movement was finished.

The Klingon leaned into the second blow, causing Fuller's blow to land behind him. The momentum of the blow put Fuller's weight forward and Kell was able to easily toss the section chief over his hip.

In the moment before Fuller got up, the Klingon wondered if his mission would end right here. If a new recruit on a Klingon vessel had embarrassed a superior in such a way, there would be severe...repercussions.

Even as Kell realized he had just made an enemy out of Sam Fuller, he realized it was unavoidable. The long hours he spent learning the *Mok'bara* had conditioned his responses.

Legends traced *Mok'bara* all the way back to the days of Kahless. Yet, few in the Empire practiced it. *Mok'bara* was a discipline of the mind as well as the body, a tool for achieving focus of spirit as much as fighting. And the standard Klingon Defense Force hand-to-hand combat training was more direct: often crude but usually effective. Though more aggressive, it did not really differ much from Starfleet training.

Kell spared a glance at the recruits behind him. They were looking at him in openmouthed surprise—a reaction that meant the same in both Earther and Klingon cultures.

Silently, Sam Fuller got up. Kell braced himself for another attack—an attack that on a Klingon vessel would likely end with the death of one of the combatants.

But Sam Fuller didn't move against him. Instead, he simply studied the Klingon for a moment.

"You surprised me, Mr. Anderson." Fuller paused for a moment. "And you threw me. Twice. A new recruit has never done that before in all the years I have been doing this."

Fuller turned his body so he could address both Kell and the rest of the officers. "In the words of the Vulcan Surak, 'the best student is the one who takes his instructor's education the most seriously.' It's clear that you have something to teach me, Mr. Anderson, something that will benefit the entire class."

Kell was more surprised than if Fuller had sprouted another head and started performing both parts in the climax of a Klingon opera.

Earthers, the Klingon thought, shaking his head.

"Are you ready to begin my education, Mr. Anderson?" Fuller asked.

"Yes, sir," Kell answered.

The Klingon left the training session physically tired. Fuller and the other recruits had been eager students, and he had taught them some basic *Mok'bara* exercises, some attacks, and some counterattacks.

To his surprise, Fuller seemed to harbor no ill-will to him and had been the best student, making sure he mastered each movement so that he and Kell could demonstrate it to the class and then supervise the other recruits' progress.

Equally incredibly, no one seemed suspicious to see him using a fighting style that they did not recognize. Though Fuller seemed to have an encyclopedic knowledge of Earther and a number of non-Earther martial arts, he had no trouble accepting that the Federation might contain styles he did not know.

Recalling the experience gave the Klingon a lightness of heart that he had not experienced since beginning the mission. He attributed that to the comforting and focused nature of the *Mok'bara.*

But there was another feeling that at first he could not identify, but was something that he had never felt during his time in the intelligence division of the Klingon Defense Force. It was what the Earthers called pride.

Kell had made sure he was the last to leave, telling

Benitez and the others that he would see them later. This gave him a moment to think as he headed back to his quarters. Thus, he was surprised to see Leslie Parrish approach him from behind.

He realized that she must have been waiting for him in the corridor. Immediately, he was on his guard.

"Jon," she said, rushing to catch up to him. Keeping pace with him, she looked at him and smiled. "I was wondering when you were thinking of having dinner. I thought we could have it together."

The Klingon stopped walking. For a moment he was unable to produce anything other than a blank look. The Earther female was undeterred. "We can trade stories to see who had the most boring childhood."

For a human female, he noted, she was attractive. Her skin was darker than most Earthers'. Her hair was dark—almost black—and hung straight, below her shoulders. He reviewed his study of Earther ethnic types and placed her as being partly or wholly Asian. With Earthers you could never be sure, though; there were many ethnic groups with many combinations of the different tribes' blood.

Trying to think of a good reason to say no, Kell was temporarily spared that task when the Klingon Infiltrator posing as an Earther named Matthews arrived.

"Jon," Matthews said. "Do you have a minute?"

Kell nodded to Matthews and then turned to the Earther female. "I can't tonight," he said, then he gestured to Matthews. "We have business."

Leslie's face did not betray any disappointment. "Maybe another time, then," she said as she walked away.

Matthews cast her a dismissive look and said, "Earther females, more trouble than they are worth. Do not bother with them." Then he started walking down the corridor. "Walk with me.

"We are very close," he continued. "I have my landing-party assignment for tomorrow morning. I beam down to Exo III with Captain Kirk. It is a rescue mission for some Earther *scientist.*" He spat the last word out with scorn. "The good news is that the landscape is rugged and there will be few around. The captain will not return from this mission. I regret that we will not share in the glory of the kill, but when he dies the ship will be in chaos. We will be able to do much to serve the Empire then. Until then," Matthews said, and headed into a turbolift.

In his quarters the Klingon who called himself Matthews straightened his uniform.

"Our first landing-party assignment," Matthews's roommate, Rayburn, said with an almost giddy enthusiasm. Rayburn had a habit of stating obvious truths. It was a constant irritation to Matthews. Yet it was not the worst of Rayburn's qualities. Their shared living quarters had given Matthews ample opportunity to study all of Rayburn's Earther failings.

"To be honest, I'm a little nervous," Rayburn said, and put on his own tunic.

There it is, the Klingon thought. *His worst quality of all, his basic Earther cowardice.*

Steeling himself, Matthews forced his mouth into a friendly Earther smile. "I'm sure it will be fine," he said.

"I'm sure you're right," Rayburn said, showing his most idiotic toothy grin.

I'm going to enjoy killing him, Matthews thought as they left the room.

Rayburn kept up his nervous chatter the whole way to the armory. The Klingon had developed the ability to hear Rayburn and even grunt responses without actually listening to what the Earther was saying.

While the Earther spoke, he calculated that, if they beamed down on time, they would be on the planet's surface in one hour. With luck Kirk would be dead and Matthews would be a hero to the Klingon Empire within two hours.

And if the planet was as inhospitable as the computer indicated, it would be easy to arrange an accident for the captain, or possibly the entire landing party. That way, he could return to the ship, with honors, and continue his work.

However, Matthews was also fully prepared to die if it meant killing the captain. The only stipulation his orders made was that he was to make every effort to destroy his own body so that an autopsy would not reveal him as a Klingon.

At the armory, the men were met by their section chief, who said, "You can have your phasers, but we're still waiting for word from Mr. Spock on whether or not you will require full environmental suits."

"Will Mr. Spock be accompanying us?" Matthews asked.

"He's on the roster," Ordover said. "Along with you two, Dr. McCoy, and, of course, the captain."

Matthews cursed his fortune. The first officer would complicate things. Vulcans were not sniveling Earthers, and Spock was half Vulcan. Though Vulcans claimed to be pacifists, Matthews knew that they were physically strong and had a bloody history. And there were many rumors about their special mental abilities. The Klingon was determined not to underestimate Spock.

Even if the Vulcan complicated things, Matthews was sure that he could get the captain before anyone, even

Spock, could stop him. If Matthews was killed in the battle, so be it. In that event, a special message would be sent to the next of kin of the Earther named Matthews. The message would contain some inane communications to Matthews' family as well as a coded message that Klingon Intelligence would decipher. In that message were some very interesting pieces of information he had gathered in his few months aboard the *Enterprise*.

The most interesting was technical information about a device called a neural neutralizer, which acted on the Earther brain directly. He had no doubt it would revolutionize Klingon interrogation techniques.

Section Chief Ordover approached them and said, "There's been a change. I have the new roster here. The captain is beaming down just with a nurse."

The Klingon cursed the captain, cursed Starfleet, and cursed the Federation, trying to keep his face neutral the whole time.

Ordover looked at him, read something in his face, and said, "You'll get your chance. You both will. Mr. Spock asked to have you standing by in the transporter room. If the captain needs you, he'll call. And the good news is that the beam-down site is in underground caves with a comfortable temperature so there will be no need for environmental suits. Before you go, remember: You have both done well in your training. And remember what you've learned, look sharp, and you'll be fine. Since there are no hostiles that we know of, the biggest danger you are likely to face is from the weather if you go outside. Dismissed."

Matthews led the way out the door. Rayburn hurried to follow. "Do you think we will get a chance to—" the Earther began. Matthews did not respond and picked up his pace. "Hey, Matthews," an indignant Rayburn said to his back.

The Klingon made it to the turbolift and got inside before Rayburn could follow. He was simply in no mood for his Earther roommate's prattle. At the transporter room, Mr. Spock waited with a transporter technician named Kyle.

"Sir," Matthews said to Mr. Spock.

"Mr. Matthews, stand by," the Vulcan said.

A moment later, Rayburn entered the room, looking at Matthews with a frustrated and confused expression on his face. Thankfully, he said nothing.

Spock said "Acknowledged" into the intercom and turned to the security men. "Please take your positions on the transporter pad. When you are ready, Mr. Kyle."

Matthews and Rayburn stepped up to the pad, and a moment later the transporter beam took them.

They materialized inside a cave. Matthews looked around and saw they were actually in a network of tunnels. The captain and the nurse were in front of him. Matthews realized that he would have to kill Rayburn first, and then the captain, but that would be easy because Kirk did not have his phaser drawn.

"Rayburn, maintain post here," Kirk said.

"Yes, sir," came the reply.

"Matthews, we'll look for Dr. Korby. You'll accompany us."

"Yes, sir," Matthews said, as an Earther smile nearly touched his lips. He would not have to kill Rayburn first after all. Of course, he would still kill the pathetic Earther, but he would take his time and enjoy it.

Kirk led the nurse along the wall of the cave. Matthews followed. On their left was a deep crevice. The fall would easily kill the captain and the female.

As if to confirm this, the female slipped and the captain had to grab her to keep her from falling.

Pity, Matthews thought. She had almost taken care of one-third of his problem for him. No matter. The female was of little consequence anyway; he doubted she would even struggle once the captain was dead.

The Klingon put his hand on his phaser as they moved forward but then thought better of it. A simple push would do the job. Their deaths would be ruled an accident. He would arrange a similar accident for Rayburn and then return to the ship a hero, the only survivor of the landing party. Perhaps he would get a promotion, which would put him in an even better position to serve the Klingon Empire.

The only possible complication was this missing scientist, who might turn up any moment and act as a witness. His death would be harder to explain.

Just then, a bright light filled the cavern. Matthews instinctively drew his phaser and noted that the captain did the same. In fact, Matthews noted that Kirk was fast, so fast that there was just a blur of motion and then the small Phaser I was in his hand.

Matthews vowed to himself not to underestimate the captain. He took a few steps back and decided to plan his next move carefully as Kirk spoke to someone up ahead.

Suddenly, something reached out and grabbed his hand, the one that held the phaser pistol. Matthews had a moment to realize that that something was a hand, but it was as unyielding as stone. The hand closed, crushing the phaser and Matthews's own hand.

The Klingon could not cry out, because another large, unyielding hand had covered his mouth. Matthews had a moment to look at the large form that had him. It was a humanoid, very tall, without any hair.

The humanoid picked up Matthews by the ruined hand and face as easily as if he were an Earther child's plaything. The figure carried the Klingon for one of its large paces, and held him over the precipice for a moment.

Matthews had a brief instant to look into the creature's eyes. They were not human and not a warrior's eyes. They were very cold.

Then Matthews fell.

Chapter Six

KELL SAT DOWN at the only empty table in the mess hall. A moment later Benitez burst in. He saw the Klingon and approached the table, a look of shock on his face.

"Have you heard?" Benitez asked.

"No," Kell said.

"About the landing party, they lost two security men," Benitez said, causing a chill to run down his spine. "I didn't know them," the human continued. "One was named Rayburn, one was Matthews."

The Klingon's face betrayed his surprise, and he cursed his lack of control.

"Did you know either of them?" Benitez said, reading Kell's reaction with remarkable accuracy.

Steeling himself, the Klingon said, "I met Matthews." He searched for an appropriate, Earther response. "He seemed like a good man."

Benitez sat heavily across from Kell. "I don't understand. It was supposed to be a simple rescue operation, with no hostiles. But the captain came back by himself, saying the men fell into a crevice. An accident, a stupid accident."

Now I have to fulfill our mission, now I must kill the captain myself, Kell thought. That thought did not bother him. Yet he wished he could do it as a Klingon warrior.

It felt wrong. Hiding among Earthers. Not showing his true face, his Klingon face. Kahless had said, "Only an enemy without honor refuses to show himself in battle."

Kell's father had died in battle and he had died well, wearing his true face. Suddenly, the Klingon was certain that when he died, it would be wearing this Earther face.

"The memorial service is tomorrow," Benitez said. "In the recreation room. Lieutenant Fuller suspended training for the morning so we can attend."

The Klingon nodded. He knew such gatherings were important to Earthers. Later in the day, there was an effort made to recover Matthews's and Rayburn's bodies. Kell did not understand that human custom. Without the spirit, the body was an empty shell.

Yet humans believed otherwise and actually risked their lives descending into the crevice with antigrav devices. Ultimately they were unsuccessful, because the men had disappeared into a molten pit deep in the planet's crust. Kell thanked Kahless for that. Any examination of Matthews's body would have revealed that he was a Klingon and no doubt raised suspicions to a dangerous level.

"Come," the Klingon said to his human roommate as he stood. "I suspect Lieutenant Commander Giotto will be early for class today."

"There's no way you could have known, Jim," Dr. McCoy said as he poured a glass of Saurian brandy from a bottle he kept behind his desk in sickbay.

Kirk took McCoy's offered glass and sat down. "But I did know, Bones. I knew something was wrong."

"Come on, Jim, you're the captain of a starship. If you *always* had that feeling, you would be right ninety percent of the time. This is a dangerous business we're in. We all know that. Those two men knew it."

Kirk shook his head. "Men. They were barely out of training, on the ship just months, and on their first landing party. Their *first* mission, Doctor."

McCoy was silent for a moment. "It's bad, Jim. Losing crewmen is one of the worst things that can happen on a starship, but it's not the worst. And while you beat yourself up over what happened down there, think about what you prevented and how many times you've prevented it. If Dr. Korby had succeeded, he would have replaced the entire crew with his androids and you would be looking at four hundred and thirty dead people, not two, and implications for the rest of the galaxy that neither of us wants to think about. Face it, Jim, you won today. Yes, we lost two men, and that hurts—let it hurt—but you won."

Kirk nodded silently. He knew the doctor was right. But he had had a bad feeling about the mission from the beginning, even if—as he had told Spock—intuition was rarely specific.

Say he had not responded to the distress call from Korby. Then another ship surely would have, and probably not a starship. If that machine that called itself Korby had succeeded in overpowering the crew and getting off-planet with the android replication technology…

A dozen scenarios ran through his mind, each one worse than the loss of two crewman. Yet, the simple fact was that those men were dead because he had ordered them down to Exo III.

Despite what the doctor said, and despite the fact that

McCoy was right, Kirk knew he had to do more than mourn his lost people—because there was still a threat to his ship and crew. It wasn't as simple as mere danger, which the doctor had pointed out was the status quo for a starship. This was something new. Something had just felt wrong with the mission to Exo III.

And that something was still out there. He could feel it.

When the yeoman brought him dinner, Lieutenant West barely looked up from his computer terminal. Then the smell hit him. Jambalaya. It was his favorite. Yet somehow, the fact that it had magically appeared did not surprise him.

Walking into the office and finding his computer tapes and some of his personal effects already there had surprised him. Learning that the rest of his things had already been moved to his new quarters had surprised him—as had finding a gold command uniform in his size waiting on a hanger in the office. The fact that these things had been accomplished before he and the admiral had finished their conversation had stunned him.

After that, having his favorite food suddenly appear at the mealtime did not faze him.

"Thank you," he said, and then Yeoman Hatcher smiled and disappeared.

West looked down at his food and realized he was hungry. He ate quickly. After an entire day of sifting through the Starfleet intelligence reports on the Klingon situation, West felt he had barely scratched the surface.

Yet he was sure of one thing: The admiral was right to be worried. The Klingons were preparing for war.

When he was finished, Yeoman Hatcher appeared and took away the plates. He dug back into the reports when his intercom beeped.

"The admiral would like to see you," said the voice.

"I will be right there," West said.

Then the door to West's office slid open.

"That will not be necessary," the admiral said, stepping inside.

"Sir," West said, getting up, immediately standing at attention.

"At ease, and have a seat," the admiral said, taking the seat next to West's desk.

He wants to talk to me and he comes to my *office,* thought West. Protocol said that meetings and discussions were held either in a meeting room or in the office of the highest-ranking officer.

Yet the admiral had come to see him. It was a sign of respect, that the admiral valued him and his work—or at least wanted him to believe so.

The fact that West saw through the maneuver did not change the fact that he was impressed by it. West's primary concern had been that the admiral had created his position to quell critics, and that in the end the admiral and Fleet Command had made up their minds to seriously consider only military options for the Klingon situation.

Perhaps this was a sign that the admiral, at least, was serious about making xenostudies a part of the fleet-level decision-making process.

Then again, perhaps not.

"The office is satisfactory?" the admiral asked.

"Yes, sir, more than satisfactory," West replied.

"You haven't seen your quarters yet, but I'm sure you will find them satisfactory as well," the admiral said.

West was sure that he would.

"You've had some time to look at the reports?" the admiral asked.

"Yes, sir, and as you indicated, the Federation is facing a very real threat. The Klingons' ship- and weapons-building program, their war games, their high state of readiness, they all point to preparation for war."

"See any quick diplomatic solutions for us?" the admiral asked.

"Not yet, sir," West said, immediately before he saw the twinkle in the admiral's eye.

"Well, it's still your first day. There's still tomorrow," the admiral said, allowing a small smile.

West found himself returning the smile. "I'll do my best, sir," West replied, marveling at the admiral's skill. *He's establishing a rapport to gain my trust,* he thought. And again, the fact that West saw through it did not make the maneuver any less effective.

"I'm going to briefing with the diplomatic corps in twenty minutes. I would like you to accompany me," Admiral Justman said.

The surprise registered immediately on West's face, and he realized that his guard was down. "Sir, I am far from ready. I would be more of a liability at this point."

"I'll be the judge of that," the admiral said, getting up. "We'll be making vital, life-and-death decisions with grossly inadequate information. Welcome to Starfleet Command."

West grabbed his data padd and followed the admiral out the door.

West followed the admiral into the large conference room at Starfleet headquarters, a room that up until now he had seen only in his first-year cadet tour of the facility.

There were perhaps a dozen chairs around an oval table that dominated the empty room. A window dominated a whole and very large wall, showing the Golden Gate Bridge.

The admiral took a place at the head of the table, and West took a seat next to him.

"What is the purpose of this meeting, Admiral? And what is my role?" West asked.

"The diplomatic team in charge of the Klingon situation is going to brief us on the progress of diplomatic talks with the Klingons. The problem is that there has been no progress, because there have been no talks," the admiral said.

"Then this will be a short briefing," West said.

"If the diplomatic team has their way, yes. The diplomatic corps does not like Starfleet meddling in their negotiations," the admiral said.

"Then what do we hope to accomplish?" West asked.

"We hope to meddle." The admiral studied West's blank expression.

"As you know, the diplomatic corps does not report to Starfleet Command, though I sometimes wish they did. The work we do together is in the spirit of cooperation. They regularly come to brief us on their progress and we regularly brief them on our status. And since neither party is responsible to the other, we can only hope to influence each other's actions and policies."

"What do we hope to accomplish today?" West asked.

"To give them some help," the admiral said.

"Have they asked for help?" West asked.

"Not at all, and that is how I know they need it," the admiral said, giving another wry smile.

Three more Starfleet Command officers arrived, one commodore and two lieutenant commanders by the braiding on their sleeves. They greeted the admiral silently.

Moments later, the diplomatic team arrived. At least,

West assumed it was the diplomatic team. They wore civilian clothes.

The admiral and the other officers stood when they entered the room. The leader of the group was clear. He was a middle-aged man who wore his authority the way he wore his civilian tunic, formally yet completely naturally.

"Ambassador Fox," the admiral said, extending his hand to the leader.

"Admiral," the ambassador said.

The rest of the diplomatic group and the admiral's staff exchanged greetings. They all clearly knew each other and were cordial but not warm, West noted.

When those pleasantries were done, Admiral Justman said, "I present my new special attaché doing a research project on the Klingon matter, Lieutenant Patrick West."

The ambassador stepped forward and shook West's hand firmly.

A look of recognition crossed the admiral's face. West knew the look well. "West…" the ambassador said.

"He is my father," West said.

"Of course," the ambassador said. "I never met your father, but of course I know his reputation. It is a real pleasure to meet you. Your father must be proud to see his son on Admiral Justman's staff. I'm sure you will give him even more reasons to be proud in your time here."

"I will certainly do my best, sir," West said.

As they sat, West felt Admiral Justman's eyes on him. For the first time, he wondered if the admiral had had some ulterior motive for hiring him, Jonathan West's son, for this job.

Wasting no time, the ambassador spoke first. "I'm afraid that this briefing will be short. For the moment the Klingon ambassador has…resisted new talks. They claim there is no need."

"Despite all of our intelligence reports to the contrary," the admiral said.

"Precisely," the ambassador said. "However, we will continue to make overtures and I'm sure that we will be successful before long."

"Excuse me, sir, but could you describe the nature of your overtures so far," West said.

For a moment, all movement in the room stopped and all eyes turned to the lieutenant. As the most junior member of the admiral's team, he knew he was probably violating every rule of protocol by questioning the ambassador that way. On the other hand, he was new and he thought that might grant him some indulgence.

"Describe the overtures?" the ambassador said, his stare boring into the new lieutenant.

"Please, and the Klingons' reaction," West said, keeping his eyes locked on the ambassador's. "It would help me with my research project," he added.

The man shot the admiral a quick glance, then began speaking. "We had three communications with the Klingon ambassador's office. The first was a subspace talk between the ambassador and myself. I asked for a meeting to discuss closer diplomatic and economic ties and he simply refused, saying that he was needed elsewhere at the time.

"In the second communication I spoke to one of his staff and made the request again, offering to accommodate the ambassador's schedule. The Klingon simply refused with no explanation. In my third communication I asked—"

"Excuse me," West interrupted. "Was your third communication with the same member of the Klingon ambassador's staff?"

The ambassador seemed surprised by the question.

"No, it was a different staff member," he said. "At any rate, I offered to make any accommodations necessary and even travel to Klingon space for the talks instead of using a neutral territory."

West nodded and the ambassador seemed annoyed. *"Lieutenant* West," he said, putting emphasis on West's rank. "Does any of that seem significant to you? We have been doing this for some time. I can tell you from experience that dealing with the Klingons is not an efficient process. Progress is rarely steady, but it does happen."

"With all due respect, Ambassador," West said, "I don't think we can call what has happened to relations with the Klingon Empire since the Battle of Donatu V progress. And yes, what you have told me seems extremely significant."

The lieutenant could see that the ambassador was maintaining control, but it was requiring an effort. West hoped he hadn't pushed too hard, because he wasn't finished.

"How is it significant?" the ambassador asked.

"Besides studying the recent Starfleet intelligence reports on the Klingon situation, I have also been reviewing the Klingon cultural database, which I also studied at the Academy. As you know, the Klingons consider themselves a race of warriors."

"And as you know, we are not in a state of *war* with the Klingons. War, in fact, is something we are trying to avoid," said the man next to the ambassador, the one Fox had introduced as his secretary.

Lieutenant West refused to be intimidated. "True, but I am not sure the Klingons see things the same way." The secretary started to speak, but West cut him off. "The Klingons have hundreds of words in their language for conflict, for war, for violence. Conflict is the context through which they see much of their lives. And every communication with an enemy—or in the Federation's case a *potential* enemy—can be seen as a form of combat."

"Your *studies* as a *student* at the Academy are very interesting," one of the other members of the ambassador's staff said. "But hardly relevant."

"I disagree, they are very relevant. Because when Ambassador Fox calls them and requests a meeting instead of demanding one, the Federation is not challenging them, as an equal would. When the Klingon ambassador insults you by having a junior staff member talk to our ambassador, we offer to make concessions—essentially conceding a victory to the Klingons," West said.

The ambassador's secretary was getting red in the face. "That is absurd," he said.

The ambassador raised his hand and the man immediately went silent. "So what do you suggest?" he asked.

"I suggest we try to understand the Klingon mind-set, and not treat them as we would expect to be treated, but as they would. And they expect conflict, they respect it. From what we know, in Klingon politics and military service, succession is a violent and challenge-driven process. We have no reason to believe they treat diplomacy any other way."

"So are you suggesting we just slap them in the face to challenge them?" the secretary said.

"Yes," West said. "If they don't immediately agree to a meeting, accuse them of cowardice. Don't offer to meet in their territory. Fight on the issue, hard, even if you let them win. They won't respect any concessions they do not feel they have won."

The ambassador's secretary looked ready to burst, but Fox silenced him with a wave.

Standing, the ambassador took a polite tone. "This has been an interesting meeting, Admiral. Your staff has given us a great deal to think about." Then the ambassador shot West a look and a dry smile.

The diplomatic team filed out of the conference room. When they were gone, the admiral turned to West and said, "I'm sure Ambassador Fox is composing his complaint to Admiral Nogura now."

"I'm sorry, sir," West said.

"No need to apologize," the admiral said, smiling. "That was the most interesting diplomatic briefing we've had in some time."

The rest of the admiral's staff smiled at West as the admiral continued, "And this is what I hired you for. Unless we start approaching this problem differently, we know what we will be facing in the next year. And Fox will complain, but he is light-years from a fool. He will think about what you said."

As he left the conference room, the admiral patted West on the back. The lieutenant was already thinking about his research for this evening. He had discovered a new thread that he wanted to follow. There was a Klingon named Kahless and he had a growing cult of followers.

The Klingon's teachings were interesting and called for a strict adherence to principles of honor. He wasn't sure, but he thought those principles might be the key to dealing with the Klingons. While not all Klingons followed Kahless, the believers seemed to be growing in number. And since the teachings seemed to codify cultural norms and rules about duty that existed almost everywhere in the Klingon culture, many of the teachings would be relevant to nonbelievers as well.

He was so excited about the research project, he declined the invitation to join the rest of the staff for dinner. And it would only be much later that he would realize that he had temporarily forgotten his disappointment at the assignment and his anger at the admiral for postponing his dream of serving on a starship.

Chapter Seven

By THE END OF his duty cycle, Karel had decided what to do. His superior officer was hiding something. And Karel was certain that no matter how long he waited, Gash would produce no information about his brother.

Checking a chronometer, he saw that he had some time before Second Officer Klak began his duty cycle. This time of morning he knew just where the second officer would be.

Karel entered the dining hall and saw that Klak was eating alone. The second officer's alert eyes tracked him as he entered the room and followed him as he sat down at the table. The officer immediately offered the traditional greeting. "What do you want, Junior Weapons Officer?" Klak barked over his bowl of squirming *gagh*.

"I have not been able to contact my brother, who serves on Qo'noS. And command does not respond to my messages," Karel said.

The second officer eyed Karel carefully, then asked, "Where does your brother serve?"

"In the intelligence division, cryptography," Karel replied.

Klak eyed him with sympathy, which the Klingon disregarded. Warriors were not the only ones to serve the Empire with honor.

"It has been months since I or anyone else has had contact with him," Karel said.

"You have spoken to Gash about this?" Klak said.

"He has failed to get results," Karel said.

The second officer considered him for a moment. "I may be able to help you," Klak said. "I have contacts at command."

"You would have my gratitude," Karel said.

That piqued Klak's interest, and his watchful eyes considered Karel carefully. Karel thought Klak was strong and an able enough officer, but there was something in the Klingon's eyes. It was not the outright lie that he saw in Gash's eyes. Still, Klak's eyes carried something else, something he could not quite place. Klak was a better commander than the brutish Gash, he was also more intelligent. But now Gash wondered if that made Klak more dangerous, not less.

"If I can help you reach your brother, I may call on that gratitude, Karel," Klak said.

Karel wondered what that service might be, but he did not ask. He simply nodded and said, "I serve the Empire."

When the Klingon and Benitez arrived at the memorial service, the recreation room was already filling up with people. A platform was erected at the far end with a podium in front. On either side were photographs of

Matthews and Rayburn. Kell recognized them as training graduation pictures.

The Klingon was again impressed by the size of the room. He had been impressed by the scale of the ship and the amount of open area when he first came on board, but this recreation space dwarfed most others on the ship.

The security staff had taken places closest to the podium. Kell and his Earther roommate made their way there and found Sam Fuller, waiting with him. A few moments later the other four members of their section arrived.

The Earthers nodded solemnly to each other. The Klingon noted that their demeanor was not unlike that of his fellow Klingons at a death ceremony. Of course, there was no death howl to warn the next world that a warrior was arriving. Kell regretted that he was not able to perform that ritual immediately after Matthews's death.

Then he realized how alone he was among these Earthers. If he died among them, as he suspected he might, who would pry his eyes open and perform the wail?

At that moment he felt someone's eyes on him and turned to see Leslie Parrish watching him. He nodded to her. She gave him a grim smile and turned away.

The captain arrived and stepped up to the platform. Immediately the murmur of the assembled crew disappeared and the large hall was silent except for the hum of the engines.

Kirk considered the assembled crew silently for a moment, then began. "Thank you all for coming, and greetings to those of you who are listening to this memorial service through the ship's com system. I know that many of you have questions about how Ensign Ethan Matthews and Ensign Edward Rayburn died. Though the details of our mission yesterday on Exo III remain classified, I will tell you what I can. But first, I would like to talk about how they lived. Ensign Rayburn was a champion runner back on Earth, an athlete who dreamed of space from early childhood. He is survived by his parents as well as three sisters. During his Starfleet training, Rayburn displayed competition-level marksmanship and earned high marks in all areas of his training.

"Ensign Matthews faced tragedy at a young age. The rest of his family was killed when raiders attacked their settlement. Matthews survived and was rescued by Starfleet personnel. From that point on, he was determined to join Starfleet's security force. The road was long and difficult for him and he struggled in some areas of his Starfleet training. But his instructors all said the same thing about him: Edward Matthews was the most committed and dedicated recruit they had ever seen."

Kell shuddered inwardly. The real Earther Matthews had survived much, reached his goal, only to be captured by the Klingon Defense Force after his Starfleet training en route to his first assignment on the *Enterprise* or on leave somewhere. Had the Earther joined Starfleet security because he himself had something of a warrior's blood in him? Was such a thing possible for an Earther?

Security was probably the closest that a member of a lesser race such as Earthers could come to exploring life as a warrior. Was that what the real Matthews was trying to do?

He found himself hoping that the Earther died well, though he knew it was unlikely, since he had no doubt died at the hands of professional Klingon interrogators—just as the real Jon Anderson had done.

"Both men reached their dreams of service in Starfleet," Kirk continued, "yet neither had the chance to distinguish himself in his short career. They died just ten weeks after joining the crew of the *Enterprise*. Yet in their lives, their training, their short service, and their deaths they honored both the Federation and Starfleet Command. They died facing an alien threat that put machines above living beings. And their deaths helped avert a threat that could have cost countless lives throughout the galaxy.

"They died in the face of a force greater than themselves, but in their deaths they served ideas greater than themselves. The idea that different peoples can band together for mutual protection and enrichment; the idea that it is better to reach out a hand in friendship than to live in fear of the unknown; the ideas that are summed up in the words of Zefram Cochrane and quoted in the Starfleet oath, which says, 'To seek out new life and new civilizations, to boldly go where no man has gone before.'

"We were unable to recover the bodies of Edward Rayburn and Ethan Matthews and return them to their loved ones. And so we commend them to the unexplored depths of a planet which will be their final resting place. They honored us in their service. We honor them in their deaths," Kirk said.

Kell felt another pang at the mention of the Starfleet oath; an oath he had taken himself while wearing the false face of a Earther; an oath he had uttered but would not honor—and he felt shame run through him.

The ultimate defeat of the Earthers demanded he make sacrifices. Even if some individual Earthers were capable of low-level courage and adherence to duty, their cowardly and treacherous leaders, like Kirk, insured that the Federation would remain a threat and an enemy to the Klingon Empire.

Kirk convincingly uttered the lies of the Federation's

principles, just as he appeared sincere when he spoke of pain at the loss of two unimportant crewmen. The Klingon was not fooled. And yet, he could see the blind admiration for the captain in the eyes of the crew around him. The coward's lies bound the crew to him.

But to Kell, the casual lies were an affront to honor.

As he watched the Earther Kirk step down from the platform the Klingon was struck with a thought that startled him in its clarity: *It is going to be an honor to kill this deceitful coward.*

The service continued with some more words from the dead officers' section chief, a man named Ordover. Then one of the men told a story about Rayburn. No one came forward for Matthews, which did not surprise Kell. After all, Matthews was not his real name. No doubt the Klingon behind that human face had taken pains to avoid social relationships that might compromise his mission.

At the end the captain came back to the podium and asked for a moment of silence for their two lost comrades. A hush fell over the assembled group.

The silence was broken by a voice on the com system that said, "Yellow alert, yellow alert, captain to the bridge."

The captain leaned forward and said, "Everyone to their duty stations," and made his way out to the door.

"Come with me," Fuller said to Kell, Benitez, and the rest of the section. Fuller headed for the door, and the Klingon followed.

"Report," Kirk said as he stepped out of the turbolift with Mr. Spock following behind him.

Uhura got up from the command chair and said, "Priority-one distress signal from System 1324—it's near the Klingon-Federation border, sir. The message says their settlement is under attack from an unknown force."

"Mr. Spock?" Kirk said, turning to his first officer, who was hovering over the viewer at the science station. Spock looked up from his console.

"System 1324 is only 37.48 light-years from Klingon space. And there are no sanctioned Federation settlements or outposts on that planet."

"A trap?" Kirk asked.

"Possibly," Spock replied. "But there are unconfirmed reports of a settlement organized by the AFL."

A hush fell over the bridge as all eyes turned to Spock, whose face was, of course, impassive.

"In your opinion, Lieutenant Uhura, is the message genuine?" Kirk asked.

"Yes, sir," Uhura responded.

Kirk did not hesitate. "Navigator, plot a course."

"Done, sir," came the reply.

"Helm, lay the course in and give me maximum warp."

"Aye, maximum warp, sir," Lieutenant Sulu replied.

Kirk searched his feelings to see if there was a warning there. For now, he felt nothing but the extra alertness that came with a dangerous mission.

"How long, Mr. Spock?" Kirk asked.

"Four hours, twenty-seven minutes, Captain," Spock replied.

"Let's hope the settlers can hold out that long," Kirk said.

Chapter Eight

KELL CLIMBED OFF the ladder and stepped onto the deck. He scanned the area in front of him, looking for possible threats. Above him was a large cylinder that was more than two decks in diameter. His study of Klingon intelligence reports had told him that this was the heart of the main sensors and navigational deflector system.

He crouched to step under the cylinder and walked to the forward bulkhead. Beyond the bulkhead, he knew, was the front of the ship's lower, engineering hull and the navigational deflector dish itself.

The quarters were tight, but Kell was able to make his inspection quickly and return to the ladder.

"Clear," he called.

Two repair technicians wearing red coveralls stepped onto the deck with Benitez trailing behind them. The technicians crouched and moved forward, examining a console.

The Klingon immediately saw the value of this drill.

In battle conditions, the close quarters and heavy machinery would make repair and rescue operations here very difficult to carry out.

"End drill," came a voice from the intercom. It was Fuller. "Anderson and Benitez, report to the theater."

Nodding to the technicians, Kell and Benitez walked toward the rear of the ship. Toward the *aft*, he reminded himself. But the Earthers had two words for the rear of the ship and the other was...stern. *Another sign of Earther waste and excess,* he thought.

Humans, the Klingon corrected himself. He doubted most of them would recognize the Klingon term for them—or understand the depth of the insult it represented. Nevertheless, he did not want to use the term Earther by mistake and risk that one of the...humans would recognize its Klingon origin.

Once on the deck, they headed for the turbolift, which took them from the secondary, engineering hull to the bottom of the primary hull, where the ship's theater lay.

Inside, he and Benitez took a place with Leslie and the other Earthers—*humans,* he corrected himself—in their security section as the theater filled up with security personnel. Once again, Kell was struck by the size of a space *humans* set aside for recreation.

Klingons valued theater as well. In fact, Klingon opera was a much more highly developed form of that art than anything humans had. Yet no Klingon warship would ever dedicate the kind of space required for actual performances on board.

When the theater was full, Security Chief Giotto took the stage, flanked by Section Chief Ordover as well as some others Kell did not know by name.

"I'm going to tell you what I know, but at the moment we do not have a lot of information and that is not likely to change as we begin our search-and-rescue operation. For those of you who are new to the *Enterprise,* welcome to security service aboard a starship," the security chief said.

The Klingon saw smiles and heard laughter among the assembled crew.

"The *Enterprise* is responding to an urgent distress call from the fourth planet in System 1324, which is under attack from an unknown force. We are to find and rescue the settlers, very likely while under fire. The problem is that there is no official settlement on the planet, but unconfirmed reports suggest that the settlers may be squatters from the AFL," he continued.

"Who?" someone from the crowd asked, articulating the question in Kell's mind.

"For those of you who don't know, the AFL is the Anti-Federation League, a political group that opposes the United Federation of Planets on the grounds that since it arms its starships, it is a military force. They also have some sort of complaint about the 'dilution of each member world's culture,' but you would have to talk to someone in the social sciences for an explanation of what that means," Giotto said.

The Klingon thought that was very interesting. So there were those in the Federation who saw through the lies on which it was built. Perhaps there was hope for some humans.

"And these anti-Federation people are asking *us* for help?" someone asked. Kell turned and saw that it was Becker, from his own section.

"Yes," Giotto said evenly.

"And we are going to give it to them?" a security officer from another section asked.

"Yes, we are," Giotto replied, waving off the ensign's

protest before the human could voice it. "For a few reasons: First, the Starfleet oath we all took requires us to give aid when asked. Period. Second, the Federation's commitment to 'Infinite Diversity' means that we will often be called on to serve and protect all kinds of people and aliens—regardless of their politics, no matter how silly those politics might seem to us. I will remind you again that your oath called for you to serve the 'Federation's highest ideas of peace and brotherhood.' "

Giotto's face set. "Any questions?"

No one spoke.

"Excellent, see your section chiefs for duty assignments," Giotto said.

Madness, Kell thought. Had the Federation been so successful in perpetrating the lies on which it was founded that the people in this room actually *believed* them? Would they risk their own lives to protect their sworn enemies? All in some strange adherence to their principles?

Then again, Kahless himself had said, "A warrior defends his principles with his own blood."

Perhaps these humans had some semblance of honor. That made the deceit on which Starfleet and the Federation were founded even more repellent.

Giotto left the stage. The section chiefs followed him and found their people. Sam Fuller approached the Klingon and his group.

"We will be one of the three sections to beam down to the planet. Standard search-and-rescue procedure. We do not yet know if the hostiles are still on the surface. Go to the armory to pick up your weapons and tricorders and meet me in the transporter room in one hour," Fuller said. Then he seemed to soften for a moment.

"I know this is your first landing party, your first search-and-rescue, and likely your first experience coming under fire, but you have trained for all of this. Remember your training, stay close to me, and you will be fine. Dismissed," he said.

As they exited the theater, Kell noticed that his entire section had moved together. They got into the turbolift together and remained silent. Even Luis Benitez was quiet.

The Klingon was lost in his thoughts. In one hour, he would likely find the first battle of his life. And he would do it wearing the face and uniform of a Starfleet officer. For now, his duty to the Empire required that he continue to act the part of a human. Thus, he would do his best to protect a group of anti-Federation humans—enemies of the Federation just as surely as the Klingon Empire was an enemy of the Federation.

Kell knew that despite the ironies, he would do his duty to the Empire. However, he was just as sure that whatever the outcome, it could not possibly be in the interests of either of his masters.

"Entering orbit, Captain," Sulu said.

Kirk watched the planet come into view on the main screen. It was a blue-green world, mostly water, with at least two fairly large continents that he could see. It was the kind of planet that was ideal for a humanoid settlement.

"Sensors, Mr. Spock?" Kirk asked.

"Multiple life-forms, perhaps twenty. Some human... some not. Energy readings in several points. There are fires and other energy fluctuations in what appears to be the settlement area on the main continent."

"Any signs of vessels?" Kirk asked.

"Nothing in orbit," Spock said. "There may, however, be landing craft on the planet."

"Find a landing site near the main settlement. Give

our people some cover, but make sure they are close to the life-form readings," Kirk said.

"Transferring coordinates to the transporter room now," Spock said after a few seconds.

"Tell the transporter room to energize, Mr. Spock," Kirk said. "Lieutenant Uhura, coordinate with Lieutenant Commander Giotto in auxiliary control. I want reports every five minutes."

Kirk stared at the viewscreen. He was once again sending his people into danger. His instincts told him to go with them, but he couldn't leave the ship unless he was certain the *Enterprise* would not come under attack in space.

For now, the security teams were on their own.

The captain quieted his mind, trying to see if there was anything he was missing. Unfortunately, this mission had so many holes and so little information that it was impossible to calculate the potential hazards. It was also impossible to isolate his concerns from his instincts; there was too much danger and there were too many variables.

"Third security team is on the planet's surface, Captain," Mr. Spock announced.

"Shields up," Kirk said.

"Aye, sir," came Sulu's reply.

For the moment, there was nothing else Kirk could do except one of the few parts of his job he truly disliked.

He waited.

Kell felt the momentary disorientation of the transporter and then he was on the ground of the planet. His eyes went to Sam Fuller, who was already talking on his communicator, presumably to the ship.

Looking around, the Klingon saw his own team around him and the other two security teams scanning the area. Reflexively, he confirmed that his mission partner, Benitez, was next to him.

They had beamed down into a clearing, which was surrounded by trees. To their right were some low mountains and ahead through the trees Kell could see smoke.

"Check your tricorders for a revised layout of the settlement," Fuller said. All the members of the security team picked up their tricorders and checked the screens. The Klingon's tricorder showed a basic diagram of the settlement and surrounding area.

"We are north of the settlement, in the wooded area. To the west are the mountains you can see," Fuller said, pointing at the mountain in the distance. "South of the settlement is the river you see in the diagram. To the east is the open land and is probably where the attack came from. Take a moment to study the map. You'll need it committed to memory when we begin.

"Meanwhile, we have some further intelligence from the *Enterprise*. There is confirmation that this is a settlement sponsored by the AFL. Sixty colonists have been living here for almost a year. The colonists brought synthesizers, agricultural and manufacturing equipment, but no weapons, so their only defense right now is us. The only contact with the colony in the last eighteen hours was the distress call," Fuller said.

Kell shook his head. Sixty people on a planet with no weapons to defend their settlement. And the settlement site had effectively trapped them inside a semicircle of dense forest, mountains, and a river. Proximity to the river made sense, but he had no doubt that proximity to the mountains was a human aesthetic conceit.

In a Klingon colony, the mountains would have been a useful platform for defensive weapons, but here they were just part of the trap the colonists had built for themselves.

He took a few seconds to study Benitez's face. Remarkably, the human did not seem surprised by the foolishness of the settlers.

Kell quickly memorized the layout of the settlement. There was a central building, which the map identified as "central structure." Then there were small dwellings to the north, just below the security team's position. To the south of the central structure, there was a building marked "heavy equipment and manufacturing." To the east was a "recreational field" and below that a "landing field." Farther east were tracts marked "agriculture."

"According to my readings, the landing field took heavy fire and I'm not showing any power sources, but I'm getting two strong energy readings from the recreational field. Those might be our hostile crafts. For now, we're going to concentrate on finding and securing the settlers. When we've gotten the survivors to safety, we'll worry about the hostiles."

Kell was once again struck by the difference between Klingons and humans. A Klingon commander would face the threat first and then effect a rescue.

"Okay," Sam said. "We'll take the right flank. Chief Brantley's team will take the left, while Chief Ordover's runs center. Look sharp, people. The humanoid life readings are all centered in the central building, about five hundred meters directly south of our position. They may be hostages. Let's move."

The Klingon was very alert; his heart was pounding in his chest and his face felt warm. He knew it was a simple physiological response to stress, but he imagined that his blood was growing hotter as he prepared for battle.

The heat of battle was descending on him for the second time in his life and the second time in two days. The first battle was a drill concocted by his human superiors. This time, he had no doubt, the battle would be very real.

He was determined, and a clarity fell over his mind. His own struggles against the lies of his mission were forgotten. Kell realized that he was entering a battle that even Kahless would find just. He would be facing a foe that preyed on the defenseless, the weak, and the hopelessly naïve.

If he never found it again on this mission, the Klingon knew he had found peace.

The lead group was coming to the edge of the trees before the clearing that contained the settlement, with the two flanking teams perhaps twenty meters behind and thirty meters to either side.

Kell knew that when they left the cover of the trees, the security teams would be vulnerable. They would be in the open for at least 150 meters before they found the shelter of the first dwellings.

The Klingon spared a look at Benitez, who was beside him. The human's face was set, and he seemed as determined as Kell felt himself. Kell wondered if that was truly possible for a human.

Checking his tricorder, the Klingon saw that they were perhaps three hundred meters from the central structure.

Soon, he realized.

"When the first team hits the open," Fuller said, "they're going to run for the cover of the buildings up ahead. Keep up."

Kell kept his eyes forward and his body tensed. He knew it would begin in seconds now.

Then the world exploded in front of him.

Chapter Nine

"EXPLOSION ON THE SURFACE, Captain," Mr. Spock said, his calm tones undercutting the gravity of what he was saying.

Kirk was on his feet immediately.

"Uhura, report," Kirk called to his communications officer.

"No response from the surface, Captain," Uhura replied. "I will keep trying."

"Sensors, Spock?" Kirk asked.

"Still showing a concentration of life signs in the beam-down area, but we are getting some interference," the Vulcan said.

"Spock, keep scanning and have the transporter room maintain locks on our people. I want to be able to get them out fast."

"Negative, Captain," Spock replied. "We cannot get a transporter lock owing to the interference." The Vulcan's eyes never left his science-station scanner. "I believe we are being intentionally jammed from the surface. It is affecting sensors and communications, and would prevent successful use of the transporter."

"Have Scotty try to compensate with the transporter, Spock. Lieutenant Uhura, you do the same with communications, we need to know what's happening down there," Kirk said.

The captain took a step closer to the viewscreen, as if by peering into it he could see what was happening on the planet's surface.

The only thing he could be sure of was that things were going wrong. Then he was equally sure that they weren't finished going wrong.

A voice called out inside his head. *Trap. It's a trap.*

Intuition. And specific this time.

At that moment, the turbolift doors opened and someone stepped onto the bridge. Without turning around, Kirk could tell it was McCoy by the sound of the footsteps.

"Did someone call for a doctor?" McCoy asked flatly.

"As a point of fact, Doctor, no one did," Spock replied as McCoy took a position over Kirk's shoulder.

"That's the problem, Captain. I have my whole staff ready to go in sickbay, with additional triage set up in the recreation room. The only thing I'm missing is patients. According to reports, we likely have some injured colonists down on the planet."

"We seem to be cut off at the moment, Doctor," Kirk said.

"Sir," Spock said, and Kirk swiveled around to face his first officer.

Spock spared a glance up from his viewer to look directly at Kirk. "A vessel is powering up on the surface," the Vulcan said.

Suddenly, Kirk was not surprised.

"Lieutenant Uhura, hail the vessel," he said.

After a moment, Uhura replied, "No response on any channels."

"The interference?" Kirk asked.

"The communications interference is limited to the frequencies our communicators receive. They hear us all right. They just don't want us talking to our people," Uhura said.

"Shields to maximum," Kirk said.

"Shields at maximum," Sulu replied.

"Red alert, prepare for battle stations," the captain said. "How long, Spock?"

"The ship will be ready to launch in a few minutes," Spock replied.

Kirk took his seat and looked over his right shoulder to Spock's science station. Anticipating the captain's question, Spock had a schematic of a ship on the viewscreen above his station. Though Kirk did not recognize the specific model, he was certain he recognized the manufacture.

"Orion vessel, Captain," Spock said, speaking Kirk's own thoughts aloud.

"It's the Orions then?" McCoy asked.

"Apparently," Spock replied. "Usual crew complement of twenty. Technically classified as a cargo ship. No weapons in the specifications."

The sleek arrowhead-shaped vessel in the schematic did not look like a practical cargo hauler. "But?" Kirk asked.

"But the ship is built more for speed than for cargo," Spock said. "Much of the ship's internal volume is devoted to the engines."

"I bet that model is popular with smugglers," Kirk offered.

"Precisely. Smugglers of high value, low mass cargo," Spock said.

"What would smugglers want with the settlement on the surface?" McCoy asked.

"An excellent question," Spock replied. "The planet is moderately rich in natural resources, but the vessel is not big enough to hold large quantities of any raw materials it might find. It is also doubtful that the colonists brought anything of sufficient value to attract pirates. The settlement is small and the only things of value I saw on sensors are synthesizers, agricultural processors, and other heavy equipment that would not be practical for that vessel to move." Spock looked up from his viewer. "There is no logical reason for them to attack the settlment."

"That's the problem with pirates, Spock, you just can't trust them to behave logically," McCoy said dryly.

"Three minutes until the vessel is ready to launch," Spock said, ignoring the gibe.

Whoever they are and whatever their intentions, Kirk thought, *they are hostile.* They had attacked a settlement in Federation space and had cut him off from twenty-one members of his crew. In just a few minutes they would learn just how big a mistake they had made.

Kell and his team reflexively turned away from the flash of light, which was fortunate. Because a moment later the sound of an explosion hit his ears, then he felt the shock wave—a hot blast hitting him in the back.

The blow pushed him forward, but gently. It had obviously dissipated in the few hundred meters between the explosion and their position. Like the other security officers, the Klingon kept to his feet.

The blast passed them quickly and Kell did not need to check his tricorder to see where it had come from.

The center of the explosion had been approximately three hundred meters ahead of them, just past the dwellings in front of them. It was the settlement's central structure and the source of all of the human life readings.

"Are you okay, Flash?" Benitez said from beside him.

The human was looking at him with concern. Kell had to remind himself that for humans, this was not an insult.

"I'm fine," he said.

The squads re-formed in their original positions. Sam Fuller leading the Klingon's section, which made up the right flank. The three squads moved forward.

"I'm still showing life-form readings from the central building, or whatever is left of it," Fuller called out. "Even if we don't come under fire, this is going to be tough."

Coming to the edge of the trees, Kell could suddenly see why. In front of them, he could see simple two-level dwellings, evenly spaced in two rows of six. They were prefabricated structures, not unlike those he might find in a Klingon settlement. Of course, he had no doubt the dwellings contained nonessentials and luxuries that no Klingon would never dream of having in a small colony.

Now, however, some of the dwellings were smashed flat, presumably by powerful energy weapons. Others were burning and the rest were smoking. None of them would ever be used as dwellings again.

He wondered if the humans had fought for their homes. Even without real weapons, Klingons would have fought, with rocks and farming tools if necessary. Of course, if the humans had fought, he would see bodies on the ground in front of him. And there were none.

Strange, he thought. *An attack of this magnitude on an undefended settlement of weakling humans and yet there are no bodies.*

"Who would do this?" Benitez asked. "And why?"

But there was no time for Kell to respond. The lead team was stepping out of the forest.

The Klingon had his phaser in his hand, alert for signs of attack. Like the rest of his squad, he scanned the air and ground around Ordover's team. They were headed toward the cover of the first dwelling, which was smoking but reasonably intact.

The team dashed across the open space without incident and took positions behind the dwelling. Then Kell saw Fuller gesture with a hand signal to the squad on the left flank, which sprinted behind another house in the same row. This one was missing its second level, and looked as if a great hand had swiped it away, leaving the first level to smoke.

In his peripheral vision, Kell could see Benitez shaking his head and staring openmouthed at the destruction. He sensed that humans did not understand aggression and realized that when the final battle with the Klingon Empire came, there would be many more wearing that expression—just before they were destroyed.

As Ordover's team tensed for their move, the Klingon again bristled at the thought of his squad being the last to go. Of course, he realized that his team was the newest. The most experienced people would have the honor of going first into danger.

In a repeat of the maneuver that brought them from the woods behind the first row of homes, they moved from their current position to the next row of houses. For a moment, Kell gave thanks that the dwellings in the center were the most intact. This gave them the best cover as they approached the central structure.

It was unusually considerate of the attackers. Actually, strangely considerate, the Klingon thought.

And then Ordover's squad prepared to approach the

central building. Peering around the side of the dwelling to give cover fire, the Klingon saw the building, or what was left of it.

It must have been large, by the amount of the rubble in the area. Some of the outer walls on the first level were still standing. Thus, Kell was able to estimate that the structure must have been a square of perhaps thirty meters wide. From the amount of the rubble, he guessed the building must have been four or five levels. Clearly, it was the most important structure to the humans. It looked like it had actually been a construction project, not a simple piece of prefabrication.

Now it was a useless pile of rubble.

"I'm still getting most of the life-sign readings," Sam Fuller called out. "They must be underground. Our job will be to get them out, and out of the line of any possible fire as quickly as possible. We'll move survivors back to this position, then back to the beam-down site in the forest. Hopefully, by then, the transporters will be back online."

Just then, someone from the squad covering the left flank called out, then all eyes watched as a flash of light appeared over the trees.

That was not an explosion was Kell's first thought. The light was not a flash. If anything, it gained in intensity; then the light's source revealed itself above the trees.

A ship slowly rose above the trees. It had a simple arrowhead design. Though it was familiar, Kell couldn't immediately place it. Not surprising, as his Klingon Defense Force intelligence work was limited to languages and cryptography.

No doubt his brother Karel, with proper military training, would be able to identify the vessel immediately.

"Orions," a voice said next to him.

Kell was startled and turned, half-expecting to see his brother Karel beside him. Instead, he only saw Benitez, who looked at him and said, "It's an Orion ship."

The ship hovered for a moment at perhaps half a kilometer. Then it fell briefly as its antigravity repulsors were switched off. An instant later the vessel's dual main engines flared and it rocketed upward in an extreme arc.

The vessel's roar hit them a moment later and the ship was gone.

"Captain, one of the vessels has launched," Spock said.

"Mr. Sulu, move to intercept," Kirk said.

"Aye, sir," came the helmsman's reply. "Interception in two minutes."

"Lieutenant Uhura, continue hailing. I want—" Kirk said.

"Captain," Uhura interrupted. "I have Lieutenant Fuller. The connection is weak, but I have him."

Kirk was immediately relieved. Sam was alive. "Kirk here, Sam. Report."

Kirk heard static, a few garbled words, then Sam's voice. "No casualties among the landing party. We're about to begin rescue operation." A few more garbled words, then, "A lot of damage, but we're still getting life signs."

"Sensors detected the explosion, Sam. Effect your rescue, but take no unnecessary risks down there," Kirk said.

"...ship launched," Sam said.

"We're tracking it now. We'll begin beam-out as soon as we can lower shields. In the meantime, see if you can locate the source of the communications and transporter signal jamming we're experiencing," Kirk said.

"Aye, sir," Sam said.

"And Sam, good luck down there. Kirk out."

Kirk was pleased to hear that the landing party was safe. Yet he knew they would have a tough time with the survivors if there were injured civilians. Without the resources of sickbay and the *Enterprise,* there wasn't much the security teams could do to treat them. And if the security people came under fire...

Whatever happened, Kirk knew that Sam would handle the situation as well as anyone could. For now, Kirk knew he had to concentrate on protecting his ship.

"Coming into range," Sulu said.

"They have come to a dead stop and are holding position, sir," Spock said from his science station.

"Helm, bring us in close," Kirk said.

"No response to hails," Uhura said.

Kirk nodded. Whatever their plan was, it didn't include talking.

"Hold us at half a kilometer," Mr. Sulu.

"Aye, half a kilometer now, sir," Sulu said.

"Ship still holding position, Captain," Spock said.

"Are you reading any weapons, Mr. Spock?" Kirk asked.

"Possibly, sir. Readings are inconclusive," Spock replied. "I'm reading high energy levels but the ship's main systems have an unusual amount of shielding from sensors, even for smugglers."

Kirk felt McCoy's hand grasp the back of his chair. It was as much a gesture of support as it was an expression of the doctor's tension.

"They're just watching us," McCoy said.

"No, not watching, Doctor. Studying us," Kirk replied.

"Captain, how can you—" Spock started to ask.

"A hunch, Spock," Kirk said. The pieces didn't fit yet,

but they were beginning to take shape. "Spock, is that vessel a serious threat to the *Enterprise?*" Kirk asked.

"No, sir," the Vulcan replied.

"Scotty, cut shields to sixty percent," Kirk said. "Have phaser control do the same with the weapons."

"Aye, sir," Scotty replied from the engineering station, but Kirk could hear the uncertainty in his chief engineer's voice.

"Increase in power on the vessel," Spock said.

"Hold fire until my mark," Kirk said.

"They're moving," Sulu added as Kirk watched the ship became larger on the screen.

"Ramming course?" Kirk asked.

"No, sir," Spock said.

A second later the ship practically filled the viewscreen and appeared to be headed straight for the bridge. Kirk tensed reflexively and felt McCoy doing the same as he continued to grasp the back of the command chair.

When the ship seemed mere meters from the viewscreen a red blast of energy leaped from it. Kirk felt the *Enterprise* shudder as the blast hit the shields, and then the ship disappeared above them.

Kirk didn't have to turn around to know that Scotty was shaking his head in disgust.

"Damage report," Kirk said.

"It was a nasty jolt at such close range, but shields are holding," Scotty said.

"What did they hit us with, Spock?" Kirk asked.

"High-energy particle beams," the Vulcan replied.

"Scotty, can you adjust the shields to be more effective against their weapon at lower power?"

"Done, sir," the chief engineer replied.

"They are heading away at warp five, Captain," Sulu said.

Kevin Ryan

"Follow them, but match speed. Do not overtake or engage yet," Kirk ordered. The captain could hear surprised gasps from his bridge crew.

"I think we're being tested," Kirk said.

"Tested? By who? And why?" McCoy asked.

"I have no idea," Kirk replied. "Call it a hunch, Bones. Nonspecific for the moment, but I'm working on it."

Chapter Ten

As THE CENTER SECURITY TEAM prepared to dash from the cover of the dwelling to the settlement's main building, Kell once again regretted that his squad was denied the honor of facing the danger first.

He glanced at Benitez and reminded himself that he was dealing with humans, who were incapable of even understanding the principles of honor as taught by Kahless the Unforgettable.

Still, they seem to know something of courage, he thought, as the center squad dashed into the clearing. There were perhaps one hundred meters ahead of the dwellings that still provided the flanking squads with cover and the remains of the central building.

The squad had covered about half the distance when Section Chief Ordover disappeared in an explosive flash.

It happened so quickly that the Klingon thought the man must have stepped on a land mine, a thought that was supported by the small crater that now existed where the section chief had stood.

When the second flash of energy came, it created a second crater but missed the rest of the squad, who had thrown themselves flat when their chief was hit. The second flash, however, betrayed its source as two small ships appeared in the distance over the rubble of the central building in front of them.

Before he had consciously registered that they were indeed ships, Kell was aiming and firing his phaser. He noted with surprise that Benitez and the rest of his section were doing the same.

The range made a hit from a hand phaser unlikely, but, nevertheless, they all made the effort.

"Pull back," Fuller called to the survivors of the group even as he fired his own weapon. Still lying on the ground, the exposed squad began to crawl to back to the cover of the trees. Another flash from the ships and another member of the squad disappeared in a burst of angry red energy.

"Move it!" Sam shouted, stepping on to the field to get a better shot. Kell found himself following suit. Incredibly, Benitez did the same.

A hail of fire from the ships struck the ground all around the exposed squad. Then the ships started moving toward them, slowly but steadily. From a distance, they had killed two members of the security team in seconds. At close range...

The Klingon knew they didn't have much time.

As the ships came closer, Kell could see they weren't ships at all. They were heavy weapons platforms, oval in shape and perhaps two to three meters wide. Each platform had a large figure standing on it manning an energy weapon that was mounted on the platform. The base itself was thick and had what looked like armored plating that came up to cover the lower half of the pilot. Overall, the vehicles looked very solid and very dangerous.

When the weapons platforms came a few meters closer, Kell could see that the attacking figures were wearing full, armored environmental suits, making them look even larger than they were.

As they reached the rear of the ruined central building Kell was pleased to see his phaser beam find its mark and flare against the platform closest to him. After his beam hit, another did, then another, each coming from someone in his squad. The Klingon was filled for a moment with an odd sense of pride in himself and his sectionmates. Yet the platform continued flying and moving as if the phasers were in training mode instead of firing high-powered blasts of deadly energy.

Reflexively, Kell checked his phaser. It was set to Full.

"They're shielded," Fuller called out. "Keep up the fire."

Continuing to fire, the Klingon was pleased to see the platform nearest to him shudder when three beams hit it simultaneously.

So they aren't invincible, Kell thought. He wished in that moment that he could get his hands on the beings in those suits.

Honorless cowards, he thought. *They strike from their armored platforms, concealed behind their suits.*

The second platform shuddered under fire and the Klingon realized they had a chance. Any type of force screen on a device that small must be drawing huge amounts of power. Maintaining flight, weapons fire, and shields would deplete any power cells quickly.

Unfortunately, the attackers did not seem content to wait for that to happen. The platform tilted up, momentarily ceasing the barrage against the squad stuck in the open. In a flash, Kell saw what they were doing as each platform trained its heavy weapon on the squad nearest it.

There was no time to move, run, or even drop for cover. The first blast came immediately and Kell was aware of a momentary flash of red light and heat on his left.

Instinctively, he checked to make sure that his partner Benitez was still standing. Seeing that Benitez was all right, he turned back to the Orion. He felt a flash of insight and took careful aim at the head of the pilot of the platform closest to his team.

His beam hit its mark and the shield protecting the pilot flared red when the phaser beam hit it. He was pleased to see the pilot visibly recoil.

"Aim for the head," he called out to the rest of his section, but before the words were out he could see the others were doing the same.

Phaser beams lanced out at the pilot's head, and though the range was long for a head shot, several of the beams found their marks.

The hits had two immediate effects. The flashes created when beams struck the force screen were blinding the pilot. And some of the energy was getting through. From time to time, Kell could see the surface of the helmet flare.

He also imagined that it was getting hot inside the shield. It wouldn't be long before the controls, if not the pilot himself, were affected.

A warrior's instincts for a distant shot were to aim for the largest target: in this case the large, heavy base of the vehicle. However, this was clearly the best-protected portion of the flying weapons platform.

No doubt, the shield was generated by the base of the vehicle and was naturally weakest near the top. It was still strong enough to repel even repeated strikes by maximum-power phaser beams, but certainly not indefinitely. Because the vehicles had high-powered weapons, the attackers probably counted on keeping far enough away from their prey to keep the pilot from being practical target himself.

Apparently, the attackers did not expect sustained resistance from the security teams. Or they did not think their coward's weapons were vulnerable. Either way, they were as arrogant as they were cowardly.

The pilot was struggling in the vehicle nearest the Klingon. Constant phaser hits were obscuring his vision and doing Kahless-knew-what to the controls.

Though the Orion was still firing his energy cannon, his blasts were going wild. It was just a matter of time.

Then the attacker made his fatal mistake.

He turned his vehicle around. In some ways it was a natural reaction. It would allow him to see, with the blasts now hitting him from behind. However, it also revealed the one place where the shields would be even weaker: the exhaust area of the vehicle's twin engines.

As the attacker lumbered away, the security team wordlessly concentrated their fire on the vehicle's engines. This was an even larger target than the pilot's head. Even as the vehicle was retreating and increasing the range, several beams hit it.

They didn't have much time, Kell realized. The vehicle's flight was steadying and its speed increasing. The pilot was regaining his bearings. When he was confident enough to retreat at full speed he would be quickly out of range.

As it turned out, he didn't have the time.

Three new phaser beams lanced out from the ground, and the Klingon saw that four of the five security officers who had been trapped in the open were now on their feet and had joined the battle. Since they were even closer to the platform, more of their shots found their mark.

Kell watched the entire vehicle shudder for a moment, its forward momentum stopped. Then two beams lanced out from the ground and there was a great flash, which the Klingon realized was the vehicle's shield finally giving out.

Sam Fuller shouted to the people in the open, "GET DOWN NOW!"

Kell dropped, instinctively reaching out a hand for the slower-moving Benitez.

The vehicle dropped for a moment, but its sudden, dramatic explosion interrupted its descent. The main force of the blast traveled upward in a bright orange flash.

Instinctively, the Klingon turned away and heard pieces of debris fly past him. When he turned back to the direction of the vehicle he could see the burning remains of it on the ground.

He could also see where the vehicle's last blast had struck. Now that the immediate danger had passed, he could see Leslie Parrish staring down at her partner Philip Becker, or what was left of him.

Kell felt a surprising stab of empathy for the human. The damage was terrible, but he consoled himself by thinking that the man could not have lived long in his condition.

By then Fuller was leading a charge toward the Chief Brantley's squad, which had made up the battle's original left flank. Kell followed, noting that some of the team was down, or missing.

The vehicle was still in the air and still facing the remains of the squad, which was focusing phaser fire on the head of the pilot. But the pilot must have seen what happened to the other attacker, because he had not turned around and was trying to back away from the security people.

Fuller's squad and the survivors from the center squad took position about twenty meters from the left flank and caught the flying weapons platform in crossfire.

The combined fire was making the shield flare constantly and the pilot seemed to be barely conscious. The security officers were able to keep up with the vehicle's slow backward movement easily on foot.

Finally the platform came to an unsteady stop about two meters off the ground, and the shield seemed to be in its death throes, fading in and out and flaring constantly.

"Cease fire," Sam called out. "We want him alive."

The officers complied immediately. The Klingon marveled that they were able to do so as he forced his own finger off the phaser's firing plate.

Fuller stepped forward and took careful aim, firing a prolonged blast at the very top of the shield. The force screen crackled weakly once and then disappeared. The section chief's next beam passed through the air in the space the shield had occupied a moment before.

Though barely on his feet, the pilot was still intact, since Fuller had taken care not to aim the beam directly at him. The section chief's restraint astonished the Klingon.

Just then a phaser blast leaped out from somewhere behind Kell and struck the pilot directly in the chest. The force of the blast threw the attacker backward and sent him in an arc to the ground below.

All eyes turned to see who had fired the blast and saw Leslie Parrish still holding the phaser out and pointed at the platform. The look on her face was cold fury, and the Klingon remembered that Philip Becker, who had taken the first platform's first hit, had been her partner.

For a moment, Kell wondered if the female was finished using her weapon. Then she slowly pointed it downward.

She met Sam Fuller's gaze and said flatly, "Heavy stun, Chief. He'll live—as per your orders."

Fuller raised an eyebrow, and then said, "Good work, Ensign."

If the Orion is alive it is only because humans cannot kill with a look, Kell thought, observing the expression set into Leslie Parrish's face.

The vehicle was listing in the air now and followed a slow arc down to the ground as it lost power.

"Sir," said Benitez, who was studying his tricorder beside the Klingon. "I'm getting a power surge from the pilot. It looks like—"

"Down!" Fuller shouted, throwing himself to the ground. The others did the same as the pilot's environmental suit exploded. After the initial blast, Kell turned up to see a small mushroom-shaped cloud of smoke above where their attacker had lain.

Apparently, the attacker did not want to be taken alive, Kell thought.

"Sir," Benitez called out again. "I'm getting another power reading. Like the one we saw before the ship launched." Benitez got up, studying his tricorder. The Klingon took out his own device and confirmed the readings.

"Do you think they know we're here?" Benitez asked.

Fuller looked into the distance, toward the hill where the recreational field lay.

"You can bet on it," Fuller said. "Let's get moving."

He walked to the open space in front of the central structure where a dead security officer lay.

Correction, the Klingon thought, as he watched the human struggle to his feet, revealing a burn, which covered his left shoulder and arm.

As he walked closer, Kell could make out a sign behind him that had hung over the main entrance of the central building. It hung at an angle, supported on only one side now.

The sign read: CULTURAL CENTER.

Kell shook his head. *Humans,* he thought. *Naïve fools. No, not fools. Children.*

"The vessel is accelerating," Mr. Spock said. "Warp 5.5…5.7. Holding at warp six."

"Mr. Sulu, match acceleration, but do it slowly. I don't want them to know what this ship can do."

"Aye, sir," Sulu said.

Kirk stood and decided not to let the question hang in the air on the bridge any longer. It was only a hunch, but he was asking his people to act on that hunch. They deserved to know what he was thinking.

"I think the capabilities of the *Enterprise* are being tested," he said. "I think we're being watched very carefully."

Kirk could feel Spock's raised eyebrow without turning around to see it.

"By who, Captain?" McCoy asked.

"By whoever is on that ship, Bones. And no I don't know why, but too many pieces on this mission don't fit," Kirk said.

"Do you think the attack on the settlement was a trap to lure the *Enterprise* here?" Spock asked.

"Someone attacked a small settlement that had nothing of real value. We arrived and they did not communicate with us or make any demands. And when we beamed down a team, they were ready with sophisticated jamming equipment," Kirk said.

"They were expecting a Federation starship," Scotty said, nodding his head.

"And they did not hesitate to engage the ship," Sulu offered.

"Captain, putting aside the question of how you reached your conclusions, I must admit that your theory fits all the available facts," Spock said.

"But Jim, that still leaves two important questions you have left out: Who would do this and why?" McCoy asked.

"Good questions, Doctor. The first priority of every person in this room will be to figure them out. Though the answer no doubt lies on that ship."

"The vessel is accelerating, Captain," Spock said. "And executing a high-speed course change."

"Follow, Mr. Sulu, but..." Kirk let his voice trail off.

"Aye, sir," Sulu said.

"Will it do any good to hold back, Captain?" McCoy asked. "The *Enterprise*'s specifications must be public record by now."

"True, but those specifications are more than twenty years old," Kirk said. "Upgrades and new systems are still classified information. Someone wants to know our current specifications."

"Someone with an interest in our tactical capabilities, no doubt," Spock said.

"That's a verra short list of suspects," Scotty added.

No one mentioned the Klingons, but Kirk was sure they were on the mind of everyone on the bridge who had been part of the briefing about the situation with the Klingon Empire.

But Kirk knew he needed more than a hunch and a theory that fit the *available facts*. He needed proof, and that was on the ship just ahead of the *Enterprise*.

"Captain, another course change," Spock said. "They are headed for a star system three light-years ahead."

"Stay with them," Kirk said.

The chase was on.

Chapter Eleven

THE LOSSES WERE HEAVY, Kell thought. His squad had lost one member; the center team had lost two people, including their section chief, and another was injured. The team on the left flank, commanded by Brantley, had lost two people.

Out of twenty-one officers, five were dead and another was seriously injured. Yet, the humans bore their losses well. They were not crushed as the Klingon would have expected.

In the seconds after the battle, Sam Fuller had assigned one member of the now-dead Ordover's squad to be Leslie Parrish's new partner. Then he merged the two remaining teams to form a new squad, under the command of the other surviving section chief, Brantley.

Kell had helped tend the wounded human, whom he learned was named McFadden. Unfortunately, the only security officer who had been cross-trained as a medic had been one of the first ones hit. Though in pain, Mc-

Fadden had not complained when his burns were cleaned and dressed.

Fuller had wanted to take McFadden deep into the woods, away from any danger of attack, but the ensign had refused.

Cross-trained as a technician, McFadden had insisted on helping check out the downed weapons platform. Jawer, from the Klingon's own section, also had technical training. Together, the two men judged that the vehicle would not fly any time soon, as many of the systems were overheated. Further, the energy cannon itself could not be removed without tools. And even if it could be removed, it would not operate without the vehicle's power cells.

Yet McFadden had insisted on staying with the platform. "Maybe I can make myself useful and salvage something," he had said. Kell had thought it was remarkable enough that the human was remaining conscious.

All that activity had taken only minutes, which was just as well, because the Klingon knew they didn't have much time.

Fuller assembled the survivors near the edge of the woods, keeping the central structure in sight.

"We don't have much time," Fuller said, seeming to pluck the thought from Kell's mind. "We're cut off from the ship, and we still have a rescue mission and people likely trapped under what's left of that building."

Just then, all of their communicators chirped at once. "Hold on," Fuller said, pulling out his own communicator. He spoke quickly into the device. Then he listened for a long moment and finished by saying, "I will have to talk to my people. Give me some time." He flipped the communicator shut.

"That was our attackers, who have asked for our immediate surrender. They say that if we surrender our weapons, we will not be harmed," Fuller said.

"Do you believe them, sir?" Benitez asked.

"Not for a second," Fuller said. By the muttering of Benitez and the others, Kell saw that they agreed with the chief.

"This has been a setup from the beginning. We were lured here by this attack on the colonists. Then the building was detonated to draw us into the open to rescue the settlers. I think we gave them a surprise, though, when we fought off the vehicles. Whatever their plan had been, that changed things."

"What now?" the Klingon found himself asking.

"Now we have a choice. We can accept their terms and surrender, or we can fight. They claim to have a ship, which our tricorders confirm. And that ship will have shields, sensors, and heavy weapons. It will be a lot tougher than those flying platforms. Now, the book recommends surrender when confronted by overwhelming force. We are supposed to preserve our lives and survive to provide intelligence to Starfleet."

"What do you say, sir?" Parrish asked.

"Well, we are badly outgunned. In fact, our weapons will probably not be able to harm the vessel. I would say we are facing overwhelming force," Fuller said.

Kell shuddered inside. For a moment, he had thought he had seen some surprising strength in the security officers, something of a warrior's spirit. But ultimately, he knew, they were only human, only Earthers.

"For me, that means only one thing," Fuller said.

The section chief paused for a moment, then said, "We attack."

For a moment, the Klingon did not think he had heard correctly; then a cheer erupted from the assembled teams. "We would be signing our own death warrants if we put down our weapons, and death warrants for the settlers we are here to help. Whatever else the attackers are after, they want us dead. I say we give them a surprise instead," Fuller said.

This time, the cheer was louder and, before Kell could stop himself, his own voice had joined in.

"Approaching warp eight, sir," Sulu said, then, "Warp eight."

"The other vessel has entered the star system up ahead and is decelerating. We will overtake them in four minutes twenty-seven seconds," Spock said.

"Ready phasers," Kirk said. "Slow to impulse speeds as we enter the system, Mr. Sulu. Report, Mr. Spock."

Kirk turned to see Spock looking up from his viewer. "No life, Captain. Two small planetoids near the sun. A large asteroid belt. The asteroids have high iron ore and nickel content. There is also a single gas giant. It is a developing star system, not yet fully mature."

"Any signs of energy or other ships?" Kirk asked.

"No," Spock said. "Orion vessel is entering the asteroid belt."

"Looks like it might make a good hiding place," McCoy added.

"I think you may be right, Doctor," Kirk said. He turned to DePaul. "Navigator, plot as many of those asteroids and objects as you can. Tie into Mr. Spock's station for data.

"Aye, sir," DePaul replied.

"Vessel reducing speed to impulse. They have disengaged impulse engines and are entering the asteroid field on thrusters."

"Reduce speed to impulse. Follow them, Mr. Sulu,

but be careful in there, Lieutenant, try not to scratch her."

"Aye, sir," Sulu replied. "I have them on screen now, maximum magnification."

A moment later, the screen showed the asteroid field, whose large and small objects formed a horizon line that stretched off in both directions, seemingly forever.

Kirk knew that besides the enemy ship, each object in the field was a potential threat to the *Enterprise* and its crew. Though the navigational deflector would easily handle the smaller objects, many of the larger ones would be navigational hazards for the ship.

And inside that mess, Kirk knew, the smaller ship would have an advantage in maneuverability.

"Scotty, maintain reduced shields and phasers until I order an increase, but keep navigational deflectors at maximum," Kirk said. "Disengage impulse engines. Thrusters only, Mr. Sulu."

"Thrusters only," Sulu said, as he slowed the ship.

"Entering asteroid zone now," Spock said.

The deflectors had cleared the area in front of the ship of small objects. As the *Enterprise* entered the system, it passed an asteroid that was small, yet still several times larger than the *Enterprise* itself, more than large enough to seriously damage the ship during even a low-speed collision.

There were too many variables again. Kirk didn't like it. And he didn't like the idea that an enemy vessel was directing the *Enterprise*'s actions.

He couldn't shake the feeling that his ship was a pawn in someone else's game.

Sulu delicately maneuvered the starship through space between three asteroids. The largest was perhaps half a kilometer in diameter; the others were about half that size.

At impulse speeds, maneuvering would have been completely impossible. Using the much slower maneuvering thrusters, it was just nearly impossible.

Kirk could see the set in Sulu's shoulders. The helmsman's concentration was written there.

"The vessel is moving," Spock said. "They have turned about and are coming toward us."

Kirk stared at the viewscreen. One large and one small asteroid obscured the ship up ahead.

"Phasers ready," Sulu said.

"Track him carefully. If they open fire, return fire at will," Kirk said.

"Vessel is charging a new system," Spock said.

Kirk spun to the right to look at Spock's science station. One of the large screens above still showed a diagram of the Orion ship. A red light was flashing near the nose of the vessel.

"A new weapons system?" Kirk asked.

"Apparently," Spock said.

The other screen above Spock's station showed a wire-frame readout of the asteroid field in front of the ship. Behind the large asteroid, he could see a blip moving closer to the *Enterprise*.

"Ready, people," Kirk said.

A moment later the Orion suddenly appeared from behind the large asteroid in front of them.

A split second later, green energy flared from the vessel, rocking the *Enterprise*. The jolt was much stronger than before.

"Return fire," Kirk said.

Kirk saw twin red phaser beams lance out at the ship. But before they made contact, the Orion vessel had disappeared behind another asteroid. So instead of hitting the ship, the phasers pulverized a large chunk of the top of the asteroid.

Though completely ineffective against their attackers, it made for an impressive display.

Kirk looked over his left shoulder to see Scotty's panel lighting up. "Damage, Scotty?"

Without turning around, the chief engineer shook his head. "Shields are down twenty percent. Current capacity is forty percent because we were running at lower power, but I could give you eighty, sir."

"I don't think we'll need it, Mr. Scott, but keep it in reserve," Kirk said, an idea already forming in his mind.

"Mr. Spock, that new weapon, was that disruptor fire?" Kirk asked.

Kirk turned and saw Spock's raised eyebrow.

"Yes, sir."

"Klingon?" Kirk asked.

"Possible, but not certain," Spock replied. Then he pointed at the wire-frame tactical display above him.

"Enemy vessel is holding position behind this asteroid. It is .83 kilometers in diameter," the Vulcan said.

"Mr. Sulu, take a position one kilometer from that asteroid," Kirk ordered. Then he stood.

"What does that look like to you, Doctor?" Kirk asked McCoy as the asteroid took a center position on the screen.

"That looks like an old-fashioned bushwhack, sir," McCoy said.

"My thinking exactly," Kirk said.

The bridge crew was silent for a moment, waiting for Kirk's next orders. He was determined not to disappoint them.

"I think we've played their game long enough. It's time to change the rules," he said.

"Sir?" Spock asked, his eyebrow rose again.

"The pawn is about to take the queen, Spock," Kirk said, allowing himself a smile.

Kirk knew just how he was going to do it.

He thought it would make a very impressive display.

"If we hit the second Orion ship while it is still on the ground, we might have a chance. And right now it is five hundred meters in that direction," Fuller said, pointing to the portion of the settlement the tricorder had labeled a recreational field. It was situated to the east of the two rows of smashed dwellings and just north of the settlers' own landing field. "My team will come at them from the landing field to the south. You will come at them from the north from behind what's left of those houses," he said to Section Chief Brantley.

"Since communicators will still be out, wait for my signal. Partners should stay together, but teams should disperse as much as possible. Let's not make it easy for their sensors to track all of us at once. Move out."

Both teams headed out at a full run.

As they started out, Kell could hear his communicator chirping.

"I got them," Fuller said, pulling the communicator to his ear as they moved. "We've considered your offer," the Klingon heard Fuller say. What followed was a string of human expletives, some of which Kell understood and some he did not. Then Sam Fuller was out of earshot.

The Klingon ran on. "It is a good day to die," he said to himself, wondering if he would be soon standing at the River of Blood, looking at the afterworld *Sto-Vo-Kor*.

They soon came around the south side of the human

cultural center, and Kell spared the rubble a glance. The Klingon wondered briefly about the humans underneath it.

Though he expected to die, he knew that meant the security force would fail in its mission and the settlers would also die. As a Klingon, he should not have been troubled by the death of weakling humans.

Yet he found that he was. Perhaps it was the cowardice of the attackers and the genuine courage he had seen in the Starfleet humans. For the moment, he reckoned, he was on the right side of this fight—even though he was fighting alongside bitter enemies of the Empire.

He did not doubt that most humans were weak and deceitful. But he had found a small number in Starfleet security that seemed to know something of honor.

For now, that was enough.

At the far end of the cultural center, Fuller ordered the team to disperse. The Klingon and Benitez took a position near the center, keeping a careful eye on Fuller.

A moment later, they were out in the open and racing for the settlement's landing site, which Kell could now see for the first time.

"Find cover," Fuller shouted.

The enemy ship came into view and Kell saw it was sister ship to the one that had taken off earlier. The Klingon waited for the inevitable weapons blasts, but none came.

Either they had not seen them yet, or they did not view the Starfleet men as a threat.

Kell led the way, with Benitez following close behind him. The landing field was littered with shuttles and transports, or what was left of them.

The Klingon and Benitez headed for a shuttle that looked mostly intact. In seconds they were behind it. Up close, Kell thought the shuttle looked like a Starfleet design, similar to the ones he had seen on the *Enterprise*.

It might have even been an old Starfleet vessel. He wondered if the anti-Federation settlers knew or cared that Starfleet had built one of their ships.

There was also a large personnel transport that looked too lightly built to be an orbital craft and was probably just for travel within the planet's atmosphere. There were other small vessels that looked like they were shuttles of various sizes and one large vehicle that must have been a construction device of some kind.

Now, of course, all of the ships were badly damaged, no doubt from an even more powerful version of the energy weapon used by the attackers. The Starfleet shuttle seemed to have fared the best, however. Though one nacelle had been blasted off and a hole still smoked on the top of the hull, the ship was basically intact. No doubt Starfleet specifications were more stringent than those for the civilian ships.

"Orions," Benitez said. "Same as the other ship."

Kell nodded. He knew what that meant. "Pirates, then?" he said.

"Maybe, or mercenaries working for someone else."

"The Romulans?" the Klingon asked.

Benitez smiled widely. "Could be. We can't rule anything out at this point." Then his face quickly became serious. "So what's the plan, Flash?"

"We wait for Lieutenant Fuller's mark, then we fight." *And most likely die,* the Klingon thought.

From Benitez's face, the human was having the same thought. And yet, the human was not cowering in fear as Kell would have expected.

"I don't know, Flash, they don't look so tough," Benitez said, smiling again.

"Perhaps we should save the others the trouble and destroy them ourselves," the Klingon said.

Benitez laughed out loud at that. "You're all right, Flash, still a little stiff, but all right."

Then the two men sat in silence waiting for Fuller's signal.

Kell felt his blood warming. It was his father's blood, the same blood that drove his warrior brother, the blood that had driven Klingon warriors since the days of Kahless and the days before those.

He spared one more look at the human beside him, who responded with a grim smile. How did his human blood drive him? What was its call?

Then Fuller's voice rang out, "Fire!"

Before he was conscious of it, Kell was squeezing the firing plate of the phaser in his hand. His first strike hit the side arrowhead shape dead center. At almost the same time, six more beams lanced out from positions nearby, and the vehicle's shield flared brilliantly.

A split second later, the Klingon could see the second team's beams hit the other side of the shield, which flared as brilliantly.

"Focus on the engine," Kell said, as he fired at the rear of the ship, where two cylinders protruded. The shield flared but was just as strong. Other beams lashed out on the engine area and other spots on the ship as the other security people tested the shield.

The shields flared slightly brighter shades of red in different places, revealing small variations in the shield strength. Despite those differences, the shield seemed more than powerful enough to repel fifteen hand phasers.

Kell shuddered as he realized that this would be a short fight.

Just then a panel opened up on the top of the ship and the Klingon could see something moving inside.

He immediately tested the shield above the panel. It was as strong as the shield covering the rest of the ship.

Then something rose out of the ship. It rose slowly, so slowly it seemed like the Orions were toying with them. Kell quickly recognized the object as a cannon of some sort, a larger sibling to the one that the weapons platforms carried.

A much larger sibling.

"Look," Benitez said, pointing to a squat, roughly oval device that sat behind the ship. The human had his tricorder out and was scanning. "That's the source of their jamming signal. They are also using it as an outboard sensor array—probably for targeting." Kell quickly turned his phaser to the device and fired. A moment later, Benitez's beam struck it as well.

The Klingon cursed under his breath when he saw the device's shield flare but hold.

Then an idea struck him, and he targeted the ground in front of the device. Dirt exploded into the air, forming a small crater. Benitez followed suit and Kell fired again.

Suddenly, the jamming device leaned forward and tilted over into the crater. Then it was lying on its side, its shield flaring and crackling.

Then at least ten phaser beams struck it at once and the device exploded with a satisfying orange blast. Since it was less than twenty meters from the Orion ship, the blast radiated straight into the ship's own shield, making a large portion of it flare bright red and, for a wonderful moment, blue.

Immediately, all the phaser fire from the two security teams was focused on the weakened portion of the shield at the rear of the ship, but the shield quickly recovered and the beams did no more damage than before.

And still the energy cannon continued its lazy climb out of the top of the vessel.

They do not regard us as a credible threat, Kell thought. *And they may very well be right.*

He doubted the *Enterprise* people had more than a few seconds before the gun came online. Just then, his communicator beeped, as did Benitez's.

The device was in the Klingon's hand in an instant, even as he maintained phaser fire with the other hand.

"Fuller here. Nice work on the jamming device, people. We'll need communicators. Now look sharp and start moving as soon as they open fire."

As the chief said, "Fuller out," the gun on top of the vessel suddenly flared, spitting out a crackling bolt of energy that exploded from the cannon and blasted one of the half-smashed dwellings on the far side of the ship.

Anyone from the other security squad who was behind that building would have been obliterated with the building itself.

Kell targeted the weapon, hoping the shield would be weaker there. Everyone else in his section had the same idea.

But the shield held and the gun began a lazy arc, slowly turning to face the other side of the ship, where Kell and his squad were positioned.

"They are in no rush," Benitez said.

"They are toying with us," he replied. Then he tried some of the human expletives Sam Fuller had used. The Klingon found them extremely satisfying.

The cannon fired and one of the small transports to their right exploded. The Klingon turned away from the flash.

The gun turned again to the other team.

Kell continued his fire, even as he saw that it was having very little effect.

Then he detected motion to his right and turned his head to see Ensign Jawer approach him. The man had obviously been close to the explosion. His uniform was torn and blackened, and he was bleeding from a superficial wound on his forehead, but otherwise he looked intact.

Jawer fell in heavily between him and Benitez. "They got Johnson," Jawer said, gasping for breath.

"We should move out," Benitez said, and Kell nodded.

"Wait, this thing still has some power," Jawer said, checking his tricorder.

"What?" the Klingon shouted.

"The shuttle, it still has some power," Jawer said.

Chapter Twelve

KIRK WALKED TO Spock's station, with Dr. McCoy following closely behind.

"Scotty," Kirk called, and the chief engineer was there in a moment.

Kirk studied the screen above that showed the outlines of the *Enterprise,* the alien ship, and the asteroid between them.

"Mr. Spock. In your opinion, what is the Orion ship waiting for?" Kirk asked.

"They are undoubtedly waiting for us to pursue them. When we come around the asteroid, they will open fire," Spock said.

"And until we do, it's a standoff," Kirk supplied.

"Yes," Spock replied.

"We could ask them to move," Kirk said.

"Ask, Captain?" McCoy said.

"In the strongest terms possible," Kirk said. "Mr. Spock, photon torpedoes are standing by?"

"Yes, Captain," Spock asked. "But it will be difficult to hit a moving target in such crowded quarters. Our chances of hitting an asteroid are much greater than of hitting the enemy vessel."

"That is what I'm counting on, Mr. Spock," Kirk said.

Mr. Scott's face lit up with understanding. "Aye, Captain, that would work just fine."

"What would?" McCoy groused.

Scotty turned to the doctor. "A well-placed torpedo detonated underneath the Orion ship could force them to run from the debris and—"

"Right into our sights, Doctor," Kirk finished. He turned to Spock, "Mr. Spock, please select an appropriate target, something that will make an…impressive display."

"Already done, sir," Spock said, and then he touched a control on his panel and the display suddenly showed a simulated *Enterprise* firing two torpedoes in rapid succession.

The first torpedo went around the large asteroid to the left, finding a target almost directly below the Orion ship. The second traveled to the right and found one below and behind it.

They struck their targets almost simultaneously and the simulated debris hit the vessel a moment later.

Kirk turned to see the rest of the bridge crew watching the exchange. From their faces, he could see that they were as pleased as he was to be turning the game around.

"Mr. Sulu, ready photon torpedoes to fire at Mr. Spock's coordinates. And ready phasers. Target their weapons first, I don't want any scratches on our paint," Kirk said.

"Aye, sir," Sulu replied.

"Fire torpedoes," Kirk said.

Sulu's finger hit the control and Kirk could see the flash of light as the torpedoes cleared the ship.

With the viewscreen aimed at the top of the asteroid, where Kirk expected the Orion to appear, he could not follow the torpedoes' trajectory around the asteroid. However, less than a second passed before light from the torpedoes' matter-antimatter explosion filled the screen for an instant.

Almost immediately, Kirk could see the debris from the explosion race up from behind the asteroid.

One of the larger pieces of debris Kirk recognized by its arrowhead shape.

"Fire phasers," Kirk ordered.

Twin red beams lanced out and struck the ship.

"Direct hit on their disruptor weapon," Spock said.

"Fire on particle-beam weapon," Kirk said, and another blast touched the Orion ship.

"Both weapons out," Spock said.

"Target engines," Kirk said.

The phasers released their energy for a third time. But this time, the ship moved with surprising speed considering the beating it had just taken from debris and phaser fire.

The twin red beams hit the space the Orion ship had occupied just a millisecond before.

"Pursue," Kirk said.

The vessel dove for the surface of the asteroid, skimming it and then darting straight up.

Kirk saw immediately what the commander was planning. The quickest way out of the belt was straight up—or perpendicular to the orbital plane. In a few hundred thousand kilometers, the Orions would be above the orbital plane, out of the asteroid field, and in open space.

They intended to run.

Inside the asteroid field, the attacker still had the advantage of maneuverability. While Sulu was doing a remarkable job of moving the *Enterprise* through the asteroid field, the Orion ship was putting more and more distance between itself and the larger ship.

However, at relatively slow thruster speeds, that difference would not mean much. They would have at most a few seconds' head start once they cleared the field.

Kirk was determined to make sure they didn't even have that much.

"Tactical officer," he said. "Keep a lock on the Orion ship. Whenever you have a clear shot with the phasers, take it. Let them know we're serious."

"Aye, sir," the officer replied.

Kirk would rather have had Sulu taking the shots, but targeting and firing phasers would take away from his efforts to guide the *Enterprise* around the asteroids and to keep it in one piece.

The phasers struck out and just missed the fleeing vessel, instead pulverizing a small asteroid.

A hit would be unlikely, but the phasers would give the other commander something else to worry about.

Another shot and another near miss.

"Captain," Spock said. "The vessel is powering its impulse engines."

"What?" came Scotty's startled reply.

Kirk was equally surprised. Even one-quarter impulse inside the asteroid belt would be near-suicidal.

"Engaging impulse," Spock said.

On the viewscreen, the Orion ship darted forward, narrowly avoiding a large asteroid. It plowed through a series of small ones, barely pushing them away with its deflector shields.

"Increase magnification on screen, stay with them," Kirk ordered.

What followed was another series of near misses with larger asteroids and many more direct hits with smaller ones, the space debris flaring brilliantly against the ship's deflectors. With a combination that was nearly equal parts good piloting, speed, and luck, the Orion ship seemed to be doing the impossible.

"If they survive, they will clear the field in forty-eight seconds," Spock announced.

The seconds ticked by and then Kirk saw the inevitable. The ship was going to make it, and when they cleared the field they would have a several-minute head start.

They had surprised him again, Kirk realized. Well, he wasn't out of surprises either.

"Ready photon torpedoes," he ordered. "And a class-one probe."

Kell looked at the shuttle in disbelief as Ensign Jawer tried to force the door open with his hands.

"It will never fly," the Klingon said.

A moment later, Benitez was helping Jawer pull at the door.

Kell wondered if they were thinking of simply hiding themselves in the vessel and hoping the enemy did not find them.

Humans. The Klingon shook his head.

Whatever Jawer and Benitez had in mind, they wouldn't get the shuttle open with bare hands.

"Would you give us a hand?" Jawer asked.

"Stand back," Kell said. "And keep up the fire."

Both men complied immediately, stepping away from the shuttle door and drawing their phasers.

Kell adjusted his own phaser, pointed it at the door,

and fired. The door glowed red for a moment. The Klingon moved quickly, forcing it open with his boot. The superheated metal gave way and the door crumpled open.

"Get in!" Kell shouted to Jawer. The ensign hurried inside, taking care not to touch the still-hot door.

Benitez was next, then the Klingon.

The interior of the shuttle was remarkably intact...if you ignored the gaping hole in the ceiling and the top of the far wall.

"Give me a minute," Jawer said, leaping for the command chair.

Kell and Benitez took positions in front of the hole in the ceiling and wall. They pulled out their phasers and began firing.

Jawer was a blur of motion that the Klingon was able to track with his peripheral vision.

"Weapons?" Kell asked.

"No," Jawer said. "No weapons on this model and the settlers didn't think to add them."

Then Jawer jumped from the seat and pulled open a panel on the floor. He reached down, studying the circuitry for a moment.

"Main drive is offline. Antigrav systems available via battery power. Navigational deflectors are also online. Oh yeah, and we have music," he said, flipping a switch. Suddenly loud noise that Kell recognized as human music filled the shuttle.

It was a disquietingly cheerful sound.

"Can it fly?" Benitez asked excitedly.

Kell turned to the ensign.

Jawer nodded. "We might be able to get airborne with the antigrav system."

"Can we ram them?" the Klingon asked.

Just then an explosion rocked the shuttle. Dirt flew up in the air. The bolt must have struck very nearby.

Kell's communicator was in his hand. "Anderson to Fuller," he said.

A long moment later came Fuller's voice, sounding surprisingly calm for a human in his situation. "Fuller here."

"Chief," Kell said. "We're in the Starfleet-surplus shuttle. We may have something here. Could you keep fire off us for a few minutes?"

"I think we can, Ensign. Good luck. Fuller out."

"We can't ram them," Jawer said. "I would need to route a self-destruct to do any damage to that ship and that would take too long. But we do have navigational deflectors."

Benitez nodded. "They work against solid objects like debris, small asteroids—"

"Or a ship," Kell finished for him.

"Yes, I could program the system for a single concentrated burst. It would make a pretty good weapon. We'd have to be airborne and we'd get only one shot."

Kell realized that both men were looking at him, waiting for his word.

"What do you think, Flash?" Benitez asked.

"Do it. Do you need help?" the Klingon asked.

"No, just give me a minute," Jawer said, already at work.

Kell and Benitez resumed fire on the Orion ship. As they did, they saw Fuller and two more officers emerge behind a transport and race toward the enemy vessel.

They were carrying small pieces of equipment that Kell did not recognize. They covered the distance to the ship quickly, and as they ran, the Klingon saw that one of the officers was Ensign Parrish.

Whatever they were doing, it was both foolish and brave.

Meanwhile, the weapon at the top of the ship was turned away from the landing field and searching for a target in the row of dwellings on the other side.

About thirty meters from the ship, the three humans stopped in their tracks and started digging. Suddenly Kell had an idea of what they were planning. It was clever.

He had read about intentionally overloading a phaser in order to make it explode in *The Starfleet Survival Guide*. Fuller had bound the phasers to something else, presumably to amplify the explosion.

Kell only hoped they had enough time to try it.

When the weapon turned to Fuller's team it would be all over very quickly. And at point-blank range, there would be nothing left of the humans.

"Ready," Jawer announced.

"Wait for my mark," Kell said.

"We'll have to be airborne first. And then we'll only have a few seconds to fire," the human said.

Kell felt the stirrings of something he had not felt since the battle began.

Hope.

Fuller and the other two took positions several meters apart and started digging under the shield.

Kell saw that they might succeed.

If Sam Fuller and his team succeeded in doing what they were attempting...and if Jawer's plan worked...

It was a lot of *if*s, but it was better than hand phasers against a heavily shielded vessel.

Fuller and the others pushed their equipment into the holes they had created and under the shield. Then they pulled back.

Pulling his hands up, the male ensign must have touched the forcefield. His body spasmed violently.

Then it began to burn.

Kell saw that it was hopeless for the man. Unfortunately, it was not quick.

Parrish ran to the human, who was between her and Fuller, but the chief pulled her away from the dying ensign, and the two began to run.

As if suddenly woken up from a sleep, the weapon on top of the Orion ship spun quickly toward the running security officers.

In a few seconds the humans would be vaporized.

But the Orions did not have a few seconds.

Three explosions from the charges placed by the team lit up the interior of the shield.

It was then that Kell realized just how clever Fuller's plan had been. The shield contained the blast within its volume, which extended about twenty meters around the ship. For a moment, the vessel was surrounded by a violent, red-orange blast that reverberated through the ground and even shook the shuttle.

Fuller and Parrish were thrown to the ground as the Klingon shouted "Now!" to Jawer.

Kell watched as Jawer hit a switch and...

Nothing happened.

The human hit it again. The shuttle whined for a moment but stayed just where it was.

"Now!" the Klingon repeated, with even more force this time.

"What is it?" Benitez asked.

"We've got a problem with the main circuit, I've got to reroute," Jawer said, his hands a blur of motion.

"Hurry," Kell said, as he watched the blast dissipate within the Orions' shield. Incredibly, the shield still held.

But more of the phaser strikes, including the Kling-on's own, were hitting the shield, which was now flash-ing blue and purple. It was weakening.

The weapon on top of the vessel was also a crumpled mess. And the ship was slanted to the ground, because two of the four landing struts that were closest to the blast had disappeared.

Fuller and the others had hurt them.

Kell watched Fuller and Parrish get up, backing away from the vessel, their phaser beams lancing out at the Orion ship as they moved.

Then the vessel began to rumble. It straightened out and the Klingon realized that they had engaged their own antigravity system.

The Orions were becoming airborne.

Up until now, Kell sensed they were toying with the Starfleet people. But the humans had given them an-other surprise. The time for play was over. The Orions meant to finish this and finish it quickly.

Unless they could give them another surprise.

"What is the problem?" Kell bellowed.

The Orion vessel rose.

"Apparently, there's been some *wear and tear* on this shuttle recently," Jawer said, defiance in his voice.

The Klingon shouted his response. "It's about to have a lot more *wear and tear!*"

Chapter Thirteen

"PROBE IS AWAY, Captain," Spock said.

A moment later the viewscreen showed the probe appear ahead of the ship, its thrusters making it look like a small comet as it traveled ahead and out of view.

"Take position, Mr. Sulu," Kirk said.

"Aye, sir," Sulu said as he guided the ship behind one of the larger asteroids. This one, Kirk knew, was more than a kilometer in diameter, more than big enough for their purposes.

"Switching main viewer to the probe's transmission," Spock said as the screen showed the probe's distant view. In the left-hand corner, the image showed a small-looking *Enterprise* hugging the surface of the asteroid. The rest of the screen was filled with the asteroid field, the edge of which was now visible.

Many of the asteroids turned and moved, catching the light from the system's star. For the first time, Kirk realized the scene was quite peaceful, beautiful actually.

"All systems ready, Captain," Spock said.

"Fire," Kirk said, without hesitation.

The probe showed seven streaks lash out from the *Enterprise* in succession. They traveled in an apparently lazy arc away from the ship, around the asteroid, and out toward the edge of the orbital plane and the end of the debris field.

Then the torpedoes diverged, taking carefully selected positions near larger asteroids. Then, virtually simultaneously, the antimatter charges in the torpedoes met the matter and they exploded.

The resulting series of explosions was remarkably bright and Kirk had to shield his eyes for a moment. The charges immediately pulverized the nearby asteroids and sent debris flying in all directions.

The resulting chain reaction of destruction was, Kirk thought, both terrible and, in its own way, beautiful. With debris racing in every direction at high speed, it was only seconds before the large debris cloud struck the asteroid shielding the *Enterprise*. For a moment, the asteroid seemed to be swallowed up, and then the image disappeared.

"Probe destroyed," Spock said.

The main viewer once again showed a view of what was ahead of the ship—in this case, the asteroid.

Kirk turned around to watch Spock, who was looking into his station's viewer.

Kirk waited. After long seconds, Spock looked up and said, "Debris cleared, no remaining significant navigational hazards on our course."

Spinning around, Kirk said, "Take position, Mr. Sulu."

The *Enterprise* turned and moved away from the asteroid.

"Deflector screens and navigational deflectors on maximum," Kirk ordered.

"We're in position, Captain," Sulu said.

The screen showed an orange-red tunnel of dust ahead of them, forming a path the torpedoes had cut out of the asteroid field.

"Ahead one-quarter impulse," Kirk said.

The ship began to move and the viewscreen immediately showed space dust and small pieces of asteroid flashing against the deflector screens. Kirk knew the navigational deflectors would push most of the larger pieces out of the way.

Most, but not all.

The deflector screens would handle the rest, but even a pebble-sized piece of debris would pack a tremendous punch when it was struck by a starship going at impulse speeds.

"Shields holding," Spock said.

"Half-impulse," Kirk ordered.

"Half-impulse, aye," Sulu responded.

Kirk sensed Dr. McCoy behind him, leaning closer to the command chair, then gripping it tensely. The doctor was nervous.

Well, Kirk thought, *he has every right to be.*

"Shields holding," Spock said.

"Three-quarter impulse," Kirk ordered.

"Three-quarter impulse, aye," Sulu said.

Kirk could hear the acceleration of the ship, while the main viewscreen showed more and more flashes of energy as the *Enterprise* picked up speed—hitting more and more debris in a shorter and shorter period of time.

Soon, the space in front of them disappeared. It was replaced by a constant and pulsing blast of energy. Kirk knew that, from the outside, the *Enterprise* resembled a fireball, like the first space capsules as they plunged to earth.

"Increasing power loss to shields," Spock announced. "I recommend that we do not increase speed."

"Agreed," Kirk said, and he could feel McCoy relax behind him.

"We will clear the orbital plane in six seconds," Spock said.

"Five.

"Four.

"Three.

"Two.

"One."

The crackling energy on the viewscreen rapidly dissipated and began to show the familiar starfield.

For a few more seconds there were a declining number of flashes against the shield, and then they were gone. They were out of the asteroid field.

"Intercept course," Kirk said. "Maximum warp, maximum acceleration."

"Maximum warp," Sulu acknowledged.

"Lieutenant Uhura," Kirk said. "Jam any transmissions from the Orion ship."

"Aye, sir," came the reply.

Kirk could both hear and feel the engines' acceleration as the *Enterprise* operated at full power. It felt good. The pretense was gone. He was no longer going to hide the ship's full capabilities.

The Orion ship had proven too dangerous to toy with any longer.

He would simply have to insure that the vessel did not report to its base. He would also have to insure that he learned who was behind the staged attack.

"Warp eight," Sulu said.

"Interception in one minute fourteen seconds," Spock said.

"Ready photon torpedo," Kirk said.

Almost immediately, Sulu announced "Photon torpedo armed and ready."

Spock appeared on Kirk's right side. "Captain," he said. "A direct hit with a photon torpedo would likely destroy the vessel."

"Yes, Spock, but I'm not aiming for a direct hit. But we need to end this now." Kirk leaned forward. "Mr. Sulu, I want the photon torpedo to detonate in front of the vessel, close enough to shake them up a little. Fire at will."

"Torpedo away," Sulu said.

Kirk watched the torpedo streak away from the ship and disappear into the starfield. A moment later the space in the distance flared for a moment.

"Lieutenant Uhura, please hail the Orion vessel. Tell them to stop and prepare to be boarded."

"No response to hails," Uhura said a moment later.

"Mr. Spock?" Kirk said.

"Vessel is maintaining speed," Spock announced from his station.

"It looks like we are going to have to do this the hard way," Kirk said. "How long until interception, Spock?"

"Twenty-four seconds," the Vulcan announced.

The ship appeared as a distant flare on the viewscreen.

"Maximum magnification," Kirk ordered and the ship took shape. "Mr. Sulu, prepare another torpedo. Detonate this one behind them. I want their warp engines offline. It's time to end this. Fire at will."

"Torpedo away," Sulu said.

Kirk watched as the torpedo approached the ship and exploded in a brilliant flash of energy.

"Vessel dropping out of warp," Spock announced.

"Impulse only," Kirk ordered. "Interception speed."

"Impulse speed, aye," Sulu said.

"Uhura?" Kirk asked.

"Still no response to hails," the communications officer said.

"They are at full impulse and are not decelerating," Spock said.

"They don't seem to know when they're beaten, Captain," McCoy offered from behind him.

"Apparently not, Doctor," Kirk said. He stood up, studying the viewscreen carefully. He felt he was missing something.

But he had no more time to waste. He had twenty-one people trapped on a planet light-years away from the ship. And he had a notion of what was happening to them.

"Phasers ready. Target their engines," Kirk said. "Fire."

"Firing phasers," Sulu said as the twin red beams lanced out, striking the ship directly.

"Engines are offline," Spock said. "They are coasting now."

"Excellent. Lieutenant Uhura, continue hails," Kirk said. "Spock, have the transporter room standing by to beam the crew of that ship on board."

Then he turned to the tactical station. "Lieutenant Giotto, please have a security team meet our guests in the transporter room and escort them to the brig."

"Mr. Sulu, bring us about. Mr. Spock, when we have matched speed with the vessel engage the tractor beam."

After a few seconds, Spock announced, "Tractor beam engaged."

"Do scans show any remaining weapons?" Kirk asked.

"No," Spock replied.

"Begin deceleration to space normal speed," Kirk said. "Prepare to lower shields and begin transport."

Kirk turned to the doctor. "Let's see if they're more talkative in person, Bones."

The viewscreen lit up with a tremendous flash and Kirk felt the ship rock under him.

He knew two things instantly. First, the Orion ship had destroyed itself. And second, they had hurt the *Enterprise.*

"Damage report," he called out.

Kell could see the security officers on the ground keeping up the fire. The shield of the Orion ship was clearly weakening. Given enough time, the ground force would succeed.

But Kell could see that time was their enemy as much as the Orion vessel.

As it rose, another cannon appeared from a hatch on the bottom of the ship. While the cannon on the top had been rendered a twisted and useless mass of metal, this one looked fully functional—and very deadly.

The ship turned slowly, wobbling slightly. They were no longer toying with the Starfleet team, however. The Klingon saw that the ship was having trouble with its stabilizers.

That would buy them a little time. If sensors and targeting systems were damaged as well, that would buy them even more.

Then the cannon exploded its deadly fire, vaporizing one of the other ships in the landing field. The gun moved immediately, turning toward the shuttle.

"Now, Ensign Jawer," Kell called out.

Surprisingly, the human called out, "Got it," and hit one of the controls. The shuttle lurched straight up in the air, rocking as it did so. The Klingon kept to his feet, barely, as did the others.

In the same instant, the enemy ship's cannon fired. The beam passed just meters beneath the shuttle, striking the ground the small ship had occupied just a moment before.

"I just need a second to power up the navigational deflectors," Jawer called out.

"I doubt we have a second," Kell replied tersely.

A beep sounded in the cabin and the Klingon thought it was an alarm. Then he realized what the sound was.

"They're hailing us," Benitez said, looking down at the control panel.

"Almost got it," Jawer said.

"Put them on," Kell said. Perhaps he could buy them the time they needed.

"Humans," said the voice on the com system. "You will die now. Your pitiful efforts would be noble if they were not so...pitiful." Kell could clearly hear humor in the being's voice.

"Let us meet face-to-face and I will end *your* pitiful, cowardly life," the Klingon said.

"Defiant, even now. Do you think you can harm this ship with your unarmed, barely powered piece of trash?" the voice asked. "Humans, so powerless and soon to be so short-lived."

"Got it," Jawer hissed.

"Perhaps not as powerless as you think," the Klingon shouted. Then he turned to Jawer and said, "Now!"

Jawer hit one of his jury-rigged controls and...

Nothing happened.

"What were you saying?" the voice asked. Then it laughed, actually laughed at them.

"What?" Kell bellowed to Jawer, who was now working furiously at his mess of wires.

"Just a second," Jawer said. "Bad connection, circuits are fried."

"I was saying that cowards like you make Denebian slime devils look like noble creatures," Kell said.

"Brave words, human, brave *last* words," the voice taunted.

"Do something," Kell hissed to Jawer.

"I need to run a patch for the circuit," Jawer said.

"No time. Do something *else!*" the Klingon said.

A light switched on the control panel blinked and an alarm sounded.

"They've got a weapons lock," Benitez announced.

"Now!" Kell shouted.

Jawer didn't hesitate. He plunged two hands into the large cables at the center of his work. The Klingon saw instantly what the human was doing. Without the time to properly patch the circuit, he was going to make the connection with his own hands.

Jawer did it and the high voltage jolted through his body, arching the human's back. The power surged for a moment before releasing Jawer, who immediately dropped to the shuttle's floor.

The shuttle itself shook only slightly, staying surprisingly stable. For a moment, Kell thought the human's plan had not worked. Then he looked outside to where an unseen hand seemed to have grasped the Orion ship, hurling it back hundreds of meters in a sudden, violent arc.

The arc slowed and Kell imagined the enemy crew members fighting for control as their stabilizers and antigrav system were overwhelmed.

At the far end of the arc, the ship had slowed almost to a stop. It almost looked like the Orions might regain control before the vessel hit the open field.

Almost.

The collision was not as powerful as Kell would have liked, but he was sure it was enough to rattle the ship solidly. Even at the few-hundred-meter distance, he could see that the two remaining landing struts were crushed under the weight of the vessel.

Then Kell spared a glance at Jawer. The human had showed courage worthy of a Klingon and had no doubt saved their lives. Benitez was alternately pushing on the human's chest and breathing into his mouth in an effort to revive him.

Kell thought it was another good effort, but hopeless.

Suddenly, Benitez stopped and looked up. "I have a pulse, and he's breathing."

Astonishing, the Klingon thought, *that a member of such a weak species could survive such punishment.*

Then a flash in the shuttle's control panel diverted his attention. He could smell the unmistakable scent of burning circuitry. Then the shuttle began to drop.

Not a free fall, exactly. The antigrav system was decaying instead of shutting off entirely. *That difference saved our lives,* Kell thought as the shuttle hit the ground. The blow was strong enough to knock him off his feet, but he was able to get up again and he thanked Kahless for that much.

"How is he?" he asked Benitez, getting back to his feet.

"Still alive," Benitez said.

Kell could see that Jawer's hands were burned, badly.

Benitez tried to lift the unconscious security officer but the Klingon pushed him aside, grabbed the man, and slung him over his back.

Kell stepped out of the shuttle and into the daylight. He quickly put Jawer down behind the vessel.

He could see the security officers converging on the Orion ship, phasers blasting.

"Come on," he called to Benitez as he took off at a run, his own phaser drawn.

Benitez appeared beside him and Kell watched with satisfaction as the other officers continued their fire on the Orion ship, whose shield blinked on and off and then disappeared.

A moment later they were in range, perhaps just two hundred meters from the ship. Kell grunted in satisfaction as his beam hit and scorched the unshielded ship.

A barrage of phaser fire met the vessel. The Orions were finished, he realized.

And then he saw the ship start to rise.

When the underside was revealed, Kell could see that the particle-beam cannon was crushed beneath the ship. However, he saw a new weapon come to life when a fixed emitter in the nose of the ship opened fire, blasting over the heads of the security people. The Klingon recognized the weapon instantly. It was a disruptor—and a very powerful one for a ship that size.

Since the gun was fixed, the ship had to turn to target anything. Though shaky and taking damage, the ship was still in the air.

Kell aimed at the cannon, but the ship moved frequently, making the shots fly wide.

"Disperse," Sam Fuller shouted.

The security teams spread out. Kell saw that it would take the Orions longer to pick them off one by one. But out in the open, it would still not take very long.

The Klingon kept moving and saw that Benitez was doing the same. Just then a blast tore a crater in front of him and Benitez, and the momentum of their bodies carried them into it.

Kell hit the ground hard and stayed down. Turning, he fired his phaser as the ship continued its game of dodge-

and-fire. Another blast came his way and the Klingon buried his head as it threw up dirt behind him.

He continued firing but he could see that the Orions had chosen him and Benitez as the next target. From what Kell could see, they would not have to make a direct hit to kill them. A near miss was still close enough with a disruptor blast of that power.

Perhaps, but until then, Kell knew he could still hurt them. He took careful aim at the cannon. Before he died, he would make sure they knew they were in a battle with a warrior.

But before he could fire a great blast flew over his head and toward the attacking ship.

The energy bolt missed, but the second shot did not. The bolt tore a gash in the side of the vessel.

Kell's head shot around to see an Orion weapons platform just fifty meters behind him. For a moment the sight did not register; then he saw Ensign McFadden on top of it. The human was keeping his injured left hand pressed to his chest and piloting the platform with his right.

It was obviously not easy, yet the human was doing it. And he was somehow managing to keep up a steady stream of fire on the ship. A surprising number of the blasts found their target.

The vessel immediately turned toward its attacker and fired a single blast that knocked out the shield, and shook the platform badly. That shaking sent McFadden tumbling backward off the platform and falling two meters to the ground. It also saved his life.

The next blast struck the platform as it sped backward, turning it into a fireball.

Then the Orion ship turned itself and its nose cannon back toward where Kell and Benitez were now standing. The Klingon fired his phaser, knowing it would be useless now. As he fired, he braced himself for what he knew would follow.

Yet nothing happened. No blasts came from the cannon. Then Kell saw why. Gray smoke poured out of the side of the ship.

"Coolant," Benitez said. "McFadden must have hit them pretty hard."

The ship began to shake visibly. Then a thruster fired on the side of the ship, forcing it sideways and away from the security teams.

"They're losing control," Benitez said. "It shouldn't be long now."

The human was right. The ship began to spin as the thruster and antigrav systems began battling each other. All the while the ship was steadily moving back over a rise several hundred meters to the east.

By the time it disappeared behind the hill, its trajectory was unmistakable. They were going down.

Kell regretted that the hill obscured the ship's final descent to the ground. Yet it could not hide the unmistakable sound of a large object hitting the ground with great force. The impact reverberated through the ground and the Klingon could feel it through his boots.

Saying a quick thanks to Kahless, he turned to see Benitez smiling broadly.

"See, they weren't so tough," the human said.

Kell found his face making a smile on its own. "Apparently not," he said.

Then the Klingon saw McFadden struggling to his feet. He barely made it to his knees when he slumped back down. Benitez headed for the man at a run and the Klingon followed.

By the time they reached him, Sam Fuller was already there, along with Leslie Parrish. Moments later, the rest of the surviving members of the three squads were there.

Fuller told McFadden to lie down. "Take a rest, son, you've earned it."

Two of the survivors showed up with a makeshift stretcher that they had fashioned from some hollow metal tubing and fabric. They gently picked up McFadden and put him on the stretcher.

"We'll need another one for Jawer," Benitez said.

Then, without a word to each other, Kell and Benitez turned to the shuttle and headed back at a trot. They found Jawer still unconscious. After a quick check, Benitez said, "His pulse is strong. I think we can move him."

Once again, Kell picked up Jawer and carried him over one shoulder. By the time they returned, the two officers were finishing a second stretcher.

Another human, a female, had her arm in a sling. The Klingon recognized her as a survivor of the center squad, who had been first hit by the weapons platform. After Ordover had been killed, she had been reassigned to Fuller's section. Now her right arm was bloodied and apparently useless.

"Jawer is injured," Benitez said, as he helped Kell put the man on the stretcher. "He's unconscious and his hands were burned pretty badly."

Nodding, Fuller examined Jawer for himself.

"Nice work in that shuttle. What did you do in there?" Fuller asked the Klingon and Benitez.

"It was Jawer, sir," Kell said.

Benitez said, "He got us in the air and used the navigational deflector as a weapon." The lieutenant studied Jawer, and then he stood up, taking a moment to gather himself. The grief was plain on Fuller's face. Kell shook his head. No Klingon commanding officer would allow his subordinates to see such a naked display of weakness.

Yet the ten surviving Starfleet crew people who gathered around him did not have pity or disgust in their eyes. They were looking at Fuller as if he were their own honored father.

"People, we got hit pretty hard today, but thanks to your courage, the special skills of ensigns McFadden and Jawer, and the lives of eight of our friends and comrades, we are still here. And we still have a mission to complete and some settlers to rescue. We will have time for our grief when those settlers are safe. Until then, we will honor our fallen friends by finishing what they gave their lives to begin.

"We beat some pretty tough odds today, thanks to some of the best work I have ever seen in the field. Be advised that I plan to recommend commendations for all of you. Please do me the courtesy of living long enough to receive them in person."

For a moment, no one spoke. Then Fuller himself broke the silence.

"Let's go," he said.

Chapter Fourteen

LIEUTENANT WEST woke with a start when his intercom beeped. After searching his desk for a moment, he found and hit the button.

"The admiral will see you in his office now," the voice on the other end said.

Shooting up from his desk, West said, "I'll be right over."

Rushing into his washroom, his *private* washroom, West splashed water on his face and ran an open hand through his hair. The result was completely inadequate but would have to do.

Less than a minute later, he was led into the admiral's office. Admiral Justman was engrossed in a data padd and waved him into a seat without looking up.

West took a seat in front of the admiral's desk and waited. A few seconds later, the admiral scribbled something on the padd with a stylus and looked up.

Studying him for a moment, the admiral said, "Sleeping in your office, Lieutenant West?" he asked.

"I...fell asleep at my desk, sir," West replied.

The admiral nodded. "Have you even seen your new quarters?"

"No, sir, but I'm sure they are fine," West said.

"They're better than fine. I insist you visit them when we are through. Acquaint yourself with your bed, Lieutenant," the admiral said.

"Yes, sir," West said.

"Now, what can I do for you?" the admiral asked.

"For me, sir?" West asked, quickly racking his brain.

"You sent me a message last night on your computer, fairly late last night. You said you had a request and said it was urgent. As I thought I made clear yesterday, I take your work very seriously. What do you need?"

West was surprised and too tired to hide it. He had not expected the admiral to speak to him so soon.

"I need information, sir. I was locked out of reports that I need for my work," he said.

"Locked out? I authorized your clearance myself. What reports?" the admiral asked.

"The reports on the final negotiations with the Klingons after the Battle of Donatu V," West said.

West saw a flash of recognition in the admiral's eyes, then something else. It lasted only a moment; then the admiral's control was back and his face unreadable.

"Negotiations you participated in yourself, I believe, Admiral," West said.

"Yes, I did, but only because I was one of the highest-ranking officers left standing," he said.

"I would like to see those reports," West said.

"What could be in them that would be of use to you now? The battle was twenty-five years ago," he said.

"With all due respect, I cannot tell you how useful the information would be until I see it. But given the seriousness of the situation, I don't think we can afford to overlook anything," West said.

The admiral's face set. "I know how serious the situation is, Lieutenant, yet it would take an act of the Federation Council to open that file," he said.

"Why?" West said. "As you said, it was twenty-five years ago."

"At the time the cease-fire was reached, experts in the diplomatic corps and in the Federation Council at the time judged it prudent," the admiral said.

"Perhaps at the time, but it creates a problem for my project now."

Pausing for just a moment to think, the admiral said, "I can't open the file for you, but emergency powers grants me the right to relay vital information in a situation that threatens Federation security. This qualifies. What do you want to know?" the admiral said.

Taking a moment to think, West decided to ask the most obvious question first. "What happened? The battle ended with a cease-fire, without a clear victor. From what I have seen about Klingons, that is unprecedented."

"That is one of the reasons the information was sealed. The experts thought that it might be a sensitive issue for the Klingons internally," he said.

West nodded. "You said it was *one* of the reasons?"

The admiral hesitated for a moment, then said simply, "The other reason is that we could have won. We had them beaten."

Taking a moment to absorb that, West finally asked, "Why didn't you finish the Klingons then, sir?"

"Maybe I should have. I know that is how you think we in Fleet Command think," he said, waving off West's protest. "As you know, I have read your papers at the Academy. I know how you feel about military solutions." He paused. "The reason was simple. We had lost too many good people over a relatively worthless sector of space. I knew we could destroy them to the last ship, and they knew it too, which is why they agreed to a cease-fire. But I also knew how many people and ships we would lose. We had lost so many already. I was not prepared to watch any more die. So I helped put a stop to it."

West was silent for a moment. He was stunned, even more than he had been when the admiral told him about the imminent war with the Klingons.

As a cadet, he had considered himself an expert in Starfleet decision-making and the fatal flaws that drove it. In this case at least, however, Justman had done something West had not thought possible: He had turned down a victory.

Perhaps this man was serious about West's project. Perhaps he truly wanted to find another way and was not simply placating critics and civilian authorities.

Perhaps there was hope.

But first he had a lot of work to do and a lot more questions for Admiral Justman.

"Damage report, Lieutenant," Kirk repeated, as he steadied himself on his feet. It took him a moment to see that the ship was listing; the floor was at perhaps a fifteen-degree angle.

"I'm getting reports from all over the ship," Uhura

said. "I'm compiling the data now. Life-support reports some fluctuations in artificial gravity and inertial dampening systems."

"I noticed," Kirk said, looking at the odd pitch of the bridge.

Behind him, McCoy was picking himself off the deck.

"What was that, Mr. Spock?" Kirk called out. "What did they hit us with?"

"Unknown at this time," Spock said.

"I'll be in sickbay, I have a feeling that business just picked up," McCoy said.

"How bad is it, Scotty?" Kirk asked.

"Sir, I'm a showing problem with half a dozen major systems. I'll have to get to engineering to make a report," Mr. Scott said.

Kirk nodded and watched as the chief engineer made his way to the turbolift in spite of the pitched deck. After an unusual delay, the turbolift doors opened and Scotty stepped inside, shaking his head and muttering under his breath. Kirk could not hear the words, but he was certain that they were nonregulation.

Taking the few steps to Spock's station, Kirk stood for a moment over his science officer's shoulder.

"Anything, Spock?" Kirk asked as the Vulcan peered into his station's viewer.

Turning away, the Vulcan raised an eyebrow and said, "A fascinating weapon, Captain. The destruction of the Orion ship hit the *Enterprise* with a directed electromagnetic pulse that shorted out systems all over the ship."

"But we're shielded against any pulses or radiation," Kirk said.

"True, we are shielded very well against external electromagnetic forces," Spock said.

"You're suggesting that this was internal?" Kirk asked.

"Yes. This was clearly designed to be a weapon of last resort to be used to prevent boarding by a vessel holding the Orion ship with a tractor beam."

"They used the tractor beam as a wave guide for their pulse," Kirk said.

"Precisely," the Vulcan said. "Ingenious and unfortunately very effective. They have overloaded primary and secondary circuits all over the ship and damaged the artificial gravity system directly because the tractor beam ties directly into it."

"Damn," Kirk said. "A sucker punch."

"A sucker punch?" Spock asked.

"Hits you when you are not looking," Kirk said.

"An apt description then, Captain," Spock said.

Kirk headed back to his chair and sat down, hitting the intercom button. "Kirk to sickbay," he said.

"McCoy here," said the doctor's voice.

"Casualties, Doctor?" Kirk asked.

"We're treating a dozen injuries, none serious. Four broken bones and eight assorted cuts and puncture wounds. And unfortunately, the ship's medical scanners are on the fritz. We're making do with hand scanners and tricorders."

"Thank you doctor, Kirk out," he said. Hitting the button again, he said, "Kirk to engineering."

"Scott here," came the reply.

"How bad is it, Mr. Scott?" Kirk asked.

"Captain, I think you better come down here," the chief engineer replied.

"On my way," Kirk said. As he stood, he immediately felt a tinge of vertigo as the tilted floor challenged his perceptions.

Muttering some nonregulation language of his own, Kirk headed for the turbolift.

Stepping into engineering, Kirk was immediately struck by the number of people hurrying back and forth and the number of open control panels. The normally neat and orderly engine room was a flurry of crew and equipment.

Kirk stopped one of the crewmen. "Mr. Scott?" he asked.

"Jefferies tube, sir," the man said.

Approaching the Jefferies tube, Kirk could hear Mr. Scott shouting orders to the engineers below him.

Kirk waited, and the chief engineer climbed out of the tube a few moments later.

"They hit us pretty hard, Captain, with an electromagnetic pulse," Scott said.

"Mr. Spock explained that to me, Mr. Scott. Where do we stand now?" Kirk asked.

Scott turned away for a moment to give orders to one of the engineers who was heading into the Jefferies tube, then turned back to Kirk.

"We have primary and secondary circuits out all over the ship. We're operating on battery power and backup systems in critical areas like life-support and antimatter containment. We can get all systems and circuits back online. Most of the repairs will be replacing blown circuit breakers and patching blown circuits. If we get everyone out of bed and borrow some personnel, we can have most of the work done in less than twenty hours," Scott said.

Kirk shook his head. "Mr. Scott, we don't have twenty hours. We have twenty-one crewmen stranded on a planet with a hostile Orion force. *They* don't have twenty hours."

"Aye," Scott said. "Captain, I can have warp and impulse engines back online in two hours if we squeeze the safety margin, but we have another problem," Scotty said. "It's the artificial gravity system that provides inertial dampening—it's down to less than five percent. It's tied in directly to the tractor beam, so the damage is the worst there. We're still trying to figure out the extent of the problem. And without artificial gravity at full power to compensate for the force of the acceleration—"

"We can't go into impulse without tearing the ship apart," Kirk finished for him.

"With gravity operating at current power levels we would need weeks to accelerate up to full impulse and weeks more to decelerate," Scott said.

Kirk understood. The amount of power needed to provide Earth-normal gravity on the ship was minimal compared to the kind of power required to compensate for the enormous inertial forces created by quickly accelerating to near light speeds.

"But you could give me warp power to get us to the system," Kirk said.

"Aye, but once we get there, we canna use impulse to maneuver into orbit," Scotty said.

Kirk thought for a moment. He could see options swirling in his head, none of them good. And all of them were disastrous for the landing party.

"Could we go into warp from our current position and come out in or very near orbit," Kirk said.

Scotty was shaking his head. "Sir, that's never been tried even in simulation. There would be no margin for error. If we come out of warp too far from the planet, we might as well be on the other side of the galaxy. If we come in too close…"

Kirk nodded. "Understood. Then we will have to be very precise." Turning on his heel, Kirk strode to the intercom.

"Kirk to Spock," he said.

"Spock here," came the Vulcan's voice.

"Meet me in the briefing room. I have something to discuss with you."

Chapter Fifteen

BY THE TIME they reached the beam-down site, McFadden was unconscious. And since Jawer had used his hands to complete the circuit on the shuttle, he had not regained consciousness.

Fuller had seen that they were made comfortable and Ensign Clark insisted on guarding them. She had been injured in the last battle with the Orion ship and her arm was in a sling. However, she could still hold a phaser and seemed glad to have a duty.

Earlier, Kell had watched in amazement when she had argued with Sam Fuller, insisting that she was well enough to join the rescue of the settlers. The Klingon had no doubt that humans' well-known cowardice was true for most of them. However, he marveled at the fighting spirit he saw in the Starfleet security people.

Clearly, a small number of humans were capable of almost warriorlike strength. No doubt, the sniveling masses needed someone to protect them. And the corrupt leaders like Kirk needed capable soldiers to support their own lust for power.

And today these humans had bested a better-armed, better-equipped foe. They had suffered losses of almost half their number and they were still determined to complete their mission.

Besides the three injured crewmen, there were ten officers left who could fight. Sam Fuller's section now consisted of Kell, Benitez, Leslie Parrish, and John Perella.

Chief Brantley also had four officers.

Each of them had one phaser. Though Fuller and Parrish had detonated theirs in the attack on the Orion ship's shield, they had replaced them by taking phasers from the injured Jawer and McFadden.

"Still showing at least twenty life signs," Parrish announced to Fuller.

"Are they moving?" the chief asked.

"No, they are staying near their ship," she replied.

"They are not so tough without their shields and cannons," Benitez said.

"Seems like it," Fuller said. "But let's not count them out. We're going in the central building with the assumption that we are in hostile territory. We may still come under fire. And we don't know how far away reinforcements for our attackers might be, so time is important. Once we get the survivors out, we're going to regroup here. With any luck, the *Enterprise* will be back and we'll have our beam-out."

"Sir, what if the *Enterprise* is not back?" Parrish asked.

"What if the ship didn't make it?" asked one of the officers from the other squad.

The group was silent for a moment.

"Not an option, Ensign. A dozen of those ships would not keep Captain Kirk and the *Enterprise* from returning to pick us up. The captain will be here if he has to tear through the Orion vessel with his bare hands."

Surprisingly, that seemed to satisfy the ensign and the rest of the group. Kell marveled at their naïveté. *They may have courage,* he thought, *but they are still children.* The Klingon shook his head. *To think the coward Kirk would risk anything to retrieve his junior crew.*

"Until then, we will continue to do what we have to do to complete our mission and preserve our lives. We have a duty to report back to Starfleet what happened today," Fuller said.

"What did happen today? Why were the settlers attacked? Why were we attacked?" Benitez asked.

"I can't give you the answer to that. Better minds than mine will have to answer that for all of us later. Our job is to report back to the captain with what we do know. Now let's move out," Fuller said.

The section chief led the way. They moved south, the two security sections sided by side. Passing through the woods, they reached the blasted dwellings and then came into sight of the central building, the one the settlers had called their cultural center.

"Chief Brantley, we will go first. You will provide cover and then follow as we cover you," Fuller said.

Chief Brantley nodded and Kell felt a sting of pride. His team would be going first into danger. Yesterday, he would have thought it impossible that he would take pride in his part of a mission with Earthers. Yet now he did not even question the feeling.

Fuller dashed out first, with the Klingon and Benitez flanking him on the right, while Parrish and her partner flanked him on the left.

They drew no fire and reached the building safely.

Parrish had her tricorder out and was scanning. "I'm

still getting approximately sixty life-form readings," she said. "Just a few meters underground."

"They must be in the basement," Fuller said, examining the site. The building had been nearly leveled, with just some of the walls of the first level still standing.

"Chief Brantley, take your team and set up a perimeter guard," Fuller said. "Keep your eyes open and your tricorders scanning."

"Yes, sir." Brantley nodded and was off. The four officers followed closely. They quickly took positions at the four corners of the building, with Brantley keeping in constant motion, circling the structure.

Then Fuller addressed his team. "We've got to get those people out. We don't know how structurally sound this building is, so we need a way in that doesn't entail blasting through the floor that is keeping the debris off those settlers. Fan out, but partners stay together."

Kell and Benitez circled the building, scanning with their tricorders. Inside, the Klingon could see furniture and equipment, some of which could be salvaged and might be useful if they had some time with it.

Less than a minute after they had started looking, Parrish called out, "I think I have something, sir."

Fuller reached her position first, with Kell and Benitez seconds behind him.

"Here, sir," she said, pointing to a ramp that led to a large service door on the north side of the building. However, the fused mess against the building's foundation was no longer a door, and the ramp had been collapsed by blaster fire.

The colonists had not been meant to escape their building, that much was certain. The Orions intended to make the cultural center their grave.

Why seal them in? Why not just kill them? Kell wondered. *Has it all really been a trap for the Starfleet officers? If it has been a trap, why not wait until the humans converged on the building before blowing it up?*

Too many questions. For now, Kell focused on his duties.

He watched as Fuller examined the top of the fused metal of the door. Perhaps a meter of it was still exposed.

"We're out of time," he said, drawing his phaser and adjusting it. "Step back," he said to the four officers as he approached the door and banged on it with his fist.

"Starfleet security," he shouted down toward the door. "Step away from the door!"

He banged again and repeated his instruction.

Taking a few steps back, he aimed his phaser and fired a short burst at the exposed portion of the door. It glowed red immediately.

The chief adjusted the phaser again and fired a sustained burst.

The door glowed more brightly this time and then disintegrated. For a moment everything was still. Then a section of the floor and wall above the place where the door had stood collapsed.

The collapsing section rumbled briefly, threw up a small cloud of dust, and was still. Fuller was at the opening immediately, calling down.

"Starfleet security. We're here to take you to safety," the chief said.

A moment later a female showed her head through the opening. She looked alert, and very wary.

"We're Starfleet security, we're here to help you," Fuller said, allowing a note of urgency into his voice. "Can we come down and examine your people? We need to move everyone out as quickly as possible."

She studied them for a moment, taking a careful look

at their uniforms and holding her glance on Fuller's phaser.

"You can put those away," she said, pointing to the chief's phaser. "You won't need them down here."

The chief turned to Kell and his partner. "Anderson, Benitez, you're with me. Parrish and Perella, prepare to receive survivors."

The Klingon and Benitez put away their phasers and followed Fuller into the opening in the foundation. Crouching down, Kell peered inside. He could see that a table had been placed under the opening. He was able to step onto it and then onto the floor.

To his surprise, the underground level of the structure had some light, though the far corner was in shadows. The space was open and surprisingly intact, with only a few places where the rubble from above had fallen through.

It was also full of people, at least the sixty that the scanners were showing. Most were adults, fairly young. But there were also older humans and, to the Klingon's surprise, a number of small children.

Then a noise rang out, like the snarl of a *targ*. Then a blur of reddish fur came rushing toward them. Kell instinctively reached for his phaser, but Fuller put a restraining hand on him.

Then the blur was grabbed around the neck and stopped by a young human that the Klingon recognized as an adolescent.

"Sorry, he's excited," the adolescent said, grasping the creature by a collar.

Taking a closer look, Kell recognized the creature as a human equivalent of a *targ*—a dog, he remembered it was called. Though it was larger than a *targ*, it was covered in the reddish fur without any of a *targ*'s tusks or spikes.

Its tail was moving back and forth. He didn't know the meaning of the gesture, but it did not look aggressive.

Benitez stepped forward and patted the creature on the head, which made it jump excitedly and try to pull away from the human who was holding it.

"Golden retriever?" Benitez asked the human.

"Yes," came a response from a small human female, who stepped forward. "His name is Spencer."

The dog creature calmed somewhat when Benitez continued to stroke him. Kell shook his head. The animal reminded him of most humans: soft and frivolous.

"Haven't you ever seen a dog before?" Benitez asked him.

"No," the Klingon said. "We…did not have them on our colony."

"Then you missed out," Benitez said.

Kell disagreed but kept the thought to himself.

Turning his attention to the people in front of him, he saw that they were looking at the security officers with shocked blank stares. Kell recognized the look, which crossed species lines—it was the look of disaster survivors.

A woman clutching her two small children broke the silence when she started sobbing. She approached Fuller as she kept one hand on each of the children.

Reaching Fuller, she released the boy she was holding with one hand and clutched Fuller's arm with it.

"Thank God," she said, and broke out in a fresh set of sobs.

"It's okay, we're here to help you," Fuller said gently to her. Then he raised his head to address the assembled crowd. "I know you have been through a lot, and now I need you to follow me. There are more security officers outside who will take you to a safe place."

"Where is that? Are they still out there?" the woman who met them outside said.

"Excuse me, who am I speaking to?" Fuller asked.

"I'm Lara Boyd. I'm…" She hesitated for a moment. "I'm the leader of this settlement."

"What happened here?" Fuller asked.

"Two ships came, they destroyed our shuttles and transports, then ordered us to assemble here. Then they killed our leader, David Sikes, and locked us down here."

"Did they kill anyone else?" Fuller asked.

"No, I don't think they wanted to hurt us. I think they wanted to insure our cooperation. And we did cooperate. We did not try to leave, and then about twelve hours later there was an explosion."

"They destroyed the building above you, as well as your homes and the other buildings," Fuller said.

The group reacted with a combination of tears and chatter. Astonishingly, they showed no anger.

"Did they make any demands?" Fuller asked.

"No, we tried to communicate with them, to negotiate, but they refused to even talk to us. They killed David and ordered us down here. Do you have any answers? Do you know what they want?"

"We don't know anything for sure, but we think you were rounded up and placed here as bait," the chief said.

"Bait for what?"

"For us. They attacked our team almost as soon as we beamed down," Fuller said.

"Did you even try to talk to them?" Boyd asked.

Fuller seemed surprised by the question. "They refused hails from our starship and seemed more interested in blowing us out of existence than talking." Then he paused and added, "We suffered some losses, but we managed to destroy their heavy weapons and one of

173

their two ships. The other blasted away when we arrived. Their only subsequent communication was to ask us to surrender, but I suspect it was another trap."

"Suspect, but you're not sure," Boyd said, with obvious distaste in her voice.

"I don't know what you mean," Fuller said. Kell could see that the chief's even tone required some effort. *Amazing that he has not struck her yet,* the Klingon thought.

"I mean that you decided to raise your arms rather than take the only opportunity you had to communicate with them," Boyd spat out.

"We decided to preserve our lives and attempt to rescue you people since you were left here to die," Fuller said, barely holding his anger in check.

"Typical Starfleet arrogance. We never asked you to come!" Boyd retorted.

"You never asked!" Fuller exploded. "Your priority-one distress call was very clear! And it didn't specify that Starfleet was not welcome!"

"We left Federation-controlled worlds to get away from your conflicts and aggression," Boyd responded.

"Well, it looks like you found your own," Fuller said.

"What we found—" Boyd started to say, but she was cut off by Leslie Parrish, who stepped forward and shoved her. Boyd was surprised into silence.

"Would you like to know their names?!" Parrish shouted to Boyd.

"What?" Boyd stammered.

"Their names. The names of the eleven people who were killed or wounded so that you could live to judge your rescuers. They have names, and families too," Parrish said. Kell recognized the look in her eye as the one she wore when she blasted the Orion off his weapons platform.

Boyd looked at Parrish uncomprehendingly for a moment, then softened. Then she seemed on the verge of tears herself. "I'm sorry. I'm sorry for your people," she said.

"You have injured people?" one of the settlers, a young man in the back called out. "I'm a doctor."

The chief turned his attention to the doctor. "We'll need you then. Thank you." Then he addressed the crowd. "Prepare yourselves. We're going to rendezvous with the rest of our team at our beam-down site. If the *Enterprise* is not there by the time we arrive, we are going to get you as far away from the attackers as we can until help arrives."

Fuller glared at Boyd. "Any objection, Ms. Boyd?"

"No," she replied evenly.

"Then let's get moving," Fuller said.

"The maneuver is theoretically possible, yes, Captain, but it is definitely not advised," the Vulcan said.

"Can you do it, Mr. Spock?" Kirk asked.

"With the computer, I can perform the calculations to within three one-hundredths of a percent accuracy," the Vulcan said.

"But?" Kirk asked.

"But that would still be several orders of magnitude below any acceptable safety margin," Spock said.

Kirk was suddenly glad he, Spock, and Scotty had the relative privacy of the briefing room.

"That is why this maneuver has never been tried," the Vulcan concluded.

"Then you will have to achieve a higher degree of accuracy with your computations," Kirk said.

"Captain—" Spock began.

"That's an order, Mr. Spock," Kirk said.

The Vulcan considered him for a moment, then said, "Yes, sir."

"We have no choice, Spock," Kirk said, softening his tone. "Our people don't have the luxury of time. I'm sure of that."

"Intuition, Captain?" the Vulcan asked.

Though the Vulcan himself maintained that he never had hunches, which were after all based on emotion, he had developed respect for his captain's.

"Yes, Mr. Spock, and very specific this time. We need to move quickly," Kirk said.

"I shall begin at once," Spock said.

Kirk stood, and the first officer immediately followed suit. "Scotty's team should have repaired the library computer circuits by now," Kirk said.

The two men headed for the door and in moments were stepping onto the bridge, which was a flurry of activity that made the engine room look sedate.

Technicians were everywhere, instructing repair teams that included people from every department on the ship, from botany to the medical staff. Deck panels and consoles had been removed to reveal conduits and circuitry. Sulu and a team had taken apart the helm and navigation console.

Kirk approached Mr. Kyle, who was directing a team that was working on the engineering station.

"Mr. Kyle, where can I help?" Kirk said.

"Lieutenant Uhura needs some help with the communications main circuit. She's in the outer accessway," he said.

Kirk nodded. The main viewscreen was dark and had been partly pulled aside to reveal the cramped circular corridor that ran around the bridge stations.

As he stepped inside, he could see the rear of the navigation console on his right and the outer hull of the ship on his left. The quarters were tight but passable.

Kirk maneuvered quickly past the people working on the defense station and worked his way around to communications, which was the last station before the turbo shaft.

Uhura was working by herself, deep in concentration as she traced a circuit.

"What can I do?" Kirk asked.

Without looking up, Uhura said, "Thank you, Captain, we need to replace the main circuit with the cable at your feet."

Picking up the cable, Kirk grabbed a sealing tool with his other hand and started to work.

Chapter Sixteen

KAREL HAD SPENT the morning at his station without incident, performing his routine maintenance on his console—which ran a cooling subsystem for the main port disruptor bank.

He had yet to fire the weapons in battle. That honor belonged to the weapons officer, Gash. And despite precedent, neither he nor any of the other seven junior weapons officers in the disruptor control room had ever fired the main weapons.

It was an honor that Gash was not willing to relinquish, even in simulations.

Near the end of the duty cycle, everyone was tired and, like Karel, was thinking of something warm and live for dinner.

"Emergency positions," Gash called out.

Karel immediately knew what that meant. Someone in command had ordered a weapons drill. He immediately shut down his maintenance routine and checked his coolant levels.

Because he had not finished the maintenance, his coolant was down to ninety-two percent. That would be enough under normal circumstances, but Karel was not satisfied. He knew there was no such thing as normal battle conditions, either in a drill or in actual battle.

"Fire disruptors," said the commander's voice from the bridge.

A split second later, the disruptor room pulsed with light, heat—and, Karel liked to think, the power of the Empire. His usable coolant level dropped another five percent. A few more full-power blasts and the levels would begin to drop exponentially.

The redundancy built into the system meant that the coolant function would be routed to the secondary system, controlled by the junior weapons officer next to Karel. Even in the event of failure of the primary cooling system, the port disruptor bank would fire. Identical redundancy in the starboard disruptor room protected that system the same way.

Yet, in Karel's entire time at his post, such a failure had never occurred, either in simulation or actual battle.

He did not intend for today to be the first failure.

The Klingon prepared to route coolant from the secondary system as another command came to fire. The room hummed and the temperature rose again as the ship expelled its deadly energy.

And Karel lost another seven percent of his coolant. Now he was down to eighty percent, uncomfortably low.

Just then, Karel felt the ship lurch violently to port, and he smashed his head against his console. The sharp pain was exhilarating and gave him a heightened awareness and clarity.

The jolt, he knew, had been caused by high-speed maneuvers at warp. It had also diverted power from the weapons systems, including the cooling systems.

The Klingon did two things in rapid succession. First, he increased the pressure of his coolant to compensate for the lower power. He knew this would use up the coolant faster but he also knew he had no choice. Second, he began diverting coolant from the secondary system.

"Fire!" came another command.

The room hummed again and Karel lost another twelve percent. He was now down to sixty-eight percent and steadily dropping.

Where was the coolant from the secondary system? He shot a glance at Torg, the junior weapons officer manning the secondary console. As the operator of the primary, Karel was in the senior position. However, he could see by the scowl on Torg's face that by the end of the drill *he* intended to be in the senior position.

It was a foolish move. He was endangering the ship to advance himself. It was also a bad miscalculation on Torg's part.

Karel acted without thinking. In one fluid movement, he stood up, leaned over, gave a battle cry, and brought his closed fist down on Torg's left hand—the hand that had been operating the manual override.

He felt a satisfying crunch of bones and heard Torg howl in pain.

The entire operation had taken mere seconds, and before Torg was finished howling, Karel was back at his station, transferring coolant from the backup to his primary system.

"Torg, increase your pressure to compensate for the lost coolant," Karel barked.

With his peripheral vision, Karel could see Torg

struggling with the controls with his one good hand. To his credit, the Klingon seemed to be managing.

After another high-warp maneuver and two more blasts, Gash announced that the drill was over.

Karel quickly reviewed his own performance. He was pleased with both his efficiency and his remaining coolant level. They might not be records, but they were good.

Satisfied, Karel turned to examine the weapons room. Only then did he see Second Officer Klak standing to the rear, observing.

It was unusual, and Karel was immediately alert.

Gash made his rounds after the drill, examining each console for both the port and starboard disruptor-bank groups. First, he examined the port primary and secondary weapons consoles, grunting as he examined the readings. Then he stood over Karel's own console, making the same noises. Then he moved on to Torg's.

Despite Gash's silence, Karel knew his group had performed well. His own readings told him so.

Turning his attention to the other side of the room, Gash stopped at the starboard primary weapons console, which controlled the firing circuits for the disruptor bank.

"Fool," he said, grabbing the junior weapons officer by the scruff of the neck. He pulled the Klingon backward, out of the chair, throwing him to the floor.

Even from the few meters' distance, Karel could see why. The screen on top of the console revealed that there had been a failure in the primary system and control had been transferred to the backup system.

The Klingon fell hard onto his back, staring up at Weapons Officer Gash. The junior officer was much smaller than Gash, yet Karel could see the lower-ranking Klingon calculating his chances.

Karel's father had once quoted a Klingon proverb to

him: "Brute strength is not the most important asset in a battle." Then his father had added, "But it does not hurt."

As it turned out, the junior officer was not prepared to challenge Gash and slowly took his seat again as Gash shook his head in disgust.

"Poor, very poor," Gash said to the junior officer. "You are demoted to the secondary system." Then he said to the room in general. "You will all be punished for his failure. An extra duty cycle beginning right now with no break for eating. Your *gagh* will have to wait."

Karel bristled. He did not mind punishment that he had earned. But punishing all for the failure of one bred conflict among the disruptor-control officers. Later, the others would seek their own reprisals against the junior officer responsible.

Then that officer would find a way to extract his own revenge by sabotaging the efforts of those around him to embarrass them or to advance himself—as Torg had done to Karel minutes before.

Gash, of course, knew this. Though he was in many ways a fool, he was not a complete fool.

Keeping the officers pitted against each other in that way insured that his own authority would not be challenged—certainly not by more than one Klingon at a time.

It was a good method of command to insure a Klingon's own power. It was, however, disastrous for battle-readiness and kept junior officers embroiled in petty disputes. For the Klingon Defense Force to maintain its full power, a warrior's first concern had to be his duty to the Empire, his second had to be his duty to his ship, and his third had to be his duty to his own fighting force, which in this case was the group in the disruptor room.

"Would you like to conduct an inspection, Second Officer Klak?" Gash asked.

"No, I have seen enough," Klak said, with disdain in his voice. The Klingon knew that Gash would make them pay further for the second officer's displeasure.

Klak turned to go, then stopped and turned back to the room. "Junior Weapons Officer Karel," he said, then paused.

Karel's senses were once again alerted to battle readiness. He saw that he was not the only one. The room went suddenly silent at the sound of the second officer addressing so junior a Klingon.

"I have made the inquiries on your behalf that we discussed," Klak continued.

That was it. The second officer had begun the inevitable, as surely as if he had handed Karel a *bat'leth* and pointed him toward Gash.

Klak had announced that Karel had gone over Gash's head. In fact, he had gone a level above Gash's own superior, the ship's defense commander.

The other junior officers in the room understood immediately.

So did Gash.

The Klingons in the room held their collective breaths, except for Gash, who turned to Karel in disbelief.

For some time, Karel had known that he would have to challenge Gash. But this was not the time or the place he would have chosen. He would have preferred to wait until he had gained more experience and advanced to the senior position at the primary port weapons console, which housed the firing circuits themselves.

But Klak had chosen the time and place for him. Karel gave a passing thought to the second officer's motives and then did the only thing he could do.

He stood.

Karel knew he had to face the consequences on his feet.

"You challenge me, your superior, in such a way, you...Earther," Gash bellowed.

No one in the room moved. Everyone knew that the only greater insult would be for one of them to hurl names at the other's mother in the open room.

"No," Karel spat back, as Gash approached him. "I do not insult my superior, I insult the *son of a female* targ!"

The battle-hardened Klingons in the disruptor room gasped. So did Gash.

Karel knew that what happened next would happen quickly. No more insults would be hurled.

There were no more.

Now there was only battle.

At the beam-down site, Kell watched as the doctor finished dressing Ensign Jawer's burned hands. Then he reached into his large medical bag and pulled out a hypospray and gave him an injection.

He had already dressed McFadden's injuries and placed some sort of a splint on McFadden's left leg. Both men lay motionless in their stretchers.

Fuller had moved quickly. He had organized the fifty-eight settlers into small groups that could keep track of each other if they had to move. The settlers had brought some supplies and Fuller had them distributed.

When the doctor was finished, Boyd appeared, as did Fuller. "I have treated their burns and abrasions. I have set Ensign Clark's arm and closed her wounds. I set Ensign McFadden's leg, but he has a fractured skull and a concussion. He also has a small fracture in one of the vertebrae in his lower back. Ensign Jawer is suffering from severe shock due to electrocution. They are stable for now, but both these men need to be in a hospital, or up in the sickbay of your starship."

"Where *is* your starship?" Boyd said.

"Engaging the enemy that attacked you," Fuller replied coolly.

"Perhaps if you Starfleet types were not so quick to engage your enemies you would not have so many," she spat, then walked away before she could respond.

"Don't let her bait you, Chief," Parrish said.

The doctor stepped forward, "Lieutenant Fuller, please don't take what she says personally. We have all had our differences with Starfleet and the Federation—that is partly why we are here—but we are grateful for what you have done for us."

"Not all of you," Benitez said, gesturing to Boyd.

"Lara has had a rough time," the doctor said. "We came here because we wanted a new way of life. Next to our leader, Lara believed more than anyone. They were...together, and she watched him die yesterday. Right now, she needs to believe in what he stood for...she needs to believe in something."

There was silence for a moment, and the doctor held out his hand. "By the way, I'm Josh Davis."

The chief held out his own hand and said, "Sam Fuller."

Suddenly all the security teams' communicators beeped at once.

"Don't answer," Fuller said, as he pulled out his own communicator.

"Fuller here." He listened for a few moments and then said, "We will consider your offer."

Putting away his communicator, the chief addressed the group.

"That was the Orions again," he said. "They would like us to lay down our arms."

"I'll bet," Leslie Parrish said.

"They say that if we do and deliver ourselves to them, we will not be harmed," Fuller added. "Does anyone think we should?" he asked the combined group of settlers and security officers.

The security people said "No!" practically in unison.

Then three boys whom Kell recognized as human adolescents stepped forward. "We're ready to fight," their leader said in a small voice. "Do you have any weapons for us?"

About half of the settlers nodded in agreement, while the others seemed undecided.

"That will not be necessary," Fuller said. "We are prepared and able to defend you until help arrives," Fuller said.

The boys looked disappointed, which was something Kell understood. They had seen their homes destroyed and knew their families were still in danger. Clearly even civilian humans would defend themselves in that situation.

Fuller saw the boys' disappointment as well, because he added, "But stay ready. Nothing about this mission has been predictable. For now, I'll need you to help us keep everyone together."

Boyd approached Fuller and said loudly enough for everyone to hear, "Aren't you even going to talk to them?"

The chief was clearly taken aback. He waited for a moment before answering, and then said, "Not in person, no."

"Why not?" she said, the challenge clear in her voice. She kept her voice loud and strong. She clearly was playing to her assembled people.

"Because the Orions murdered one of your people, destroyed your colony, and left you to die underneath its rubble. They attacked my people and killed nearly half of them. I intend to stay as far away from them as possible," he said, with equal strength in his voice.

"Perhaps there's something they want. Perhaps we could negotiate," she said.

"Well, they were not interested in negotiation when they arrived, were they? And they refused to speak to my ship when we arrived. And if there was something they wanted they could have taken it and left, but they stayed and waited to ambush anyone who came to rescue you," he said.

"Haven't you even thought about why they are doing what they are doing?" she said.

"Not really," Fuller replied. "I have been too busy trying to keep my people and your people alive."

By now three other adults had taken places next to Boyd.

One of them, a male, said, "What can it hurt to meet with them?"

"Because I think anyone who does will be killed," Fuller replied evenly.

"You don't know that," Boyd said. "Perhaps if your training included peaceful negotiation instead of just how to use a phaser, you would not resist so strongly."

"For your information, Ms. Boyd, a Starfleet officer receives extensive training in peaceful contact and negotiation, before he or she ever picks up a phaser. But we are not trained to walk into the arms of murderers," Fuller said.

Leslie Parrish appeared at Fuller's side. She was holding her tricorder. "They're assembling, sir. At least eighteen of them. I think they're getting ready to move."

"What now, Lieutenant Fuller? Are you going to fight or are you going to talk?" she asked.

"I'm going to move this group to a safer position and then defend it if necessary," Fuller replied.

Then Boyd stepped right up to Fuller, pressing her face nearly to his.

"Well, that is not what I'm going to do," she said.

Astonishingly, the chief allowed the challenge to his authority.

"I am going to settle this directly with the Orions, and I'm going to do it peacefully," she concluded.

The shock Kell felt registered on the chief's face. "Absolutely not," he said firmly. "I can't allow it."

"Allow!" she replied. "I didn't ask your permission. You have no authority over this *civilian* settlement. We wanted to get away from the Federation because we wanted no part of your endless conflicts and your rules. On this planet, we make our own rules and I will not answer to a Starfleet officer with blood on his hands."

"Impossible," Fuller said evenly.

"How do you intend to stop me? Are you going to shoot me with that weapon? Are you going to shoot all of us?" she said, gesturing to the other settlers.

Kell noted, however, that only three of the settlers were standing with Boyd. The others, he was certain, would not follow her. She must have seen that, yet she continued.

"You live by the regulations of your Starfleet, Mr. Fuller. What do your regulations tell you to do?" Boyd said.

"My duty tells me to do my best to talk you out of any self-destructive course of action," Fuller said.

"Well, then consider your best done," she said. "I'm going."

"We're going," said the man next to her. The other two humans nodded as well.

Fuller stared at them in uncomprehending silence for a moment. When he spoke, he did it softly. "Don't do this to make a point."

"I'm not making a point, Mr. Fuller."

"Think about what you're doing," Dr. Davis said to her.

"I know what I'm doing. I'm living by the principles that this colony was founded upon. I'm living by the principles David died for. I'm going to communicate with them," she said to the doctor. Then she turned her attention to Fuller. "We wanted a society not where violence was the last resort, but where it is never a resort. We vowed to approach all others in friendship, without exception."

"That is a wonderful philosophy, Ms. Boyd," Fuller said, "and closer to Starfleet's than you might believe, but it only works if all parties want peace. And if there is one thing I've learned, it's that for some races and some beings violence and conflict are just part of their nature. For some, violence is the only thing they understand."

Kell thought that the chief might well have been describing the Klingon people.

"Then it's time someone tried to change their understanding," she said. "Watch what an open hand can do, Mr. Fuller. It might surprise you."

"Ma'am, I see surprises every day in my job, but they are almost never pleasant," Fuller said.

Then the chief addressed the other three humans standing with Boyd. "I would not recommend that anyone with children accompany Ms. Boyd," he said.

The three exchanged looks, and one of the men stepped back, looking at Boyd, who simply nodded and said, "Of course, I understand." The man walked away and joined a woman who was holding a small child.

Silence fell over the combined group of colonists and security personnel. Fuller and Boyd merely looked at each other. Something was passing between them, some sort of understanding.

Leslie Parrish stepped forward and said, "Sir, you can't let them."

"I can't stop them, Lieutenant," he replied.

"We can stun them right now and apologize later," she said.

For a moment, Boyd looked concerned that Fuller might do just that, but the security chief shook his head. "Suggestion noted, Ensign. Please bring me McFadden's communicator." Turning to Boyd once again, he said, "Keep the communicator's channel open so we can hear what happens. If you get into trouble, we'll help you if we can."

"If I succeed then you won't have to," she said.

"Talk only to the one who identifies himself as the leader. Never turn your back on him. If he shouts, shout louder. If he pushes you, push back harder," he said.

She nodded in a way that Kell thought was almost respectful. Moments ago, they were arguing bitterly. Now that they had found no middle ground or points of agreement, their battle of wills had just ended—and ended without a victor.

The more time he spent among the humans, the more alien they seemed to him.

Yet they did hold to their own principles. The security officers believed they had a duty to protect all who asked their assistance. Today they had been called on to defend a group of humans who publicly declared their hatred of the Federation. And the Starfleet officers had defended them, and paid for the settlers' lives with their own blood.

The settlers, these Anti-Federation League members, shared the Klingon Empire's hatred of the Federation. Yet Kell understood them less than he understood the Starfleet officers he had met.

A life without conflict, completely without violence? As far as he was concerned, they were as mad as wild *targ*s.

And yet, as Boyd and two other humans were proving, they were not without courage to go with their convictions.

"Good luck to you," Fuller said to Boyd and her two companions.

"Thank you, Lieutenant Fuller," Boyd replied.

The two humans stared briefly at each other. Something passed silently between them again. This time Kell saw it clearly: respect.

There had been no battle, no champion who could claim victory over the other. Yet there it was anyway.

As mad as wild *targ*s, the Klingon reminded himself.

The humans made their good-byes to the other settlers, and then Boyd spoke into her communicator.

"Orion commander," she said. "This is Lara Boyd. I and two of my companions wish to speak with you in person to see if we can settle our differences."

Kell doubted that was possible. The Orions, he suspected, wanted her and the other humans simply to die. And he doubted they were willing to negotiate on that point.

"We will come to you," she said, then closed her communicator.

"They are going to meet us about a kilometer past the recreational field," Boyd said. Then she and the others set off.

As soon as they were gone, Dr. Davis approached Fuller. "What now, Lieutenant?" he asked.

The chief directed his response to the doctor, but he kept his voice loud enough that the rest of the settlers could hear him.

"Now we need to find a safe place, a place we can defend if we have to," Fuller said.

Benitez stepped forward. "What about the manufacturing building? There might be something in there we could use."

"I thought about that, but I doubt we would have much time for improvisation if the Orions move quickly. We can't risk getting trapped inside. I think we should head that way," he said, pointing to the hills to the east of the settlement.

The Klingon approved. The high ground of the hills would give them a defensive advantage. They could also fall back down the other side if they had to.

"What is on the other side of the hills?" Fuller said, seeming to read Kell's mind.

"Grasslands and a few trees," the doctor replied.

"There are also caves," one of the humans offered. Kell could see that he was one of the adolescents who had shown the will to fight earlier.

"Caves? Large enough to accommodate everyone?" Fuller said.

"There's a large tunnel system that runs under the mountains," one of the adolescents said.

"You boys know the caves?" Fuller asked.

"Pretty well," the first adolescent said.

"What's your name, son?" Fuller asked.

"Anthony, Anthony Steele," he said.

"Okay, Mr. Steele, you are going to be our guide." Fuller turned to the group at large. "Let's get ready to move out."

The doctor approached the chief. "Lieutenant Fuller, I have treated the critically injured in your party, but there are some other people with wounds that need attention."

"Who?" Fuller asked.

"Well you, for one," the doctor said.

"Me?"

"Your shoulder, that cut," the doctor said, pointing to a bloody tear in the left shoulder of his uniform.

Fuller seemed surprised that he was hurt and reached up to feel the cut.

"Thank you for your concern, but it will have to wait, Doctor."

The group headed for the mountains. The humans, even the older ones who Kell thought would slow the group down, moved quickly. He was also impressed that all of them insisted on carrying some sort of supplies, either lighting units, or food, or medical kits.

A combination of adolescents and adults insisted on carrying the stretchers that held McFadden and Jawer.

He doubted all of them would fight, if it came to a fight, but at least they all wanted to contribute to their own survival.

As they walked, the dog insisted on weaving in and around Kell and Benitez. To his great annoyance, the dog nudged him repeatedly.

"He wants you to pet him," Benitez said.

"I...would rather not," Kell said.

"Not a dog person, Flash?" his roommate asked.

"No," the Klingon said.

A moment later a female human child came over. "Spencer!" the girl shouted and ran ahead, the dog chasing her.

She could have been a child at play anywhere, on Earth, or even Qo'noS, for that matter. Playing with her animal, with no sense of the danger that she had narrowly escaped and even less sense of the danger that Kell felt sure was still to come. That, he supposed, was just as well. She and all of them would face that danger soon enough.

The Klingon noticed that she kept herself close to Benitez and himself. Thus, the animal stayed close as well. Finally, she spoke to them.

"Where is your starship?" she asked.

"Nearby," he said. "It will be here soon." He saw no reason to tell her the truth.

"Will it come before *they* come back?" she asked lightly, but he could sense the anxiety behind her question.

He weighed telling her the truth or an outright lie. In the end, he decided to do neither.

"We will make sure they do not bother you," he said.

The girl seemed satisfied with that.

"That's your phaser," she said, pointing to the weapon at his side.

It was not a question so he did not respond.

"Did you ever shoot anyone with it?" she asked.

Before Kell could answer, an adult female appeared, took her by the arm, and said, "That's enough, sweetie. Do not bother them any more."

The female tugged the girl away.

Benitez shot Kell a look. "Just because they were happy to see us doesn't mean they like us."

"Apparently not," Kell said.

Though the girl had disappeared, her animal was determined to stay with them. Benitez did not help matters by reaching out a hand and stroking the animal from time to time.

"We've got a shadow," he said.

The Klingon simply grunted.

Chapter Seventeen

KIRK GAVE THE CIRCUIT a final pass with the sealer. "Got it," he said.

"Stand back," Uhura replied.

Kirk took his hands from the console as Uhura hit the main switch. Instantly, the console hummed to life. Though they were behind the communications console, Kirk could imagine the lights coming on at Uhura's bridge station as the systems came back online.

The communications officer ran a quick diagnostic with her tricorder. "All systems online," she said. "Thank you, Captain."

Kirk nodded, and headed for the exit. Though he was in the accessway for less than an hour, the bridge was already looking more normal. There were still open panels and deck plates, but there were fewer than before and the helm station was back together with Sulu and DePaul already at their stations.

As he took his first step onto the deck he could see

that Scotty had sorted out the artificial gravity and the bridge now appeared level.

Before he reached the turbolift, Uhura was at her station.

"Lieutenant Uhura, please have Mr. Scott and Dr. McCoy meet me in the computer room," he said as he entered the turbolift.

Less than a minute later he entered the computer room. Scotty was already there, conferring with the first officer.

"Gentlemen," he said. "Are we ready?"

Scotty spoke first. "Sir, warp and impulse engines are online. We have repair crews getting more and more systems back up every few minutes, and we'll have transporters in less than an hour."

"Artificial gravity and inertial dampeners?" he asked.

"We lost our primary generators. The book says we will need a starbase facility to replace it." Scotty read Kirk's expression, then said, "But we can manufacture our own in a few days."

"Will the backups be enough for our warp maneuver?" Kirk asked.

Spock answered. "The backups were designed to provide gravity under normal conditions. The amount of gravimetric power required to keep us all on the floor is small fraction of what we need to hold the ship together at acceleration to impulse speeds, let alone maneuvering at full impulse."

"Will they be enough for the warp maneuver you are planning?" the doctor asked.

"Theoretically, yes, Doctor. If we maintain a perfectly straight trajectory through warp space. Engaging and disengaging warp speed puts far less strain on the ship than impulse acceleration maneuvers do," he said.

The doctor seemed relieved, until the Vulcan continued. "However, the real danger remains in the flawless execution of the maneuver."

"Are you comfortable with the safety margin?" Kirk asked.

"No," Spock and Scotty said in turn.

"Would *I* be comfortable with the safety margin?" Kirk asked.

"Yes, sir," Scotty said.

"No doubt," Spock replied.

"We know what the stakes are, gentlemen. We have stranded people, so we have no choice but to succeed," Kirk said. "Dismissed."

"I'll be in sickbay if anyone needs a doctor," McCoy said, heading for the door.

Scotty started after him. "I'll be in engineering," he said.

"Please join me on the bridge, Mr. Spock. You will either make a name for yourself by developing point-to-point warp travel, or Starfleet will hold a fitting memorial in your honor," Kirk said, as they exited the lab.

"Vulcans do not seek out notoriety, sir," he said dryly, "but I would prefer to live to file the report."

At the base of the mountains, Fuller called for the group to halt. Perhaps three hundred meters high, the mountain was covered with grass and small scrub brush.

Kell noted that it also had many outcroppings and large boulders that would make ideal cover. The mountains that the humans had placed their camp near might well save their lives.

Fuller flipped open his communicator and said, "Fuller to Boyd." Then he listened carefully.

Within seconds six of the adult settlers, including Dr. Davis, had approached.

"Is that Lara?" the doctor asked.

"What's happening?" asked another.

Fuller looked up and said, "She has made contact with two of the Orions. She is being escorted to their commander."

"Is there any way we can hear what happens?" one of them asked.

Fuller thought about it for a moment and called Kell and Benitez over. "You two are with me," he said.

He instructed the others to continue to the top of the small mountain and wait there.

Then Fuller, the Klingon, and Benitez turned up the volume on their communicators. They each held out their communicators so that two of the colonists could listen in.

Kell was assigned a human male and female, who seemed nervous to be near him. He wondered at the irony. They were nervous because they thought he was a Starfleet officer, not realizing that as a Klingon he was far more dangerous than they imagined.

"I can see the ship now," Boyd said.

"How bad is the damage?" Fuller asked.

"Bad. The hull is...cracked in a number of places and it's smoking. I don't think it is going to fly again. There are a lot of people outside. They are Orions, tall and green-skinned."

"How many?" Fuller asked.

There was a pause, then, "Fourteen that I can see, but they are moving quite a bit, going back and forth behind the ship."

"Does it look like they are ready to move out?" Fuller asked.

"I don't know, maybe. They seem busy. Now we have reached some sort of sentry point—" Her voice was cut off. Then Kell could overhear her conversation with the guards.

"No, it's a communications device. We are here to *communicate,* with your leader," she said, indignation in her voice.

Then another voice said, in Orion-accented English, "It is correct, this is a Starfleet communications device. You can have them," he said. Then, after some rustling, the voice said, "We will take them to the commander."

After a long pause that was punctuated by the sounds of movement, Boyd's voice whispered, "We're going behind the ship."

A few moments later, the Orion voice returned and said, "They are here, Commander."

Then another Orion-accented voice said, "Leave them with us."

"I am Lara Boyd, we are here to negotiate a truce and put an end to this...situation. Are you *four* authorized to have this kind of discussion?"

Boyd had made a point to mention the number of the Orions there. That four plus the fourteen outside meant there were at least eighteen, not including any who were inside the ship. That information would be helpful later. Kell approved. Boyd might have been crazy—even by the relatively loose human standards of sanity—but she was not stupid.

"What do you want?" the Orion said.

"I want to end this senseless hostility," Boyd said. "What do *you* want?"

To her credit, Boyd's voice was strong. If she was afraid, she was not showing it to the Orion.

The Orion ignored her question. "Do you speak for the Starfleet people?"

"I speak for my people, the settlers who live on this

planet. But the Starfleet people are reasonable. Let us go back to them with a reasonable proposal," she said.

"What are you offering, Lara Boyd?" the Orion said. Even through the accent, his condescension was clear.

"We are a small settlement. Most of the equipment we had was...destroyed, but it is a big planet, we could share—"

Boyd was interrupted by the Orion's bellowing laughter.

"We have no use for this useless rock of a planet," the Orion said.

"Then what do you want?" she said, anger creeping into her voice.

The Orion's voice went cold. "I want you to know I'm serious." He paused for a moment and then said, "Take them."

"Lara," called the voice of the woman who had accompanied Boyd. "Lara," she said again, clearly frightened.

"You've shown us that you are serious," Boyd said, keeping her voice level, barely. "What do you want with them?"

The Orion didn't respond, but a moment later Kell could hear a distinct weapons discharge and then Boyd and her male companion's anguished cries.

The humans listening to the Klingon's communicator groaned in shock.

"No!" the male cried. Then another discharge sounded and silenced his voice.

"Why!" came Boyd's anguished scream. "Why are you doing this?"

"Why?" the Orion repeated. "To show you what I want. And what I want is to have no witnesses. That is the promise I made to my employers. And my employers are not to be trifled with. I now have two less of you to worry about. In a moment it will be three."

Kell had little doubt that Boyd's errand would meet this end, but he had found himself hoping that she would succeed. As misguided as she was, there was something honorable about her willingness to put her own life at risk for her principles. Whatever deficiencies there were in Lara Boyd, courage was not one of them.

And whatever strengths the Orions possessed, honor was not among them.

Through the communicator, they heard a strangled cry, and then the sound of an Orion weapon discharging. Finally, the Orion's voice returned.

"Do you hear that, *Starfleet?* Even if your ship returns, you will not live to see it."

Kirk hit the intercom button on his command chair, allowing him to address the crew. "Attention. This is the captain. I want to thank you all for your hard work in repairing the damage the *Enterprise* suffered in the recent attack. While we still have more work ahead of us, your efforts until now will allow us to attempt a standing jump to warp speed and straight into orbit of the fourth planet of System 1324, where twenty-one of our shipmates and friends await our assistance.

"This maneuver will be just one of many firsts for this ship, for this crew. Kirk out."

Kirk turned to Spock, who simply nodded.

"Mr. Sulu?" he said.

"Course laid in," the helmsman said.

Kirk hit the intercom. "Kirk to Mr. Scott," he said.

"Scott here," came the near-immediate reply.

"Ready, Scotty?" the captain asked.

"We're transferring all available power to the inertial dampening systems now," the engineer's voice said.

Suddenly Kirk could feel the ship loosen its hold on him slightly as gravitational force decreased. The captain guessed the gravity was now less than half of normal.

"We're ready, sir," Scotty said.

The tension on the bridge was palpable, and Kirk imagined that he could feel the same anticipation throughout the ship. That was good. His people needed to stay sharp.

He knew from experience that the unknown had a way of surprising even those who expected surprises.

"Mr. Sulu, warp speed now," he said.

"Warp speed, aye," the helmsman said, his calm voice belying the gravity of what they were doing.

As Kirk watched, Sulu hit the controls, and Kirk felt the ship move, actually felt it move.

At one time or another, Kirk had flown in virtually every type of atmospheric or space vessel, with virtually every type of drive system.

This felt like none of them.

The combination of lower gravity and the building shudder of the ship gave Kirk an odd feeling in this stomach. Yet the feeling of power was there. The massive energies of the ship's warp engines reverberated through the deck.

For that brief time, he had the physical sensation that the *Enterprise* was flying.

"Status, Mr. Spock," Kirk said.

"We have successfully made the transition to warp speed," Spock said, as the shaking of the ship quieted.

"Warp factor one," Sulu said.

Allowing himself a smile, Kirk could feel the relief of the bridge crew.

"Accelerate to warp factor six," Mr. Sulu.

"Accelerating to warp six, aye," Sulu replied, his own relief coming through in his voice.

The gravity returned to normal and Kirk noted that he did not feel the acceleration to high warp. That made sense; the physics of warp dynamics meant that the greatest stresses were during the initial transition to warp speed.

"Estimated time to planet, Spock," Kirk said.

"Forty-seven point four-five minutes, Captain," Spock said.

"Lieutenant Uhura, please let Security Chief Giotto know that I will need his team ready to go in about forty-seven minutes," Kirk said.

"Aye, sir," Uhura replied.

Chapter Eighteen

KAREL KNEW he had to strike the first blow against his superior. The bigger and stronger Gash already had two advantages. First blood would be a third.

But Gash obviously had the same thought and he was faster than Karel had anticipated. His large fist reared back and Karel saw instantly that he would not be able to dodge the blow, which was aimed squarely at his head.

So he did the only thing he could. He slammed his head straight into the fist. The result was exhilarating.

Gash's closed fist connected with the wound on Karel's forehead, which was precisely where it had been aimed. Karel had, however, been able to reduce the force of the blow by meeting it early.

Thus, the pain burned white-hot in his head, but he was not incapacitated, as Gash had intended.

Using his forward momentum, Karel pushed into the larger Klingon with both hands, forcing him back. Already off-balance from the incomplete blow, Gash fell backward, hitting the deck with a loud crash.

This gave Karel precious seconds for his vision to clear.

Even with his momentary disorientation, Karel clearly heard Gash's howl.

Had an opponent managed to push Karel to the ground in such a way, he would have used the momentum of the fall to propel him into a roll that would put him back on his feet.

But Gash had obviously never studied the martial art of *Mok'bara,* and he wasted precious time struggling forward to his feet. Karel caught a glimpse of Gash leaning forward to get up, but the blood running down his forehead now obscured his vision.

He sensed more than saw the opening Gash had left him. Karel's father had once told him the story of a warrior friend he had known. His friend was hand-fighting a larger Nausicaan when he saw an opening in the Nausicaan defenses and struck.

It was then that the warrior knew he was nearly at the end of his usefulness. Just a few years before, he would have struck before he saw the opening. Now, his instincts had been dulled to the point that he had to wait for his eyes to tell him what his blood should have been screaming.

Karel didn't wait for his eyes. He struck out where he sensed Gash's head would be and felt his closed fist make a solid and satisfying contact with his superior's face.

Gash recoiled and Karel took a moment to wipe the blood from his brow. With his now-clear vision, he watched Gash roll sideways. Reaching up, he used a single hand to pull himself up on the console there, keeping the other hand free to fend off any attack.

Again, Karel didn't wait. Using a *Mok'bara* combination, he struck once with his left and then with his right hand. But Gash was surprisingly quick and was on his feet before the blows reached his head.

Though he made solid contact with the bigger Klingon's side, the combination did not incapacitate Gash as Karel hoped it would. Instead, Gash just absorbed the blows and pushed at Karel. The move was clumsy but effective, and Karel was forced back.

Now the two Klingons were facing each other from less than two meters' distance—each with his back to a weapons console.

Karel would have preferred more room to maneuver. *Mok'bara* could be an awesome weapon and allow a warrior to defeat much bigger and stronger foes. But the fighting art required room for its most devastating blows. In fighting would work to Gash's strengths, his size and brute force.

To control the fight, Karel would have to move forward in the weapons room. Past the consoles, there was more open space just before the door. If he allowed himself to fight Gash's fight, he would soon be overwhelmed.

Karel spared a glance at the room. Second Officer Klak and the weapons-room officers were watching with interest. Usually, in a dispute of this nature a good commanding officer could expect some help from his subordinates. That was just. In Karel's mind, loyalty was a kind of strength.

Fortunately, Gash was not a good commanding officer.

The larger Klingon looked intensely at Karel, who could see hatred burning in Gash's eyes. Hatred and something else—Gash did not intend to defeat Karel, he intended to kill him.

Then Gash did something that surprised Karel. He smiled.

Before the smile faded, the larger Klingon launched his attack. Throwing not a fist or a kick at Karel but hurling his whole body at him.

Karel knew many techniques for keeping his balance and turning away such an attack by using the attacker's momentum against him. Putting one leg behind him, Karel braced himself and prepared to swivel when Gash struck him.

The move would have worked if he did not have the console right behind him, keeping his leg from finding a good position.

So instead of performing a simple throw, Karel only succeeded in twisting his own body. When Gash struck him, he hit Karel's side, forcing his hip into the console and his body back.

Karel's breath left him in a rush and a moment he found himself doubled over the console with one of Gash's large arms around his throat.

Struggling for breath, Karel found he could not draw any. Gash pulled tighter on his throat and the Klingon knew he had very little time left to live.

Cursing himself for allowing such a clumsy foe to get the better of him, Karel thought of his father, who had lived and died with his honor intact, and flailed at Gash. But he was striking backward and only able to reach the Klingon's lower body.

Then Gash leaned down to whisper in Karel's ear, his face touching Karel's own.

"Pathetic, how you die, *Earther,*" he said, squeezing tighter.

As consciousness started to give way to darkness, Karel's blood screamed out Gash's mistake. What Karel did next, he did without thinking.

Knowing he could not reach Gash with a proper blow,

he merely extended his thumb and brought it straight up into the gloating Klingon's face.

It was not a strong blow but it found its mark perfectly and within a fraction of a second, Gash was off Karel.

Karel's first act was to draw a large breath, then another. Then another.

As the darkness receded, Karel could hear Gash howling. Straightening to a standing position and turning, Karel saw Gash on the floor, his hands covering the right side of his face.

Karel looked down and saw the remains of Gash's ruined eye on his thumb. Kneeling, he wiped his thumb on Gash's uniform and stood up to face the other Klingons in the room to see if any would challenge him.

No one did.

Klak approached him and said. "Well done, *Senior Weapons Officer* Karel."

By now, Gash had quieted down and was struggling to his feet.

Then Klak turned to Gash. "Before you tend your injury, remove your things from Senior Weapons Officer Karel's new quarters and move them to *your* new quarters with the newly enlisted Klingons," Klak said as the officer stood in front him, covering his ruined eye with one hand.

As the Klingon left the weapons room, Klak said, "You have done him a favor. He was a terrible officer. But he is a good fighter and will be useful among the troops."

When the first officer left, Karel saw that the junior weapons officers were still looking at him in surprise.

"Back to your posts!" he shouted.

As they took their positions, Karel considered canceling the second shift that Gash had ordered them as punishment. It was a foolish and unfair move, but Karel decided to let it stand.

It was unusual for Karel to be promoted from his post at the cooling system console to senior officer—skipping a position at one of the proper weapons consoles.

He could not afford to allow the Klingons under his command to think him weak.

"Let's move," Fuller's voice called out.

Before he could, Kell had to help the male human to his feet. "I don't understand it...how could they," the man muttered.

"We have to leave now, we have to get you to safety!" Kell shouted. The woman, who the Klingon presumed was his mate, helped pull him up.

"We have to hurry," she said.

The man was in shock.

All of the people there had a lost look on their faces, even more lost than when Kell had first seen them underneath their ruined building. Yet he understood. They had just had their beliefs crushed.

It was a bitter lesson.

Yet they did not lie down in despair and die as he would have thought. They moved, heading up the slope with remarkable speed.

The walk up the mountain took just a few minutes and they soon joined the larger group just over the top on the other side.

Dr. Davis met them. He wore the question on his face. Fuller simply shook his head.

Then Fuller addressed the assembled crowd of settlers and security personnel.

"Lara Boyd and her party were killed by the Orions," he announced.

There were startled cries from the civilians. Kell

could see that they were frightened. He wondered if they would be able to continue, or would just give up now.

They had lost their leader. They had nearly lost their lives. And the attackers might win no matter what they did.

Looking at the settlers, he realized that they were looking at Fuller with expectation in their eyes. For now, they had decided he was their leader.

Everything depended on what he did next.

"Lara Boyd lived and died by her beliefs. She lived and died for peace. And before she died she gave us valuable information that we can use to defend ourselves," Fuller said.

Though Kell had heard the information Boyd had passed to them, he doubted that it would be very useful. The Starfleet team was outnumbered and outgunned, and they had to protect a large number of noncombatants. Yet the lie seemed to give the settlers hope.

"I am often asked by civilians if Starfleet trains us to die for our beliefs," Fuller continued. "The answer is no. We are not trained to die. We are trained to do our jobs. Sometimes those jobs put us in harm's way, but we accept risk. Sometimes we have to accept death, but we never seek it. To those of you under my command, and to those of you we are here to protect, I am not asking you to be prepared to die for duty, or for your beliefs. I am asking you to live for them. The principles on which Starfleet and this settlement were founded demand it."

The crowd looked at Fuller in silence for a moment. Then Kell saw a change come over them; he watched it happen. A few seconds ago, they had the beaten look of survivors who had nearly lost the will to continue. Now they were standing straighter and had the look of hope in their eyes.

"What do you want us to do?" Dr. Davis asked.

"I need you all to make your way down this slope and wait outside the entrance of the caves. Stay together and stay with your groups. Chief Brantley and two of our people will escort you. We have a good defensive position here, but in the event we have to fall back, you will need to enter the caves on my signal. Bring nothing but the portable lights and water. Who knows the caves?"

Three of the adolescent males stepped forward. "We do," their leader said.

"Two of you stay with the main group to guide them through the caves, but I need one of you to stay with us if our group gets separated."

The leader stepped forward immediately. "I'll stay with you," he said. Kell remembered that his name was Steele—an ironic name for a human, he thought.

Fuller conferred for a moment with the three humans; then the doctor and the group moved out.

Fuller turned back to his team and three more from Chief Brantley's team that didn't go to escort the settlers.

"How long?" Fuller said to Parrish.

"They are hitting the edge of the recreational field now," she said. "A few minutes, sir."

"Are you reading any heavy equipment?" he asked.

"No, sir," she said. "Just multiple life signs and the power readings you would expect from hand weapons...large hand weapons."

"Maybe this will be a fair fight," Benitez said.

"That doesn't seem to be their style," Parrish said.

"No, but neither is blowing themselves up before they're captured. There is something else going on here," Fuller said.

Kell spoke up. "The leader did mention that he had

employers who were not to be trifled with. Perhaps the Orions fear failing their masters."

Fuller nodded. "That may be, and that might make them prone to mistakes."

Parrish checked her phaser. "And if that's true, it's not just their masters they have to worry about."

"Remember, we don't need to defeat them ourselves to win this," Fuller said. "If we can hold them here until the *Enterprise* comes then everyone will be safe. If we have to fall back, we can head into the caves. They'll be even easier to defend than this open hill. Once we're underground we can continue to fall back to buy time."

Kell heard Fuller's words, but did not understand. Why a strategy of retreat? Better to die facing their enemy directly.

"We could stand and fight," the Klingon said.

"And when we die the settlers will be unprotected," Fuller said.

"But why prolong the inevitable?" Kell said.

"Because *nothing* is inevitable. We need to hold out just until the *Enterprise* gets here," Fuller said flatly, as if he were stating an inalterable fact.

"You really think they are coming, sir?" Benitez said.

"The captain will be here," Fuller said with the same foolish certainty.

As Kell had seen, Fuller had great courage. But his devotion to his cowardly and honorless captain was misguided.

Perhaps when the Federation came under Klingon control, men like Sam Fuller would find leadership worthy of their loyalty and courage, which he now saw clearly in Fuller and the others.

Yet for all that he saw that was honorable in humans,

he still shook his head at their obsession with the idea of preserving life—their own and the lives of their fellows.

At first, Kell had thought it was a form of weakness. A fear of approaching death. Now he knew that that was not true.

They preserved life because they valued it, in the way true warriors valued their honor.

Ultimately, he had almost believed, had almost become caught up in Sam Fuller's words. He had thought they might indeed live, the humans for their beliefs, the Klingon for his honor.

Now they would all likely die.

Fuller looked into the distance and Kell turned his head to do the same. The ruined settlement stood before them. He made out the burned out and destroyed dwellings. He could also see the individual craters where some of the Starfleet officers had died from weapons blasts that came from the Orions' cowardly weapons platforms.

He saw the rubble that was the colonists' pride: their cultural center. The smoking manufacturing building. The ruined landing field.

Less than a day ago, these few square kilometers had been filled with the settlers' lives. Even though he thought their beliefs foolish and incomprehensible, he saw that they valued them as much as a Klingon valued duty.

And wasn't their dream of a secure, peaceful life what the Klingon High Command wanted for its own people? Freedom from threats, freedom from those who would take what was theirs, freedom from those who would take their lives?

Defending against the treachery that smashed the lives of these weak but harmless people was an honorable cause. It was a cause worthy of his father, his brother, and his family name—even if he took the cause wearing the face of a human.

"There they are," Fuller said next to him.

Then Kell saw them. They were not dispersed into groups or teams. The group of Orions moved as a single, arrogant whole. Or a swarm.

The security people and the Klingon himself had taught them two lessons in humility—once when they defeated the weapons platforms and once when they destroyed their ship.

Kell thought this would be a good time for a third lesson.

"Teams disperse, but stay with your partners. Find cover and wait for my signal to open fire. I want to wait until they are close and end this quickly," Fuller said.

The people nodded and started looking for cover. Kell and Benitez found a large boulder a few meters down the slope and took positions on either side.

"What do you think our chances are?" Benitez said.

"We do have the high ground," Kell said. "They will have to charge us from the open."

The Klingon watched them cross the recreational field.

"They don't look worried," Benitez said.

No, Kell thought, *they do not.*

The Orions stopped at the far side of the rubble that was the cultural center and seemed to be busy at something.

Within less than a minute he saw a flash of light and realized what they were doing.

"Move," he said to Benitez, who turned at the command and started up the slope toward the peak.

"Mortars!" Kell shouted.

They were barely meters from their hiding place when the projectile exploded downslope.

Even though the flash was behind them, it temporarily blinded the Klingon, and the ground shook under his feet.

He saw Benitez stumble and grabbed the human by the uniform and pulled him up. Then they raced to the summit. Just on the other side Fuller and the settler named Steele were waiting.

Fuller was barking into his communicator, "Get everyone into the caves."

Another mortar shook them again as Parrish and her partner arrived. Remarkably, everyone was accounted for.

"Sir, the caves, they could seal us in," Parrish's partner said.

"We have no choice," Fuller said. "And I think they will want to be certain they have killed us all. At least underground, their mortar will be useless. Now let's move!" he shouted to the group.

Another uncomfortably close explosion rocked them.

The Klingon did not hesitate. He turned with the others and at a full run executed a strategic withdrawal.

Chapter Nineteen

"Now, Spock," Kirk said.

"Transferring helm control to the computer," Spock said.

Now they simply had to wait.

The captain did not relish the idea of turning over control of the ship to a machine, even as well-designed a machine as the ship's computer. However, in this case it was necessary. The shift from warp speed to the planet's orbit was too precise to be handled by verbal commands and manual controls. As Spock had pointed out, the safety margin was just a few millionths of a percent.

Kirk trusted Spock's computations. If something went wrong, it would more likely be an equipment or system failure. On the other hand, if there was a critical failure in the inertial dampening system, he would have no time to worry about it.

And when Starfleet salvaged the ship, they would find it in very small pieces.

"Scott to captain," said the intercom on his command chair.

"Kirk here," he said.

"Captain, we have transporters online," the chief engineer said.

"As good as your word, Mr. Scott, thank you. Kirk out." Turning to Uhura's station behind him, he said, "Lieutenant Uhura, please have Lieutenant Commander Giotto assemble his team in the transporter room."

"Aye, sir," she said.

The bridge crew waited, but Kirk knew they wouldn't have to wait long.

Mr. Spock broke the silence.

"Transition to normal space in ten seconds," the Vulcan said. There was silence for a few seconds; then he began the final countdown.

"Five.

"Four.

"Three.

"Two.

"One.

"Mark," the science officer said as Kirk felt the now familiar sensation of movement and lower gravity. Kirk counted off the seconds in his head, knowing the deceleration would take precisely as long as the acceleration maneuver.

When he judged the maneuver was just past halfway though, he felt a strong shudder in the deck and found himself pitching forward. Jumping to his feet, the captain felt the shudder pass. Then the viewscreen showed that they were in normal space.

But something had gone wrong.

The fact that he was having that thought told Kirk that

there hadn't been a critical failure. But something had gone wrong just the same.

For one, the planet was not on the viewscreen.

"Spock, what happened?" Kirk said.

"Minor fluctuation in the inertial control system," he reported coolly.

"Where are we?" Kirk asked.

"We are within the target solar system, one point six-eight astronomical units from the planet," Spock said.

Kirk felt his heart sink into his stomach. They were just over one and a half times the distance from the Earth to its sun. Under normal circumstances that trip would take minutes for the *Enterprise* at full impulse speed.

However, these circumstances were anything but normal and they would not be able to use impulse speeds for days.

"Time to planet using maneuvering thrusters," Kirk asked, knowing he would not like the answer.

"One hundred and fifty-four years," the Vulcan replied.

Kirk's next words were only to himself and decidedly nonregulation.

At the mouth of the cave, Fuller turned to the young human named Steele and said, "Take us to the rendezvous point."

Steele nodded and started inside.

"Grab a lighting unit and stay inside," Fuller said, motioning Brantley's squad to follow.

The security officers grabbed one of the lighting units on the floor at the mouth of the cave and started inside.

Kell and Benitez waited with Fuller until all of the others were inside.

"Let's go, Ensigns," Fuller said, handing the Klingon a portable light, and nearly pushing them inside.

The mouth of the cave was narrow and had obviously been created by the movement of rock that had formed the mountain. Yet once they were inside it opened up and had the smoother appearance of caves created by moving water.

They followed a tunnel for perhaps thirty meters and came to a fork. There was a single large passage to the left and a smaller one they would have to crouch to get through on the right.

"Which way?" Fuller asked.

Steele pointed to the smaller passage and leaned down to pass. The rest of the group followed quickly.

As Kell crouched down he noted with satisfaction that the relatively large Orions would have trouble getting through there.

Once again the passage opened up and Kell made his way around the various stalagmites and stalactites. He had to stay close to Benitez, because they had only the one light between them.

After a few more turns and twists, the tunnel opened into a large room, which was perhaps one hundred meters across and half that high.

The settlers were huddled inside. A few large lighting units illuminated most of the cavern, while other, smaller portable units played on the walls.

On the left side of the cavern, there was a pool of water.

"We call this the beach," Steele said to Fuller, who examined the pool.

"Do you know if the water leads anywhere?" Fuller said.

"No," Steele said. "It's fed by a small opening in the wall."

Kell noted that the area near the water was littered with beverage containers. The young humans had also constructed a fire pit nearby. *So human adolescents consume beverages near fires?* the Klingon thought. On Qo'noS he had done the same many evenings of his childhood. He suddenly knew exactly what kind of beverages they consumed. Curious that humans and Klingons would share that activity. When he was young, he felt like he and his friends had invented it—they could scarcely have imagined that other Klingons, let alone humans, might do the same.

By now, Kell had accepted that he had things in common with the security people he fought with. Yet it still surprised him to share something with this human, *civilian.*

Fuller conferred with Chief Brantley and gestured the security teams closer. Kneeling down, he picked up a rock and drew a quick diagram in the earth of the cave. Pointing to a spot about halfway to the entrance of the cave, he said, "My team will take a position in front of here. We'll hold them as long as we can."

Fuller looked up at Brantley. "If we have to fall back, your team will provide cover. Then, we'll take a position behind you to cover you. We'll continue in this manner until we work our way back to the settlers. We'll mount our last defense there."

"What about me, sir?" said Ensign Clark, her right arm in a sling. It had been set by the doctor and its open wound closed. But it would be days or weeks before she could fight properly.

"You will remain here with the settlers," Fuller said. And before the female could protest, he added, "If none of us make it back, you will be their only defense. If none of us remain, you are to use your phaser to seal this cavern from the inside. It might buy you some time until the captain gets here."

Ensign Clark nodded, and Fuller motioned Dr. Davis over to them.

"Doctor, you will be the leader here—"

"Lieutenant, I'm a doctor—" he began.

Fuller waved the protest off. "These people are looking to you, Doctor. You *are* their leader, whether or not you feel up to the job. Keep them calm and keep their spirits up."

"All right," Davis said. "I'll do my best. And Lieutenant, thank you." Then he addressed the security officers. "Thank you all. We will never forget what you have done for us today."

Fuller nodded at the man and turned to go, Kell and the others following.

They had only gotten a few steps when Steele and the other two young humans stopped Fuller.

"We want to help. We're ready to fight," Steele said.

"Stay here with your friends and family," Fuller said. "If we don't make it back, you'll be the only thing between the Orions and these people. Talk to Ensign Clark, she'll tell you what to do."

The humans seemed satisfied with that and turned back to their people. Before the security teams could get moving again, the female human child came running up to the Klingon with her dog behind her.

"Take Spencer with you," she said.

"I do not think so," Kell said.

"He's very brave," she said. "And see, he wants to go," she added, pointing to the fact that the animal was moving its tail enthusiastically and sniffing around the Klingon's feet.

Looking at the human child, he could see that it was important to her. Like the injured Ensign Clark, like the adolescents, she wanted to contribute. She wanted to help.

"I'm sure he will be a great...asset," the Klingon said as the group started moving, the dog staying close to his heels.

He wondered if all of their efforts and the deaths of all the security people would matter. Or would the Orions be victorious in the end?

Kahless had said that honor did not demand victory, but it did demand a warrior's best effort. Today honor would have his best.

Moving quickly through the caves, they put Chief Brantley's team into position and moved on to their own position.

Fortunately, the cave's stalagmites and outcroppings of rock provided excellent cover. Kell and Benitez took positions on the left-hand wall of the cave, while Fuller, Parrish, and Perella took positions on the right. The dog lay down, unconcerned, on the cave floor by the Klingon's feet.

"Lights out," Fuller ordered, and Benitez and Parrish extinguished their portable lighting units. The cave was immediately cast into pitch darkness.

"Anything, Parrish?" Fuller called out.

"I think they are close, sir, but there must be some interference. The tricorder is giving me conflicting readings," she said.

That was good, Kell knew. It meant that Orions would have trouble finding them via portable sensing equipment as well.

The security teams also had the natural advantage of a defensive position as well as the darkness for additional cover. If the Orions carried lights, then the Klingon and his companions would see them first.

Kell listened carefully for any sound coming from the cavern. None came.

The only noises came from the humans and the dog around him. Though the security officers had been trained to be silent in a hostile situation, they still breathed and there were the occasional sounds of movement.

And in the complete darkness of the cave, with his eyes useless and his other senses heightened, the sound of his own breathing and the beating of his heart seemed unimaginably loud. He even imagined he could hear the rushing of his blood through his body.

How could the Orions miss such a symphony? he wondered.

Yet only silence answered him.

He remained highly alert. The blood that coursed through his veins burned with purpose, with the deeds of his father and ancestors, with the promise of honor fulfilled. His blood burned with readiness and tuned his senses even higher.

He knew that special equipment would let the Orions see in the dark and skulk toward them. There were even devices that would mask the sounds they made.

No honorable foe would sneak around in such a manner. And certainly no Klingon warrior would hide his purpose. Yet, the Orions had shown they had no honor.

So Kell called on his warrior blood to warn him of treachery, to warn him of attack.

His blood burned hot, but it was silent.

The dog, however, was not.

It began to twitch, and draw unusually loud breaths. Then it grunted.

Weighing his options, Kell considered blasting the animal, but decided against it—such an act would call even more attention to them than the dog.

The animal sniffed and snorted again, then it began

growling. When it barked loudly, Kell decided to just go ahead and blast it.

Raising his phaser, Kell stopped himself for a reason he could not explain. When he sniffed the air himself, he realized what the dog was telling them and which of its senses was guiding it.

"Turn on the lights," the Klingon shouted as they found and hit the switch for the lighting unit beside him. The sudden flair of bright light in the narrow cave blinded him for a moment.

The stink of the Orions was so strong that Kell wondered that he didn't notice it before. It screamed their treachery, their cowardice.

The Klingon's blood answered that call. He did not wait for his eyes to adjust. Pointing his phaser toward the entrance of the cave, he fired, trusting Kahless and the call of his own blood to guide his aim.

They did not fail him.

His eyes had adjusted enough for him to see the phaser beam find a target. It flared a brilliant red against the figure of an Orion who was perhaps seven meters in front of him.

It was a direct hit at close range, and the phaser had been set on full—Kell did not need clear vision to know what happened to the Orion.

By the time his first beam had hit the target, the others had begun firing. A few seconds later, his eyes adjusted to the light and he could see Orions scrambling for cover.

Kell did not doubt that the second or two advantage that the dog had given them had saved their lives.

Not all of their lives, he realized, as a beam from an Orion weapon passed a few meters to his left. In his peripheral vision, he saw Parrish's partner John Perella take a direct hit to his chest.

Before his body hit the floor, a blast from Parrish's

phaser sought and found the Orion who had killed Perella. Blasts from Benitez and Fuller found targets of their own. Less than ten seconds after the Klingon fired the first shot, there were four Orion bodies on the ground.

"Hold your fire," Fuller shouted, as he repositioned the lights to shine down the cave.

Taking a closer look at the Orions, Kell could see that the enemy was wearing the same sort of armored suit that the weapons-platform pilots had worn. The fact that the two Orions Kell and Parrish had hit were lying on the ground and had not been disintegrated by the phaser beams testified to the fact that the suits offered them some protection. Yet it was not enough to save their lives after a direct hit at close range.

For a moment, the cave was quiet. Kell could see the lights shining through the cave's now-smoky interior. Taking a quick inventory, he saw that Perella was their only casualty.

Parrish had her tricorder out, but shook her head at Fuller's signal. Clearly, there was too much interference for the tricorder to get a lock on their attackers.

A moment later, the only sensing device that seemed to be immune to interference sounded. The dog barked.

Kell and the others did not delay for an instant. They fired down the cave.

This time, the Orions were more careful and were not caught out in the open. At thirty meters, they were also not as close this time.

As far as the Klingon could see, none of the security team's shots had found an Orion target.

Yet.

The smoke created by rock and cave walls being pounded by weapons fire started to get thicker. In a few moments, they would not be able to see the Orions at all, even if the attackers were in the open.

Tracing the origin points of Orion weapons blasts, Kell could see that the enemy was advancing. Slowly. But they were advancing.

The ferocity of the attack surprised him. Though they had the advantage of greater numbers, it was not an advantage on the scale of the edge the weapons platforms and the starship had given them.

And the thirty meters became twenty-five.

Then twenty.

In seconds the two groups would be on top of each other. At that range the weapons of each side would find their marks quickly.

If Kell and the three others fought well, they would kill an equal number or more of their attackers before they fell. But enough of the sixteen attackers would survive to continue on toward Brantley's team, then to the settlers.

"Prepare to fall back," Fuller shouted, his voice barely carrying over the sound of the nearly continuous fire.

In that instant, Kell saw a flash of an Orion's suit and took the shot. He thought he saw the beam flash against a shoulder. However, he could not be certain, because in the next instant Sam Fuller fired a blast into the cave ceiling above the attackers' heads.

The beam struck a large stalactite hanging there and sent it, as well as a satisfying amount of debris, raining down on their attackers.

"Now! Move!" the chief shouted.

Without hesitating, Kell reached out a hand to grab the light beside him, turned, and headed down the cave, the dog following closely at his heels.

Keeping Benitez in his peripheral vision, the Klingon

moved quickly. A few meters away, he rounded a corner and saw the air clear somewhat.

Sparing a glance around him, he saw Parrish and Fuller just ahead of Benitez and himself. Beyond them was Chief Brantley's position, though he could not see Brantley or any of his security people...

...until he was past them. Turning around, he saw Fuller conferring with Brantley while the rest of the team stayed in their hidden positions.

"Heavy fire," Fuller said to the other chief. "When they get too close, pull back to behind our position."

Then Fuller was moving again as Kell and the rest of his team followed.

At the end of the shift, Karel took his *gagh* with his weapons group. It was something that Gash never did, preferring to eat alone.

The Klingons in his group seemed to regard him skeptically. That was just, in Karel's mind. Gash was an incompetent officer, but Karel had yet to prove himself.

After the shift, Karel went to his former quarters and picked up his few things. Though the room had been his home since he was posted to the *D'k Tahg,* he would not miss it.

He was proud of the effort it took to win the better of the two top bunks, but he had grown tired of meeting the challenges from his five roommates.

As a senior officer, he would now share a room with only one other officer. As such, he would be able to concentrate more on his work and less on his personal safety. He had plans for the weapons room and was determined to make it an example for the rest of the ship and fleet to follow.

Placing his few things into a small crate, Karel left

the quarters and turned down the corridor. Behind him he heard a click that he instantly recognized.

It was the two outer blades of a *d'k tahg* snapping into place. Karel had a *d'k tahg* in his crate. That knife had an honored history—his father had owned it.

Judging that he would not have time to fumble for the knife, Karel dropped the crate and spun to face his attacker. The Klingon in front of him with the knife was M'bac from the disruptor room.

M'bac was the most experienced of the junior weapons officers. He ran the primary firing console and had no doubt considered himself the natural replacement for Gash.

Karel knew he would be challenged, but he did not expect the first one to come so soon.

Not wasting any time, M'bac lunged forward with the knife. The long double duty shift and the battle with Gash had depleted Karel. Yet he had no trouble sidestepping the clumsy and direct attack.

Clearly M'bac had no training beyond the standard fighting techniques taught to all officers in the Klingon Defense Force.

By striking at M'bac as he passed, Karel was able to force the Klingon sideways into the corridor wall. M'bac grunted as he struck with his shoulder but kept to his feet and spun around.

Since it was late in the evening and most of the Klingons on the ship were asleep, the corridor was empty. The relatively spacious corridor gave Karel more room to operate than the cramped disruptor room did.

Focusing his energy, Karel found the peace that *Mok'bara* always brought him. The pain of his injuries and his own exhaustion melted away.

Though M'bac was clumsy, Karel refused to allow

that to bait him into overconfidence—which had cost Gash both his post and his eye.

M'bac began his next attack immediately, slashing back and forth with the *d'k tahg*. It was another clumsy attack that dishonored the traditional weapon after which the ship they both served was named.

Pushing forward, M'bac obviously intended to back him into the far wall and then strike.

Feinting a blow with his left hand, Karel waited for M'bac to try to slash him. When M'bac did, Karel launched a hard blow with his right hand, striking the Klingon on the side of his head.

Momentarily disoriented, M'bac continued trying to slash at Karel's left hand, which had pulled back from its feinted blow. Pulling the left hand up, Karel swung out, striking M'bac's face with the back of a closed left fist.

As any Klingon would, M'bac would see the backhanded blow as a great insult, but it could not be helped. Karel could not let the fight continue much longer.

With surprising speed, M'bac recovered and launched another straight attack, leading with the point of the weapon, which was now aimed at Karel's chest.

Rather than dodge the blow completely, Karel decided to end the battle quickly. He twisted so the blade shot under his arm, mere inches from his chest. Pulling his arm down, Karel pinned the attacking arm and the knife it held.

Karel simultaneously twisted his body, slamming M'bac backward into the corridor wall, while still keeping M'bac's hand trapped between Karel's body and arm.

Bringing his free left hand down, Karel struck hard on the junior weapons officer's wrist, which immediately released the knife.

For a moment, Karel considered breaking the man's arm, but he resisted. He did so for the same reason he resisted killing the Klingon: M'bac was a good officer and Karel did not want to lose him in the disruptor room.

So he pushed the now kneeling Klingon aside and picked up the knife.

"Stand," Karel said.

M'bac did, slowly, watching Karel's eyes for signs of what he would do next.

But Karel made sure his face betrayed nothing. He would let the junior officer sweat for a moment.

After a long moment, he said, "You forfeit your *d'k tahg*. Make sure you are the first one at your post tomorrow morning."

For a moment M'bac did not understand and seemed to be waiting for the fatal blow that Gash certainly would have delivered in the same situation. But Gash was a fool who was more concerned with his own position than the effectiveness of his disruptor room.

"You are dismissed!" Karel shouted at the Klingon.

Finally understanding, M'bac nodded and left.

Picking up his crate, Karel was glad to have that inevitable conflict out of the way. He would not have respected M'bac unless the Klingon had moved against him. Perhaps now he could get his weapons group focused on their work.

Chapter Twenty

ABOUT FIFTY METERS farther along the cave, Kell and the others stopped and looked for cover. Fuller and Parrish found an outcropping on the right side, while Benitez and the Klingon found a large rock on the left.

They waited.

Behind them, Kell knew, there was the fork in the cave. Their next fallback position was just beyond that—close to the entrance to the cavern that held the settlers and the injured security officers.

The entrance to that cavern would be the final battlefield, a very small battlefield where the combatants would be able to feel each other's breath. It was what the Klingons called a killing box.

Even if the humans fought bravely, the Orions would overwhelm them with their numbers in those close quarters. And then the attackers would have the settlers, because even if they succeeded in sealing themselves inside the cavern, the Orions would blast through soon enough.

Inside, the attackers would meet a single, injured security officer with a single phaser, and perhaps a few brave settlers with rocks.

Their end would not take long.

Kell knew that honor, courage, and strength did not guarantee victory. Kahless himself had said, "There is nothing shameful in falling before a superior enemy."

The end might be honorable for Kell and the humans, but that thought did not comfort him. His blood rebelled against the notion.

Or was it his blood? Perhaps he had been contaminated by his contact with humans.

Then the sounds of phaser blasts and Orion fire interrupted his thoughts.

In less than a minute, the sounds ceased and the Klingon heard the footfalls of running people.

Chief Brantley's team came running around the bend in front of them—not the whole team but what was left of it. Kell saw two people and then Brantley himself. That meant two more did not make it.

"Hold here, Mr. Brantley," Fuller said.

"Lost Heller and Wright, I think we got two of them," Brantley said between gasping breaths.

Fuller put a hand on the man's shoulder.

"Request permission to stay with your team, sir," Brantley asked.

Fuller considered the other chief for a moment. The lieutenant and the surviving security people knew what Brantley was really asking.

He wanted to make his stand here.

He was requesting permission to die.

Along with everyone else, Kell waited breathlessly for Fuller's response.

Was there an end to how often humans would retreat?

Was there a point where the differences between Klingon and human would completely disappear? Was there a time when humans would prefer to die like warriors and take the faces of their enemies with them into the afterlife instead of showing those enemies their backs?

If humans were even capable of such an act, was that moment now?

For Sam Fuller, the answer was yes.

He nodded and said, "Take positions."

A silent thought passed through every human in the group and the Klingon himself.

For all of the humans' talk about living for their beliefs, they were about to die for them. They would die here, together.

Yet something in Kell rebelled again. Perhaps his blood really had been tainted by humans, or perhaps the face he wore had worked deeper changes inside him.

Surprisingly, the notion did not trouble him greatly.

Kell stood. "Sir," he said to Fuller. "Perhaps there is another way. If the rest of you fell back to the cavern's entrance I could lead the Orions down the left fork," he said, pointing down the cave behind them.

After a pause, he added, "It might buy some time."

Benitez and Parrish stood up at the same time. "I'll go, too," they said, nearly in unison.

The chief thought for a moment, then nodded.

Fuller stood and addressed the others. "Let's go. We'll make our stand in front of the cavern."

The security people disappeared nearly silently behind them as Parrish crossed the cavern to join Kell and Benitez. She did not need to explain. They had no reason to use crossfire for this tactic.

They would only engage the enemy long enough to show their position.

The dog barked and Kell knew the Orions were close. He fired into the cave and the others followed suit.

Then the Orions started moving in force.

Though there were fewer of them now—perhaps eleven or twelve—they were moving with the confidence of a *targ* who had already tasted a prey's blood and was preparing for the kill.

Part of the Klingon wanted to stay and show one or two of them the price they would have to pay for that kill, but he resisted the impulse and said, "Move when I do."

Turning to the rear of the cave, he kept firing behind him and then leapt to his feet and headed down the cave, with the dog and the others close behind him.

In seconds they stood at the fork. Pointing to the left, he said, "Get inside."

"But—" Parrish started to protest.

"Now," he said. "I will be right behind you." To his mild surprise, she listened and headed into the cave with Benitez behind her.

The dog, it seemed, was determined to stay with him.

Kell waited in the open, his phaser ready. Three Orions appeared at once and his phaser was firing before he was conscious of willing his hand to do it.

One of the Orions fell and again he was tempted to stay and see this battle through to the end and straight to the River of Blood.

Again he resisted and turned to run down the corridor, certain that the Orions would be behind him in seconds. He had traveled perhaps sixty meters when he saw light up ahead. There was a small opening in the cave's corridor. Kell threw himself into it...and very nearly into the opposite wall.

Stopping himself short, he saw the small compartment—the small *sealed* compartment. Benitez and Parrish were lying on the floor, behind a rise that was the compartment's best covered firing position.

Grunting, the Klingon took a position between the two humans and said, "It will not take them long to find us, finish us, and track the others."

"It was a good effort," Parrish said gently.

Kell grunted again. He had seen that humans often praised efforts, even when they failed. Klingons, however, held that the only victory was victory.

Kell cursed himself. He had felt a pang of almost human hope when he saw the Orion fall to his last blast. For a moment, he had thought there was a possibility that the three of them could even the odds a bit before they died.

Then perhaps when the Orions reached Fuller and the others there would be a chance.

The dog barked from his position on the side of the chamber.

"Hold fire until you see them," he said.

The Orions' beams announced their approach.

The Orions appeared a few seconds later, and the three security officers fired nearly in unison. Another Orion fell to Benitez's phaser, but the others kept firing, their weapons aimed directly at Kell and the others, yet flying harmlessly over their heads.

It had not occurred to their attackers that the Starfleet people might be on the ground. Up until now, they had fought from crouching or standing positions.

It would be only seconds before they figured it out. Kell hoped that those seconds would allow them to even the odds some more.

One of Parrish's beams lanced out, hit an Orion on the side, and threw him out of sight.

Then both Kell and Benitez's beams found targets as well.

The Klingon grunted his satisfaction, but then an Orion beam hit the rock in front of him, kicking up debris.

They wouldn't last seconds with the Orions firing on their thin cover. Pushing Benitez to the side, he tugged on Parrish's tunic. The others understood and rolled to the left.

Getting to his feet inside the chamber, Kell took a few deep breaths. Benitez and Parrish stood up next to him.

Since the chamber opened up a several meters on either side, it would be a few moments until the Orion blasts could come close to them. In fact, to fire, the Orions would have to step inside the oval chamber to engage them.

They would have to enter the killing box.

"Any more ideas, Flash?" Benitez asked. Kell could sense the grim smile on his roommate's face.

Before he could say that there weren't, he realized that was not exactly true.

"When I move, follow me," he said.

Orion energy beams struck the back wall of the chamber. They were testing, waiting for return fire.

The dog was growling steadily now. Reflexively, Kell put a steadying hand on the animal, the way he would to stay a hunting *targ*. He wondered briefly if the animal might give the Orions one last surprise before it fell.

When Kell could hear the footfalls of the attackers and judged them just a few meters away, he adjusted his phaser, aimed it across the chamber, and fired directly into the wall.

For a moment, the wall glowed red, and then a section of it disappeared. Rock fell from into the opening as Kell raced across the chamber, shouting, "Now!"

He fired to his left and sensed the others were doing the same as he threw himself into the opening created by the phaser blast.

For all he knew the opening was only a few feet deep and he would hit the wall in two steps. Yet he did not hit it after four steps. Then he shined the light ahead and saw what he had hoped to see.

Benitez and Parrish were next to him.

"Is this the way to the cavern?" Benitez asked, pointing to the right.

"Yes, just a few meters around that rock," he said.

"Amazing," Benitez said.

"We'll rejoin the others," he said, pulling out his communicator.

"Anderson to Fuller," he said.

"Fuller here, where are you?" the chief asked.

"Just a few meters away. Don't fire, we're coming in," he said. Kell led the way, and once again he did not see the security people until he was past them, nearly inside the entrance to the cavern.

"What happened?" Fuller asked, frank surprise on his face.

"We engaged the enemy," Parrish said.

"How many are there now?" Fuller said.

"Fewer," Kell said. "They are right behind us."

The Klingon found cover. Benitez and Parrish took positions on either side of him again.

This time, when the Orions came they rushed into position so quickly that their first shot rang out as the dog let out his first bark.

Return fire answered them.

As Kell fired and searched for targets, he tried to estimate how many of the attackers remained. *Eight? Ten?*

Did the Klingon and the five humans have a chance?

As if to answer, one of Chief Brantley's people took a direct hit.

Then another fell.

As far as he could see, none of the Orions had been hit yet.

It is just a matter of time now, Kell realized.

Then a blast hit Sam Fuller's position. Kell did not see it strike the man, but no more phaser blasts came from the chief's direction.

The Klingon felt the urge to give a death howl, to warn those in the other world that a warrior was coming.

He thought of Sam Fuller and his belief in his great leader, his captain. It was a shame for such a brave and honorable warrior to waste his loyalty on an Earther like Kirk. Again, Kell found himself hoping that when the Empire ruled this space, honorable humans would find leaders worthy of their loyalty.

With that thought, the Klingon stood—taking his head and shoulders above the cover of the rock.

"What are you doing?" Benitez shouted.

"We are facing overwhelming force," he said. "I'm going to attack."

He did not wait to see Benitez's expression.

The Klingon howled. It was part battle cry, part death howl for Sam Fuller, and part death howl for himself.

Racing toward the Orions' position, he stopped in the open, with Orions on both sides of him. For a moment he saw that his tactic had surprised the enemy, who had stopped firing for an instant.

And instant was all Kell needed. Turning to the right, he picked one target, then another.

From behind him, he sensed motion and saw a golden ball of fur fly into the air and throw itself on an Orion taking aim at him.

The Orion's aim went high, striking the ceiling above Kell's head.

Rock flew in all direction. The Klingon briefly saw the piece that struck him straight on the head.

He fell.

Kell knew he was on the floor. He fought to keep his eyes open. The battle raged above him and he guessed that he had bought the humans some more time. Perhaps only seconds. Yet he judged it worthwhile.

Then there was silence above him. He knew his time was short as his eyes closed on their own. The next time he opened them, he had no doubt, would be at the River of Blood.

Would he see Kahless there? His father? Would they recognize him wearing his human face? He knew they would not accept him as he looked now. Yet perhaps he would be granted a glimpse of his father before *Sto-Vo-Kor* was denied him forever.

Even as the silence fell, he fought against it.

Then the silence was broken. Noise. Not noise. Voices.

Kell forced his eyes open. He didn't see the River of Blood.

He saw the ceiling of the cave.

Turning himself over, he looked down the length of the cave and saw a figure through the smoke, illuminated from behind by strong lights. It carried a long weapon. A *bat'leth?*

For a moment he thought it was Kahless or his father coming to take him.

Kell struggled to his knees, then to his feet.

The figure came closer and the Klingon could see that

the weapon was not a *bat'leth*. The silhouetted figure carried a rifle of some kind.

He immediately dismissed his thoughts of Kahless and his own father as a fevered dream.

Yet what he saw was no less incredible than what he had imagined. As the smoke cleared, he saw a gold Starfleet uniform, a phaser rifle...and a face.

It was the great coward. The betrayer.

It was James T. Kirk, holding the phaser rifle alertly.

There were sounds. The Klingon knew they were words, human words, but could not decipher their meaning. It took all of his effort to remain on his feet.

Kirk had seen him, was saying something to him.

Then the captain was raising the phaser rifle, pointing it straight at him. Then the Klingon understood that everything he had been taught about this human was true. The Earther was working with the Orions; he had betrayed his own crew.

Kell met the captain's eyes with his own. He would take the face of this enemy with him when he died.

Taking careful aim, Kirk fired.

The Klingon felt nothing.

Then he heard a thump. Turning his head, he saw an Orion resting on the ground barely a meter from his feet.

Then Kell fell himself. He fell backward. It seemed to take forever. He waited for the cave floor to rise up and strike him, but the blow did not come. Someone had caught him, he knew, but he could not tell who it was.

Then darkness came.

Chapter Twenty-one

WHEN KELL WOKE, he saw the cave ceiling again. But it had receded farther into the distance.

It took him a moment to realize that he was in the cavern now. There were voices around him and he felt water dripping on his head.

His first thought was that the humans had dishonored him by immersing his body in water. Then he opened his eyes and saw that one of the settlers was simply running a wet cloth over his forehead.

"His eyes are opening," the woman said. He recognized her as the mother of the girl who owned the dog, Spencer. The dog had saved him somehow, but the details were cloudy.

His mind was clouded, smoky. He remembered the smoke in the cavern and the dog jumping at an Orion.

Something hit his head, and then he remembered...

...Kirk.

Kirk had arrived and had saved him.

The Klingon bolted to a sitting position.

"He's awake," the woman said.

Suddenly, Benitez and Parrish were looking down at him.

"Jon," Parrish called out.

"Flash, are you okay?" Benitez asked.

"Stay there, the doctor is treating the seriously wounded first. He'll be with you in a moment," Parrish said.

Doctor? It was impossible. The doctor meant failure, the end of his mission.

"No," Kell said, brusquely, struggling to his feet.

"It's over," Parrish said gently. "Rest and wait for the doctor."

"No," the Klingon repeated. "I feel fine," he said, knowing that it was not true. His head throbbed.

Using all of his concentration, he steadied himself on his feet.

Benitez grabbed his shoulder. "It's okay. The captain is here. Everyone's safe."

Everyone?

"Fuller?" Kell asked.

"We don't know yet. Dr. McCoy is working on him now," Benitez said.

"Dr. Davis will see you in a minute," Parrish said.

Kell smiled, attempting to make it seem casual.

"A *civilian* doctor? I would rather wait and go to sick-bay back on the *Enterprise*," he said, knowing he never would, knowing it was impossible.

Yet Parrish seemed satisfied.

"I'm not sure how soon we'll be going back to the ship," Benitez said.

"The Orions?" the Klingon asked.

"No, but there's some sort of problem. The captain,

the doctor, and the rest of them came here on a shuttle-craft," Benitez said.

Looking around him, Kell could see the settlers milling around. And the children were...playing.

Not all of them, he saw. The girl who had offered him her animal was hovered over it as it lay on its side.

Kell stepped over to her.

Closer, he could see the animal's chest rise and fall slightly. He could also see that its side was bloodied and at least partially crushed in.

The animal would not breathe for long. The animal had earned his wounds in battle and had earned an honorable death. As a Klingon that thought did not trouble him.

But the girl was no Klingon and she wept for her pet.

"Son, let me take a look at you," said a voice behind him.

Turning, Kell saw Dr. McCoy with a medical kit in his hand.

"I'm fine," the Klingon said.

"I'll be the judge of that," the human replied—not pleasantly, Kell noted.

"He needs your attention more," the Klingon said, pointing to the dog.

The doctor looked down and said, "I'm a doctor, not a veterinar—"

Seeing the weeping child, the doctor stopped himself.

"He saved my life," Kell said.

"He warned us when the Orions first hit. He may have saved all of us," Benitez added.

"Can you help him?" the girl pleaded.

Kneeling, the doctor ran a scanner over the beast and said, gently, "I will do everything I can."

Kell hoped the dog would live, though he knew it was

unlikely, especially if he did not receive more intensive treatment than he could get in the cave.

The dog had warned them of the Orions' first attack and the subsequent ones as well. He had leapt on the Orion who was aiming at Kell. And he had just saved the Klingon again from the doctor's scanner, which would have meant death just as surely as the Orion's weapon.

Kell had received surgery and other treatments to make him look like the human Jon Anderson, but his internal anatomy was still Klingon. A single scan would tell the doctor that.

Yes, the dog had saved his life more than once. A Klingon did not forget such a debt easily.

Scanning the cavern, Kell saw Captain Kirk standing over Sam Fuller, conferring with the Vulcan.

Somehow, the humans had produced another stretcher, on which Fuller now lay, unconscious. He could not see the chief's injuries and hoped they were not fatal.

Reaching his hand up to his own forehead, he felt the wound and the drying blood. Pulling his hand down, he was startled by the blood's red color...its human color.

He had known the Klingon surgeons had altered the color of his blood from the proper Klingon color—what the humans called lavender. Yet seeing the red liquid on his hand had startled him.

Klingon blood carried more than oxygen and nutrients. It carried the call of a Klingon's ancestors, and some said his very honor. It was what made him a Klingon.

And now his blood was human's blood.

Yet human only in color. A simple medical test would prove that.

In an instant he realized that he was neither human or Klingon.

Adolescent Klingons used the term "bloodless" as a

taunt, almost as bad as "Earther" or an insult to one's mother.

What was he? Kell wondered. What was the call of this red blood on his fingers?

His thoughts were interrupted by the captain, who addressed the small crowd.

"Now that the injured have been stabilized, we need to move everyone out of the caves. Unfortunately, we will not be able to transfer you all to our ship immediately. It was damaged in an attack by one of the Orion vessels that attacked you and will take a few days to repair. In the meantime, we will use shuttlecrafts to transport you to the ship."

"Will we be safe outside?" one of the settlers asked. "Are they all gone?"

"Yes, they are all gone," Kirk said. "And we will be ready for them if any more come," he said with confidence. The settlers seemed satisfied.

"Once the *Enterprise* is under way again, we will take you to the nearest starbase, where Federation officials will be able to assist you," Kirk continued.

The settlers made no mention of staying with their homes. That did not surprise Kell. He had seen that humans were often foolish, yet they were not stupid.

They were also stubborn and he wondered if some of the settlers would find their way to another new planet, one closer to the safety and protection of a more densely inhabited sector.

The captain and the Vulcan led the way out of the caves. Kell noticed a small scuffle erupting between the young settler named Steele and one of the fresh security people from the *Enterprise*.

Steele, his friends, and a small group of settlers had insisted on carrying the stretchers which held Jawer,

McFadden, and now Fuller. Finally, the security officer judged the argument too much trouble and let them.

Turning he looked to see Dr. McCoy injecting the dog with something. By the doctor's face, he could see that the animal's injuries were indeed grave. He could also see that moving the animal would be a problem. Ideally, they would use a stretcher, but there were no more.

Striding over, Kell said, "I will carry him." He leaned down and picked up the animal to whom he owed his life. The beast grunted, but remained still.

On the way out of the cavern, the group passed the scene of the most recent battle.

The cave walls were scarred and blackened by weapons' fire. The remains of some of the Orions, including the one who had nearly shot him, were scattered about.

The scene replayed in Kell's mind. The dog—which he had thought as frivolous and soft as a human—jumping at the large Orion. The enemy's shot barely missing him. And then Kell seeing Kirk pointing a phaser rifle at him.

Captain Kirk had saved his life.

Kell was now indebted to him in a way that no Klingon could be indebted to a human—particularly to a human who was an enemy to the Empire.

He owed the same honor debt to the animal in his arms. He owed the same debt to the dead security people with whom he had fought. He owed the same debt to the unconscious Ensign Jawer, who had turned a scuttled shuttlecraft into a powerful weapon. He owed the same debt to Ensign McFadden, who had used the Orion weapons platform to finish the job on the Orion ship.

Going into this mission, he had had expectations. He had expected to bring honor to his family. To serve the Empire. To destroy its enemies. And finally, he had expected to die.

He had not expected to find himself owing so many honor debts—debts that he could never repay and remain a Klingon.

Kell was nearly outside when he realized that Benitez and Parrish were at his side, and had been since the cavern.

Outside, the Klingon saw the humans collecting in front of the cave. He didn't know how long they had been in the caves, but the system's sun was hanging low in the sky.

Kell placed the dog next to the stretchers carrying the other three wounded. Ensign Clark, who looked like she needed a stretcher herself, was arguing with Dr. McCoy about something. The doctors were staying close to the injured and taking a look at the shuttlecraft, which sat nearby.

Just then a familiar hum sounded in the air and a lone figure materialized on the planet's surface

"Commander Scott," Kirk said, pleasure in his voice. "It is a real and unexpected pleasure to see you."

The ship's chief engineer smiled.

"You'll nae be please when you see the new damage reports. We blew out a few more systems to get here."

"Do we have transporters?" Kirk asked.

"Aye," Scott replied with another smile.

"Then let's stop wasting time. I have injured people here," Dr. McCoy said gruffly.

As the stretchers were placed closer together for beam-up, the Klingon was surprised to see Captain Kirk approach.

"You have all done very well today," the captain said, looking over Kell, Benitez, and Parrish. "I want to thank you."

"You saved my life, sir," the Klingon said, surprising

himself. "I owe you…" He could not finish. He did not know how to explain it so a human would understand.

"You owe me nothing compared to what I owe you," Kirk said, putting a hand on Kell's shoulder. "You completed your mission in an overwhelmingly hostile situation, cut off from your ship and taking heavy losses. No, Ensign, you owe me nothing," the captain said, his voice tightening.

Kirk turned and walked away.

The injured, including the animal, were transported first. Then the settlers. In the end, only the four security officers, Captain Kirk, and the Vulcan remained.

The captain insisted that the security people beam up first.

Stepping off the transporter back on board the ship, Kell saw Lieutenant Commander Giotto, who looked at them and said, "Well done and welcome aboard. You are off duty until the morning. We will debrief then."

Before he reached the door, a yellow-haired woman wearing a medical insignia accosted the Klingon. He recognized her as a nurse.

"Dr. McCoy told me to escort you to sickbay," she said.

Without hesitating, Kell said, "The civilian doctor, Dr. Davis, examined me on the surface."

The nurse looked skeptical. Benitez stepped forward. "It's true, the doc said he was fine."

"All right," she said. "But the doctor is going to want to see you first in the next round of physicals."

In the corridor, Parrish asked him, "Why don't you just go see Dr. McCoy?"

"It wouldn't kill you to go to sickbay, Flash," Benitez said.

"I do not like doctors," Kell said truthfully.

When they reached the deck, they reached Parrish's

room first. The female seemed to want to say something to them, but could not.

The Klingon understood, better than he had understood any human since he had begun this assignment.

Benitez broke the awkward silence. "So long, Parrish. We'll see you tomorrow."

"Yes, good-bye," the Klingon said.

She nodded, shot Kell a last glance, and entered her quarters.

Back in their own quarters, Benitez was uncharacteristically but thankfully quiet. The Klingon quickly disinfected and bandaged his wound. He could not afford an infection, which would draw more attention to him. Kell considered himself fortunate that it would not require sealing, which the doctor would no doubt insist on doing.

As Kell sat on his bunk, he thought that he felt surprisingly good. After the day's long battle, he would have thought exhaustion would claim him immediately as he noticed it had done to Benitez—who was already asleep on his bunk.

Recognizing that he needed rest, Kell lay down on his own bunk. He thought he would rest for a few minutes then perhaps get something to eat.

But before he completed the thought, darkness took him.

"Join me for lunch, Lieutenant," the admiral said, pointing to the chair facing his desk.

Lieutenant West was not surprised to see a place set for him there, directly opposite the admiral's own setting. He was also not surprised to see blackened catfish, one of his favorite dishes, on the plate.

After only a few days on the admiral's staff, he didn't think he would be surprised by anything again.

Less than a week ago, he had graduated near the top of his Academy class. He was convinced he knew everything and his only concern was which starship he would be assigned to. He was hoping for the *Enterprise* but was prepared to compromise.

Within five minutes of meeting the admiral, his dream of starship service had been dashed. Just a few days later, that dream seemed brittle, hollow, and selfish.

Now the entire Federation was headed toward something terrible, something that just days ago he had believed he would be able to help prevent. The admiral had believed it too. Lieutenant West had had his doubts when he met the man, but he was sure of that now.

But he was no longer sure it mattered.

"What's bothering you?" the admiral said, and West was struck with the notion that the admiral had somehow listened to his private thoughts.

West didn't hesitate. He was dreading the conversation enough. He would not draw it out any more than necessary.

"I wanted to speak to you before I filed my first report," West said.

"Even if we had time to stand on ceremony around here, I prefer the simplest route, Lieutenant. I prefer to leave repetitive communication to politicians and diplomats," the admiral said.

"I know that, sir, but because of the sensitive nature of my preliminary findings—" West began.

"You wanted to give me a warning before you embarrassed someone," the admiral finished for him.

"Yes, sir," West said.

"Will Nogura be getting another complaint from Ambassador Fox?" Admiral Justman asked.

"No, sir, this does not involve the ambassador..." West said.

For a moment, West could see that the admiral was surprised, genuinely surprised. After studying him for a moment, the admiral said, "It's me. You've found something you think would embarrass me."

"It does involve you, sir," West said. "Since you were involved—"

"You can stop right there, Lieutenant. You never have to worry about embarrassing anyone in your work, especially not me. The only thing that would embarrass me would be to enter into and lose a large-scale conflict with a hostile race. Is that clear?" he said.

"Yes, sir," West said.

"What is your analysis? I presume it involves the peace settlement. You've come to the conclusion that I should have finished the job at Donatu V. If I had, the Klingons wouldn't be strong enough to threaten us now. Believe me, that is a question that has kept me up nights these last few months. But frankly, I'm surprised that you would think that, after your papers favoring xeno-studies-based diplomacy over military options."

"Sir, my analysis does trace our current problem with the Klingons to the Battle of Donatu V, but not for the reasons you think. And I used xenoanthropological and xenosociological models to arrive at my conclusions. I'm confident that I understand the Klingons much better than I did before," West said.

"But you have seen that understanding doesn't necessarily improve the situation," the admiral said, once again showing an uncanny insight into what West was thinking. "Explain, Lieutenant."

"As we have discussed, the Klingons are a proud warrior-based people for whom conflict is seen as a natural part of their lives and relationships. In many ways, expansion is necessary to keep their aggressive impulses from turning groups of them against one another. In that respect, Starfleet was right to see their interest in the Donatu V system as a threat. The battle fought there kept the Klingon Empire from trying to expand toward Federation space for twenty-five years," West said.

"So what has changed?" the admiral asked.

"Nothing, sir, and that's the problem. The kind of work I do requires that I try to see a race of people as they see themselves. In the Federation, we see ourselves as peaceful. War and conflict are seen as interruptions to our status quo. You saw an opportunity to stop the fighting at Donatu V and took it. You made the correct moral and ethical choice according to our values," he said.

"Somehow I don't think I'm going to like the punch line here," the admiral said.

"The problem is that the Klingons see themselves in a completely different way. For them, conflict is the natural state of being. They fight because it is their nature. They fight, as one of their leaders said, 'to enrich the spirit.' We look back over the last twenty-five years and see peace. They see a temporary suspension of hostilities."

"Would that have changed if we had beaten them?" the admiral asked.

"Yes. Because fighting is a way of life for them, they readily understand both defeat and victory. What they don't understand is peace based on a negotiated truce. For them, it is worse than defeat because defeat would have earned us respect in their eyes. For the Klingons, the unfinished battle and the last twenty-five years of peace are a stain on their honor—a stain that must be avenged," West said.

For a long time, the admiral was silent. During that

time, he seemed to shrink in his chair and age ten years before West's eyes.

"Sir, you made the right decision at the time. You saved lives. And you didn't have the information—"

"But that's what we do here, Lieutenant, we make vital, life-and-death decisions—"

"With grossly inadequate information," West said, finishing for him.

"And while we have spent the last quarter century exploring, colonizing, and building, they have spent it preparing to finish a battle that should never had gone beyond one star system but may now swallow all of us," the admiral said.

"I'm not convinced there is not another way. With more study—" he began, but the words sounded hollow to his own ears. He was not writing a student paper criticizing Starfleet policy, or second-guessing decisions made decades ago and tens of light-years away. He was contemplating the end of the Federation and a loss of life on a scale that the galaxy had never known.

And suddenly, for the first time since he had applied to Starfleet Academy, he was speechless.

Chapter Twenty-two

THE NEXT DAY Kell awoke slowly. Before he opened his eyes, he took a quick inventory of his body. His head ached but no longer throbbed. He was sore in places but felt well enough.

Finally opening his eyes, he saw that Benitez was stumbling around in the room already.

"What time is it?" Kell asked.

"After eleven hundred," Benitez said.

"What?" the Klingon asked.

"It's tomorrow, Flash," the human said.

Pulling himself to a sitting position, Kell shook himself fully awake. Then he was on his feet.

"Fuller? The others?" he asked.

"Fuller is going to make it. Jawer is awake. McFadden is still unconscious," Benitez said. "We'll have to wait until after the briefing to see them. Giotto wants us in the briefing room by twelve hundred.

Kell realized he was hungry. He showered quickly and joined Benitez.

"Ready for breakfast?" Benitez asked.

"Yes," the Klingon said, realizing he was more than ready. He felt like he could eat a whole *targ* himself.

In the deck's mess hall, he found Parrish eating with Clark, Chief Brantley, and the other survivor from Brantley's team.

The room went silent when Kell and Benitez entered. They took trays and went to the synthesizer. Unfortunately, *targ* was not on the menu.

A few moments later, he sat with the others and ate his meat loaf. They ate in silence, a silence that was maintained by the rest of the room.

By unspoken signal, they moved as a group to the briefing room. A yeoman with yellow hair asked them to wait and disappeared inside. A moment later, she reappeared and said, "Ensign Anderson, you can go in now."

She put a gentle hand on his arm and led him inside.

The captain was sitting with Mr. Spock and Lieutenant Commander Giotto.

The last time he had entered this room, the captain was sitting in it alone and Kell was certain that he had been discovered.

This time the captain and the others stood, and he realized he was being honored.

"Have a seat, Ensign," Kirk said.

Only when Kell had sat at his end of the table did the others sit.

"How are you feeling, Mr. Anderson?" Kirk said.

"Well, Captain," he replied.

"Have you eaten since you returned?" he asked.

"Yes, sir," he said.

"If you need anything at all in the next few days,

please contact me directly. If I'm not on the bridge, Yeoman Rand will know where I am," he said, indicating the yellow-haired yeoman who had shown him in and was now standing by the door.

"Yes, sir...thank you, sir," he said.

"I want you to know that what you and your fellow crew members did yesterday is appreciated by myself and the senior officers of this ship. It will be indicated in my report and figure prominently into your Starfleet record.

"I have already interviewed Section Chief Fuller so I know the basic events of yesterday and have an idea of the courage you showed under fire. Now I would like you to tell us what happened from your point of view. After that we will have some questions for you. Later, after we have interviewed the others, we would like to talk to you as a group."

The Klingon spoke; then he answered their questions.

He was dismissed while the others were debriefed and went straight to sickbay.

Inside, he was met by Dr. McCoy, who took one look at him and groused, "Not another one. This is a sickbay, not a trading post."

Kell did not know if a response was required.

"Perhaps I should come back," he said finally.

The doctor shook his head. "No, Fuller wants to see you. He seems to have no respect for his doctor's orders."

Stepping through the outer examination room, the doctor found Fuller on one of the three beds in the intensive-care room. The other two beds were occupied by Jawer and McFadden, who were both unconscious.

"Chief Fuller. Are you," he said, searching for the correct human idiom, "all right?"

"Fine," Fuller said, though Kell could see that his torso was heavily bandaged.

"Fine!" the doctor repeated from behind the Klingon. "If by fine you mean recovering from a badly punctured lung and multiple rib fractures, yes, then you're fine," he concluded as he left the men alone.

Fuller smiled at the doctor's outburst.

"See, even the doctor says I'm fine," Fuller said.

"Jawer and Benitez?" Kell asked.

"Jawer is just asleep. The burns on his hands will heal." Fuller was silent for a moment. "McFadden is still in a coma. He had a bad blow to the back of his head. Dr. McCoy is going to operate when he's a bit stronger."

Nodding, the Klingon turned to go. "I just wanted to see that you were well," he said.

"Ensign," Fuller said, and Kell turned back around. "That was some fine work you did back there."

"Everyone fought well," the Klingon said.

"Yes, that is true, but I want you to know how much I appreciate what you did for all of us and for the settlers. You showed real courage and real leadership, Anderson. You are a credit to this ship and her name."

The Klingon was not comfortable with such praise. It was not his people's way. "Thank you, sir," he said finally, hoping that ended it.

"I only wish I could take credit for your training, but I have had you for only a few days," Fuller said, smiling.

Taking that as a dismissal, Kell made a smile of his own and turned to go. As he was walking out, Fuller's voice called out, "You have a real future in Starfleet and a real future in security if you want to pursue it."

With those words ringing in his ears, the Klingon left sickbay.

It was late afternoon before he was summoned back to the briefing room. The others were outside waiting for him. The yellow-haired yeoman named Rand came out a moment later and ushered them inside.

The survivors of the mission sat around the table. The captain thanked them again, making Kell wonder. As a rule, Klingons did not praise one another in such a way. And few commanders would admit being indebted to an inferior officer for fear of appearing weak.

Yet Kirk did not appear weak in Kell's eyes.

The Klingon had heard many things about Kirk, just as he had heard many things about humans. Still, he had seen human courage and honor for himself—just as he had seen them risk themselves for principles that any Klingon would think insane.

Kell had seen the human Kirk risk his own life for the lowest and apparently most expendable members of his crew.

Kell's brother had taught him the proverb that their father had often repeated: "The best witness is a Kling-on's own eyes."

This human had honor *and* courage. Kell knew that saying that aloud to his own superiors in the Klingon command would gain him nothing but death. Yet it was the truth, and he would not deny it.

He trusted his eyes, and what he felt in his blood.

After they were dismissed, the survivors of the mission moved together to the mess hall. Kell had meat loaf again. It was not alive, but it was surprisingly satisfying.

He noted that Benitez also had meat loaf. Seeing the deference the others gave him, he wondered if it was an unconscious sign of respect.

Kell wondered at the idea. The ones most deserving of respect had been lost on the planet, or were lying now in sickbay.

They passed the meal quietly, for which Kell was

grateful. To his surprise, he was also pleased to be in the presence of the people with whom he had fought.

He was pleased to be in the presence of these *Earthers,* these humans.

That thought should have troubled him, but it did not.

He knew that personal relationships with humans were a great danger to him and to his mission for the Empire. Increased contact meant an increased chance for his exposure as a Klingon serving the Empire.

Yet he would not deny himself the company of fellow warriors—and warriors they were. Though they fought for reasons that no Klingon would be able to fathom, they fought with all the courage and honor of true disciples of Kahless. As far as Kell was concerned, they were as worthy a company as an honorable Klingon could desire to keep.

As they finished their meal, Kell looked forward to going back to his quarters. As a Starfleet officer, he had a duty to perform that he had neglected. He would neglect it no longer.

He sensed that his time on this mission was growing short. And it was not a task he wished to leave unfinished.

Kell had begun to rise when a group of settlers entered the room. The little girl who owned the dog saw him first. She squealed and ran for him. Before he could react, she had wrapped herself around the Klingon's leg.

"Here they are!" she shouted. "I found them!"

Looking at the door, Kell saw that settlers were still coming through the door. He noted that they kept coming.

And coming.

For a moment he thought all sixty of them might try to cram themselves into the already half-full mess hall. Then he was sure. That is exactly what they were doing.

And by the way they were looking at Kell's table, they had not come for food.

Benitez and the others were standing by now, receiving pats and handshakes from the smiling human civilians. Hands grasped his shoulder, his arms.

An old woman took his face in both of his hands and kissed him straight on the lips. All the while, the human girl clutched his leg tightly.

Glancing at the other security officers for cues, Kell could see that they were smiling but were also uncomfortable with the attention. He resolved to just bear it.

"Spencer is going to be okay!" the girl yelled up at him. He could barely make out her words over the din of thanks from the other settlers.

"What?" he said.

"Spencer is going to be okay. The doctors fixed him!" she said, beaming. "I told you he was brave."

"He was," Kell said. "He saved my life. He may have saved us all."

The girl seemed to physically swell with pride. For a moment, the Klingon thought she would certainly burst in front of him.

Finally, the girl's mother removed her from Kell—with some effort, he noted.

"We wanted to thank you," she said, reaching out to touch his face.

"We all wanted to thank you," Dr. Davis said, stepping forward and to shake all of the security officers' hands.

"We tried to visit Lieutenant Fuller, but your doctor would not let us in," one of the men said.

"And I had to agree with that," Davis said. "At least until he and the others are stronger."

In the next few minutes it seemed that each of the settlers tried to pat, prod, or touch each of the surviving security officers. Finally, after what seemed like an entire shift, the doctor began ushering people out.

"We just wanted to thank you," he said.

These humans and their thanks, Kell thought. *It is a wonder they have time for anything else.*

"We will see you tomorrow," the doctor said.

When they were gone, the officer stood in silence for a moment until Benitez broke it. "Well, they seemed pleased," he said.

The others smiled and they moved as a group to the corridor. Benitez was the first to break off. He headed for a turbolift, inviting any of them to join him in the recreation room.

None of them did. Finally, it was just Parrish and Kell. She stopped in front of her quarters and said, "Jon, could we talk in private for a moment?"

Immediately on his guard, the Klingon said, "Perhaps tomorrow."

"This will just take a minute, why don't you come in," she said. By her tone, he could tell that it was not really a request.

Estimating that it would be more trouble to refuse, he followed her.

Inside, her quarters were empty.

Nodding, Kell waited for her to speak again. She did not. Instead, she merely met his eyes with a level gaze. Then she leaned into him.

The Klingon sensed the danger a moment before she acted, but she moved quickly, too quickly for him to react. Reaching around behind his head, she pulled him to her and met his lips with her own.

Kell saw that she was initiating perhaps the most dangerous kind of personal relationship—the kind most likely to end in his death and in the failure of his mission.

To his surprise, that thought did not trouble him at the moment. He pulled her closer, and she responded with a kind of ferocity in her attack that he thought was beyond human women.

She was a worthy opponent, he judged. But then so was he.

Chapter Twenty-three

KELL ENTERED HIS QUARTERS and found Benitez asleep. He moved quietly through the room and got into bed without making a sound.

Before he could close his eyes, Benitez's voice called out, "Have a good night, Flash?"

"It was...fine," Kell said. "I am very tired." He hoped that would end the discussion.

"I'll bet, the night is half over. So, how is Ensign Parrish?" the human said. The Klingon had known his roommate long enough now to clearly recognize humor in his voice.

"Ensign Parrish?" Kell said.

"Come on, I'd have to be blind not to see it. The way she looked at you..." Benitez said.

Interesting, Kell thought. *He* had not seen it. Looking back, he realized there were signs—humans and Klingons were not *that* different. Yet he had been preoccupied.

Thoughtful, Kell realized he had been quiet for several seconds. As usual, Benitez was happy to break the silence.

"It's okay, I think she's great. And she's good with a phaser. That might come in handy if you run into trouble on your honeymoon," Benitez said. The human laughed out loud at his own joke, which the Klingon did not understand.

He would have to look up the term *honeymoon*.

"She is a capable officer," he said evenly.

The human thought that was extremely funny and said, "Good night, Flash."

The next morning, Kell was amazed at the flurry of activity on the ship. Civilians were everywhere. Empty staterooms, storage, and cargo space had been converted to temporary housing for the displaced settlers, who seemed to be everywhere.

Kell had thought he had been beyond surprise at human lunacy, but he was again amazed to see the settlers given virtually free rein on the ship. As a result, they were everywhere. And Kell saw them in the corridors, at breakfast, and at sickbay—where he had learned that McFadden was due for surgery later that day.

The civilians never failed to stop him or any of the other survivors from the mission and express their thanks. Kell was as patient as he could be with them, but he looked forward to the day when the ship would be unloading its passengers.

Unfortunately, the captain had ordered the *Enterprise* to remain in orbit for a few days while the crew effected repairs needed after the ship's encounter with the Orion vessel in space. And even those repairs would not begin in earnest until the following day.

First, there was the matter of the memorial service.

This was larger than the one given for Matthews and Rayburn, which had been held in the recreation room.

This service was attended by virtually the entire crew, including those who were supposed to be in a sleep period. Barely twenty people remained at their posts to crew the ship.

The remaining four hundred-some crew and nearly sixty settlers gathered in the shuttlebay for the service.

The survivors of the mission stood together. And to Kell's surprise, both Sam Fuller and Ensign Jawer joined them. Neither man looked well, but both insisted on remaining on their feet. However, the Klingon noted that Dr. McCoy and another, dark-skinned doctor whom Kell did not know stayed close by, watching the men carefully—as protective as *targ*s watching over their young.

When the service began, Captain Kirk spoke about each of the fallen people as he had spoken of Ensign Rayburn and Ensign Matthews, whom Kell alone knew as a brother Klingon.

Kell had seen much of the settlers' gratitude toward their saviors, but he was surprised to see the captain include Lara Boyd and her mate in the service. Yet the civilian leaders of an unsanctioned Anti-Federation League settlement were honored with the fallen crew. And the captain spoke of their commitment to their ideals and fellow settlers as he spoke of the records of the honored security people.

The captain spoke well of them and Kell had seen enough of Kirk to know his words were sincere.

The Klingon had thought humans were as mad as wild *targ*s before. Now he was certain of it. But it was a madness that made its own odd sense and held its own honor.

Kell had seen Parrish at breakfast and then at the service. They exchanged polite words, and he was pleased to see that she treated him no differently than she had the day before. He had been concerned that their evening together would needlessly complicate his position and his mission.

He was pleased that it would not. He hoped that in a few days she would forget the encounter entirely. They had fought together and had found each other attractive. Their companionship could be explained as a natural reaction to the intense battle.

After dinner, she had surprised even him by getting up before he was finished with his meat loaf and bidding the table good night.

Perhaps she had forgotten already.

Yet he doubted he would be that lucky and had half-expected her to seek him out in his quarters.

When she did not, he found himself concerned. Perhaps the battle on the planet had taken a toll on her frail human constitution. And while she was a human, he still respected her as a warrior.

Because they had fought together and he respected her as a warrior, he decided to seek her out—to insure that she was well.

When her door opened she took one look at him and her face flushed in pleasure. "Jon," she exclaimed.

As he stepped inside, he decided not to insult her by admitting his concern for her. Instead, he simply said, "I thought you might want company."

As it turned out, she was open to his company.

And by the time he left her later that night, he was convinced that there was nothing frail about her constitution.

The next day, ship's repairs were delayed further when the captain announced a recovery effort for the settlers' personal effects on the planet's surface. Security teams, engineers, and technicians would help the settlers find and repair whatever could be recovered.

Days before, the AFL were sworn enemies of the Federation and of Starfleet.

It was madness, and still shocking though Kell had thought himself beyond surprise at anything the humans did now. But perhaps the greatest surprise came when he found himself volunteering for the duty.

Before they beamed down, Kell, Benitez, and Parrish stopped by sickbay to see McFadden. Jawer was visiting there as well, his burned hands still in bandages, as was Fuller, who was obviously in pain but stayed by the ensign's bedside.

McCoy seemed to barely notice them, seeming preoccupied, until Benitez asked, "How is he, Doc?"

Kell did not need to hear the answer. McFadden was not well. His cheeks had fallen and his skin was an ashen gray.

"He's going into surgery soon," the doctor said. "He's got some pressure in his brain that I need to relieve. He knocked himself pretty good down there."

Klingons, he knew, would make no such effort on behalf of so badly injured a warrior. Instead, when a warrior was unable to face his enemies, he would be allowed to die so his spirit would be freed.

At Klingon Intelligence, he had learned that humans' tendency to fawn over the sick and injured was one of the things that made them weak. But he now knew that this was not true.

For humans, preserving life was a fight against death. As he had seen, humans fought for different reasons than Klingons, but they fought well and with their own kind of honor. They also succeeded far more often than he would have thought.

Kell hoped that Kahless would look well upon the fight the doctor was about to undertake.

When Kell and Benitez left sickbay, Fuller and Jawer remained by McFadden's side.

On the planet, Kell watched as security teams, technicians, scientists, and officers of virtually every rank as well as the settlers themselves pored over the wreckage of the settlement.

Much of what they recovered seemed frivolous to the Klingon, yet he saw a strong sentimental attachment to what seemed to him worthless artifacts of a failed settlement. Photographs, computers, and children's playthings were all treated respectfully.

Back on the ship, Kell knew that other technicians and engineers were repairing everything that could be repaired.

While that effort was ongoing, Lieutenant Commander Giotto and a team examined the settlement and the site of the battle for evidence of the Orions' motives and possible employers. Unfortunately, the Orion ship had self-destructed automatically and little could be recovered from it.

Kell thought that was truly unfortunate. He would have liked the *Enterprise* to pay a visit to the ones who orchestrated this cowardly attack on the weak.

The survivors of the mission worked together, helping settlers pull equipment from the basement and sifting through the rubble of the upper floors.

"Do you know who is really responsible?" Benitez asked him while they worked.

Without looking up, Kell said, "I presume it is the Romulans."

"No, not the Romulans, but I have a friend who has a cousin that works in the records department over at Fleet Command. He says it's the Klingons," Benitez said.

Kell was glad that he was not turned to the human, because the surprise on his face would have betrayed him.

"I heard the Klingons are planning something big," Benitez said. The human leaning closer to whisper, "There's been a lot of...activity, but Fleet is keeping it quiet for now."

Kell said nothing and, thankfully, Benitez did not pursue the matter.

Though he had been surprised when Benitez first mentioned his people, he rejected the idea. Klingons did not attack defenseless beings. And they did not employ others to do their fighting—even those Klingons who did not follow Kahless's path to honor had their pride.

Yet Kell was troubled for the rest of the day and into the evening. They ate on the planet and finally returned to the ship when it was too dark to work any more.

Kell and the other survivors beamed up together. They found section chiefs Fuller and Brantley waiting for them. He knew what Fuller was going to say before the human spoke.

"Ensign McFadden died in surgery," the chief announced.

That night, Parrish and Kell sat together in her quarters. In his mind he sang the Klingon dirge for fallen warriors.

They passed the evening quietly and had nothing to offer each other but company. Yet the Klingon found that company extremely...acceptable.

Chapter Twenty-four

THE MORNING AFTER their encounter in the corridor, M'bac was in the port disruptor room when Karel arrived. Saying nothing, Karel took Gash's former position at the front of the room.

The next to arrive was the new officer who would take Karel's position as the primary cooling system panel. Then came the others, including Torg, who was wearing a splint on the left hand that Karel himself had broken the day before.

When the whole group was there, they replaced the officers from the previous shift and took their places.

Karel watched as the weapons officers performed their routine maintenance tasks, paying special attention to the performance of his own replacement. When that was done, he shouted, "Klingons! Listen! As your new commanding officer I will now warn you about what to expect. Understand that I am not Gash. He was my com-

271

mander since I was posted to this ship and I am glad to be rid of him."

There were grunts of approval from the disruptor group. "Gash pitted us against each other to keep himself from being challenged by more than one warrior at a time," Karel continued.

The faces in the room betrayed the Klingons' surprise. Clearly, they did not expect such honesty from a commander—but they had never been commanded by a follower of Kahless before.

"I expect you all to work together. The success of any of you will depend on the success of all. I will not tolerate sabotage of another warrior's effort to further your own career," he said, glancing at Torg, who had done just that the day before.

The Klingon was looking at him with the same rapt wonder as the other Klingons in the disruptor room.

"And if any of you wish to challenge me, one or two at a time, you are welcome. I am a warrior and will answer all," he said, making sure he caught the eyes of everyone in the room.

He did not linger on M'bac's eyes, nor did he mention the challenge in the open room. M'bac's defeat the previous night was enough. Karel did not need the Klingon humiliated, he needed him to do his job well.

"However, I expect you to do your plotting and planning on your own time. Anyone who disrupts the smooth running and battle-readiness of this disruptor room will be dealt with severely." Karel paused for emphasis, then shouted, "Back to work!"

The Klingons turned to their stations.

He spent the first half of the shift supervising them and correcting mistakes. Later in the shift he arranged for a drill. The results were not exceptional, but he did see that the performance was improved from recent history.

Most important, no effort was wasted on petty jockeying between officers. As far as Karel was concerned, that was great progress.

In time, he had no doubt that he would get the results he wanted. Then the Empire's enemies could beware.

At the end of the shift, he was summoned to Second Officer Klak's quarters. The second officer was alone. He stood when Karel entered the private room.

"Congratulations on your promotion and on the performance of the port disruptor room today. You have already improved on Gash's numbers," Klak said.

"Thank you, sir. I hope to improve them further. And I thank you for the *opportunity* you gave me yesterday," Karel replied.

Klak studied him for a moment. "I also reviewed the surveillance data from the corridor outside your former quarters yesterday. You fought well," Klak said.

"I prevailed," Karel said simply.

"You let him live," Klak said, making it a question.

"He is a good officer," Karel said.

"True," Klak said. Karel had the impression that the second officer was studying him carefully. Finally, the Klingon seemed satisfied.

"I have news for you," Klak continued. "Your brother is dead," he said flatly.

For a moment, Karel was sure he had not heard the second officer correctly.

"My brother serves on Qo'noS, in Intelligence," Karel said.

"Not anymore. He is dead. He was killed in a raid," Klak said.

Then it came. Rage and grief rose in Karel's blood.

His brother Kell as a young Klingon, trying hard to prove himself a warrior to his older brother as he studied *Mok'bara*. His brother facing the manhood trials. His brother's disappointment at being denied a position in the Klingon Defense Force.

Karel swallowed it all. "How?" he spat out.

"He was part of a classified mission, operating on the edge of Klingon space," Klak said.

"Who?" Karel asked.

"Earthers," Klak replied coolly. "They attacked in secret. All warriors were lost."

Earthers? Klak could not believe it. First his father, now his brother. They would pay. By Kahless and his honored father, the Earthers would pay.

By his honor, they would pay dearly.

"Why is the Empire not at war with the cowards?" Klak said.

"It is not yet time," Klak said, waving off Karel's protest before he could utter it. "But the time will come, and soon you will be able to use your rage against the Empire's enemies. Wait and take your vengeance. We will smash the Earthers to the last one. Can you do that, Senior Weapons Officer Karel?"

"I serve the Empire," Karel said, his blood burning.

Ensign McFadden's service was the following morning. It was held in the shuttlebay again, and again virtually the entire crew and all of the settlers were there.

After the afternoon meal, another ceremony was scheduled in the shuttlebay, this time to honor the survivors of the mission. On his way with the others in his section, Kell wondered that humans celebrated and mourned in the same place on the same day.

It was almost Klingon of them.

Captain Kirk took the podium with the Vulcan and the other senior officers at his side.

"In these last two days we have joined together to pay tribute to our friends and crew members who made the ultimate sacrifice. Through their efforts and their sacrifice, they have honored the Starfleet oath and the United Federation of Planets we serve.

"Today we are here to honor those still among us who honor that oath and that Federation, and who honor us with their courage and their commitment to duty.

"The first person we will honor is Ensign Jon Anderson. Ensign Anderson, please come forward," he said.

For a moment, the Klingon was frozen in place. Then Parrish and Benitez pushed him gently forward. When he reached the podium, Captain Kirk addressed him with a straight and clear gaze.

"Ensign Jon Anderson, as your commanding officer, I am honored by your service. Though you have served on this ship a very short time, you will be long remembered as a distinguished part of her legacy. In the name of Starfleet Command, I award you the Starfleet Citation for Conspicuous Gallantry."

Kirk handed Kell a package, which he accepted without looking.

"And after a very strenuous recommendation from your section chief, Lieutenant Sam Fuller, and testimonials from your fellow officers, I award you the Starfleet Medal of Honor," Kirk said, handing him another package.

For a moment, Kell was too stunned to accept the second package, but his hand found it on its own.

To hear the word *honor* fall so easily from the captain's lips was almost too much for him. Yet he said, "Thank you, sir," and returned to his place in the crowd, barely registering the congratulations of his section-mates.

As the other awards and citations were awarded, the Klingon watched, his blood in an uproar.

His own Empire judged him unfit to fight as a proper warrior. Instead, he had been sent as an assassin, forced to hide his true face and live among his people's enemies. Yet his enemies were now honoring and decorating him.

And he had to admit that the respect of these Earthers—these humans, as they called themselves—meant something to him.

They were not honorless cowards. He knew that now that he had learned to see them as they saw themselves.

He wondered how the Klingons at Command would react to that insight. He did not have to wonder for long. He knew.

Listening to the captain speak, he realized that he was not looking forward to killing this man.

Chapter Twenty-five

KIRK STRODE THROUGH dimly lit and nearly empty corridors. This late in the evening the ship was usually quiet, but not this quiet. Kirk knew that everyone felt the recent losses.

He was glad to have the civilians aboard and to have so much that needed to be done on the planet's surface. Helping the settlers would keep up morale. It would remind the crew why they were out here and would remind them what their friends' sacrifices had accomplished.

It often felt like thin comfort, but it was all they had.

Stepping into the engineering lab, Kirk was struck by the bright lights. When his eyes adjusted, he saw Mr. Scott and Mr. Spock supervising the engineering team as they worked on a new artificial-gravity generator.

"How does it look, Mr. Scott?" Kirk said.

"The new generator will be ready tomorrow, but I will

need at least three days to test it before I would want to use the impulse engines."

"You have your three days, Mr. Scott," Kirk said.

The engineer's face betrayed a mild surprise, but he said nothing.

Kirk was in no rush. There was work to do on the surface. The settlers needed time to say good-bye to their homes, and the crew needed time to come to terms with their losses.

There was always the possibility that another Orion ship would come looking for the two that were lost, but Kirk did not think it would happen. In fact, he felt sure of it.

Kirk was just as sure that whatever had happened on the surface and in space with the Orions was not over. Something had begun here, something big.

Kirk felt sure that the next move would be somewhere else. He vowed to himself that if the *Enterprise* was there when it happened, he would be ready.

"Gentlemen, I would have thought that repair of this nature would require a starbase facility," Kirk said finally, snapping himself out of his reverie.

"According to regulations, yes," Scotty said.

"But logically, we will not be able to visit a starbase until the parts are constructed and the repair is completed," Spock said. The Vulcan's tone and body language told Kirk that the Vulcan was not immune to the mood on the ship. He would have denied it, and he doubted anyone else on the ship would notice the change, except for possibly McCoy, yet there it was.

"Then carry on as logic requires," Kirk said, turning to go.

Back in the corridor, he headed for a turbolift. He had one more stop to make.

Less than a minute later, he was standing outside of sickbay.

When the doors opened, he noticed that sickbay was darker than the corridor. At first it looked empty, but Kirk knew better.

He found the doctor sitting at his desk, looking into the viewer. Kirk would have bet a month's pay that the doctor had been staring at the same image for some time.

McCoy looked up and Kirk saw that the doctor carried the patient he had lost in his eyes.

"Hello, Jim. I was just catching up on some work." McCoy started to get up. Kirk stopped him with a hand on his shoulder.

Sliding aside the semitransparent panel, Kirk took down the doctor's bottle of Saurian brandy and two glasses and then poured.

Sitting opposite McCoy, he put the glasses down and said, "There was nothing you could have done, Bones. You saved Jawer and healed the rest of them. You won more than you lost today."

For a long moment, McCoy didn't speak. Then he said, "Does that sound so damned thin when I say it to you, Jim?"

"No," Kirk lied.

"I thought so," the doctor said.

McCoy picked up his glass and said, "To absent friends."

Kirk raised his own glass and repeated, "To absent friends."

After the ceremony, Kell did not remain with the humans in his section; he took his meal in his quarters. Later, he told Parrish that he was unable to join her that evening.

Sensing that his time was drawing short, Kell knew he still had some small but important matters to attend to before he could fulfill his final duty.

Picking up a data padd, the Klingon began composing his communication. Fortunately, the real Jon Anderson was in the custom of sending text messages to his mother. As good as his Klingon surgeons had been, he did not trust their work to come under the scrutiny of Anderson's own mother in a visual message. Even if his appearance passed notice, his voice would not.

His work in intelligence helped him. By reviewing Anderson's previous messages, he was able to quickly distill the human's style of writing. Still, he tried too keep his own message simple and direct.

He began by acknowledging her previous messages and apologizing for not writing sooner. He told her of his brief service on the ship and his recent commendations. He hoped that news would bring her pleasure.

Soon enough, Kell's real mission would be complete, and he did not expect to survive long after that. Then Anderson's mother would learn of her "son's" death. Kahless willing, he would complete his mission for the Empire and die with his true nature undetected. It would spare Anderson's mother unnecessary anguish. The thought of her pain should not have troubled him, but it did, and he was beyond questioning such things now.

For the first time, Kell realized that he did not want to die on this mission, despite the fact that it was all but inevitable. The thought of his own death had never troubled him before. Yet, now he found it did. This was not because of any contamination by humans, he knew.

This was a very Klingon response.

Kell knew what his duty to his people demanded. And he knew he would do it, and probably die doing it. But for the first time, he realized that doing his duty would likely cost him his honor.

It was a bitter price. Yet he knew he would pay it.

Look for STAR TREK fiction from Pocket Books

Star Trek®

Enterprise®

Star Trek®: New Frontier

Star Trek®: Stargazer

The Valiant • Michael Jan Friedman
Double Helix #6: The First Virtue • Michael Jan Friedman and Christie Golden
Gauntlet • Michael Jan Friedman
Progenitor • Michael Jan Friedman

Star Trek®: Starfleet Corps of Engineers (eBooks)

Have Tech, Will Travel (paperback) • various
  #1 • *The Belly of the Beast* • Dean Wesley Smith
  #2 • *Fatal Error* • Keith R.A. DeCandido
  #3 • *Hard Crash* • Christie Golden
  #4 • *Interphase, Book One* • Dayton Ward & Kevin Dilmore
Miracle Workers (paperback) • various
  #5 • *Interphase, Book Two* • Dayton Ward & Kevin Dilmore
  #6 • *Cold Fusion* • Keith R.A. DeCandido
  #7 • *Invincible, Book One* • Keith R.A. DeCandido & David Mack
  #8 • *Invincible, Book Two* • Keith R.A. DeCandido & David Mack
  #9 • *The Riddled Post* • Aaron Rosenberg
  #10 • *Gateways Epilogue: Here There Be Monsters* • Keith R.A. DeCandido
  #11 • *Ambush* • Dave Galanter & Greg Brodeur
  #12 • *Some Assembly Required* • Scott Ciencin & Dan Jolley
  #13 • *No Surrender* • Jeff Mariotte
  #14 • *Caveat Emptor* • Ian Edginton
  #15 • *Past Life* • Robert Greenberger
  #16 • *Oaths* • Glenn Hauman
  #17 • *Foundations, Book One* • Dayton Ward & Kevin Dilmore

Star Trek®: Invasion!

#1 • *First Strike* • Diane Carey
#2 • *The Soldiers of Fear* • Dean Wesley Smith & Kristine Kathryn Rusch
#3 • *Time's Enemy* • L.A. Graf
#4 • *The Final Fury* • Dafydd ab Hugh
Invasion! Omnibus • various

Star Trek®: Day of Honor

#1 • *Ancient Blood* • Diane Carey
#2 • *Armageddon Sky* • L.A. Graf
#3 • *Her Klingon Soul* • Michael Jan Friedman
#4 • *Treaty's Law* • Dean Wesley Smith & Kristine Kathryn Rusch
The Television Episode • Michael Jan Friedman
Day of Honor Omnibus • various

Star Trek®: The Captain's Table

#1 • *War Dragons* • L.A. Graf
#2 • *Dujonian's Hoard* • Michael Jan Friedman
#3 • *The Mist* • Dean Wesley Smith & Kristine Kathryn Rusch
#4 • *Fire Ship* • Diane Carey
#5 • *Once Burned* • Peter David
#6 • *Where Sea Meets Sky* • Jerry Oltion
The Captain's Table Omnibus • various

Star Trek®: The Dominion War

#1 • *Behind Enemy Lines* • John Vornholt
#2 • *Call to Arms...* • Diane Carey
#3 • *Tunnel Through the Stars* • John Vornholt
#4 • *...Sacrifice of Angels* • Diane Carey

Star Trek®: Section 31™

Rogue • Andy Mangels & Michael A. Martin
Shadow • Dean Wesley Smith & Kristine Kathryn Rusch
Cloak • S. D. Perry
Abyss • Dean Weddle & Jeffrey Lang

Star Trek®: Gateways

#1 • *One Small Step* • Susan Wright
#2 • *Chainmail* • Diane Carey
#3 • *Doors Into Chaos* • Robert Greenberger
#4 • *Demons of Air and Darkness* • Keith R.A. DeCandido
#5 • *No Man's Land* • Christie Golden
#6 • *Cold Wars* • Peter David
#7 • *What Lay Beyond* • various
Epilogue: Here There Be Monsters • Keith R.A. DeCandido

Star Trek®: The Badlands

#1 • Susan Wright
#2 • Susan Wright

Star Trek®: Dark Passions

#1 • Susan Wright
#2 • Susan Wright

Star Trek® Omnibus Editions

Invasion! Omnibus • various
Day of Honor Omnibus • various

The Captain's Table Omnibus • various
Star Trek: Odyssey • William Shatner with Judith and Garfield Reeves-
Stevens
Millennium Omnibus • Judith and Garfield Reeves-Stevens
Starfleet: Year One • Michael Jan Friedman

Other Star Trek® Fiction

Legends of the Ferengi • Ira Steven Behr & Robert Hewitt Wolfe
Strange New Worlds, vol. I, II, III, IV, and V • Dean Wesley Smith, ed.
Adventures in Time and Space • Mary P. Taylor, ed.
Captain Proton: Defender of the Earth • D.W. "Prof" Smith
New Worlds, New Civilizations • Michael Jan Friedman
The Lives of Dax • Marco Palmieri, ed.
The Klingon Hamlet • Wil'yam Shex'pir
Enterprise Logs • Carol Greenburg, ed.

About the Author

Kevin Ryan is the author of two novels and the co-author of two more. He has written a bunch of comic books and has also written for television. He lives in New York with his wife and four children. He can be contacted at Kryan1964@aol.com.